Dust Bunnies and Dead Bodies

Janis Thornton

Cup of Tea Books

An Imprint of PageSpring Publishing
www.cupofteabooks.com

Published in the United States by Cup of Tea Books, an imprint of PageSpring Publishing
www.cupofteabooks.com

ISBN: 978-1-939403-27-8

Cover design by Sarah Allgire
Interior design by Rebecca Seum
Author photo by Madilyn Mann

For my parents, June and Bill Thornton, my son, Matt Geas, and my surrogate moms, Ruth Illges and Mary Ann Doggett

James Thornton

Acknowledgments

Had it not been for the patience, indulgence, encouragement, and thoughtful feedback from my treasured friends and fellow members of the Aubrey Writers group—Bob Beilouny, Chip Mann, Kathy Smith, Larry Sells, Margie Porter, Mary Marlow, and Tim Byers—I might never have finished this project. I am eternally grateful *to* and *for* them. I also am deeply indebted to my editor/publisher, Rebecca Seum, for inviting me to join the PageSpring family, scrubbing and polishing my manuscript until it glistened, and for the opportunity to fulfill my decades-long dream of becoming a published novelist.

1

FUNNY WHERE YOUR MIND GOES when you're staring into the face of mortal danger. The night I stepped through Gertie Tyroo's dark back door, uninvited and all alone, my mind conjured up an old movie, starring me as the classic damsel in distress—fragile, frazzled, and befuddled, desperate for a white knight to gallop in on horseback and rescue me.

Crystal Cropper, I thought, revolted by the helpless self-image, *you are pathetic! You don't need a white knight. You're your own white knight. Now get on with it.* And get on with it I did. Without further hesitation, I drew a deep breath and called out, "Gertie! It's me, Crystal. You okay?"

That's when the living room light went out, somebody screamed, and all hell broke loose.

Rapid-fire footsteps scurried toward me through the opaque darkness, prompting my Ladies' Kick-Ass training to kick in. I stiffened in a defensive stance—feet fixed at forty-five degree angles, knees bent, one hand clamped around my can of mace, the other poised to strike a crippling blow. I thought I was ready to rock 'n' roll, but I was quickly proved wrong when a solid

1

shoulder slammed into my chest. It bulldozed me toward the open doorway and knocked the mace from my grip. I screamed "Noooo!" and swung my right fist, hoping it would connect with the assailant's face.

Yes! My knuckles delivered a solid blow, and my attacker gasped. Invigorated, I pressed on, determined to further stun my assailant with a head butt to the chin. Unfortunately, the plan was stopped when two strong hands grabbed my upper arms and shoved me with a force that dislodged my hairpins. As my topknot unfurled, the thug grabbed a handful of my hair and yanked me out the door. Before I could rebound, I found myself tumbling down the back steps and onto the patio, where, winded and dazed, I landed hard on my left butt cheek.

The intruder took my temporary incapacitation as an exit cue and bolted through the carport. My fears for Gertie pushed me up the steps and back into the dark house. I groped the walls for a light switch, found one in the kitchen, and flipped it on. An overhead fluorescent halo flickered to life, spilling light through the doorway to the front room.

"Gertie!" I called again. "Where are you?" Still no answer.

Thinking I might catch a glimpse of the fleeing intruder, I rushed for the front door. But as I rounded Gertie's sofa, I stubbed my foot on something large and doughy. I nearly tripped and was set to give what-for to the poorly placed object, expecting maybe a hassock. But. Oh. My. God.

It was Gertie.

The squeal of spinning tires resonated from the street, followed by the grinding roar of a souped-up engine. I scrambled for the front door, but my attempt to throw it open was stymied by the dead bolt. The louder the rumbling, the more my tangled fingers floundered over the stubborn lock. Finally disengaging the bolt, I threw open the door and dashed onto the sun porch as a light-colored pickup truck rocketed past. Although I couldn't read the license plate, I took note of the truck's taillights—the left one was red, the right one orange.

With precious time wasting, I rushed back to Gertie. She was sprawled on her left side, wrapped tightly in her leopard-print coat. Her left arm extended unbent in alignment with her body, and her hand rested on her tattered wool scarf. Her right arm, which gripped the strap of her straw handbag, jutted out before her at a ninety-degree angle.

I grabbed a pillow and tucked it under her head. That's when I discovered the blood soaking into the carpet. Its source was a deep wound on the back of her skull. I unbuttoned her coat and gently probed for her carotid artery with my fingertips. She had a pulse. It was weak, but it was there.

A table lamp lay on the floor within arm's length. I set it upright and clicked it on. The room was chaos. The phone was off the hook and bleeping incessantly. I picked it up, tapped its plunger to get a dial tone, and punched 9–1–1.

2

WITHIN MINUTES OF MY CALL, two EMTs—the Minnear twins—arrived with the ambulance. Soon after, the Elm County sheriff, Verlin Wallace, flung open the front door with his bare hands and walked in without stopping to wipe his muddy boots. Halfway into the room, he paused to bark orders at the twins and assess the situation.

The entire living room was in disarray. The drawers of Gertie's desk and end tables had been pulled out and their contents scattered. A sizeable antique wardrobe also had been ransacked, its drawers extended to varying degrees, its double doors swung open, and a jumble of wire hangers and garments scattered about its base. Dozens of books and knickknacks had been knocked off the shelves of several floor-to-ceiling bookcases. Cushions from Gertie's sofa and chair had been pitched every which way.

"Darrell, Darlene," Verl said to the EMTs, "be careful what you're doing. Don't go touching things you don't need to be touching. I oughtn't have to remind you that this is an active crime scene, and potentially everything is evidence. So I'd

4

appreciate it if you'd—"

"Hello, Verl," I said.

His focus spun to the back of the room where I stood, out of the twins' way as they worked feverishly to stabilize Gertie. His bushy gray eyebrows converged in a deep V. "What the Sam Hill . . . ?" he grumbled.

To outsiders, Verl and I seemed like archrivals, always bickering and bossing each other around. The truth is, despite appearances, no two people could be closer. The complicated, gnarly relationship we enjoyed began the day we met in Mrs. Stroup's Elmwood Elementary kindergarten class. We were both only children—bullheaded, overbearing, independent, and never the other kids' first choice for anything. The kindred spirit that drew us together had taken its lumps over the years, but bottom line, Verl was my best friend. He was the only man I could ever count on or spend long periods of time with—in a purely platonic way, of course.

I flicked my tangled hair off my face and grabbed both sides of my unbuttoned flannel shirt and flattened them across my chest.

Verl's chubby cheeks reddened, and I braced for a chewing out. "Are you all right?" he said. His apparent concern surprised me. "Tell me you're all right."

"I'm all right."

His color deepened. "What the heck were you doing here? This could have been you," he said, waving toward Gertie, "and you could have been killed."

"Good grief, Verlin, relax before you blow a gasket. I was supposed to meet Gertie at Bud's just before midnight—"

"Midnight? What on earth would two old women be doing out by theirselves at mid—"

5

"—but . . ." I ignored his affront to my age, not to mention to my virtue. ". . . when she didn't show up, I got worried. I dropped by to check on her, and it was a good thing I did."

"You find her just like this?" Verl said.

"Yes, and the intruder was still here—"

"*What?*" Verl croaked. "You barged in while a crime was in progress? I gave you credit for being smarter than that. Don't you know what—"

"Listen, Verl," I said. "I don't need a lecture from you, especially not after what I just went through. If you'll keep quiet for a minute, I'll tell you what I know. Is that okay with you, boss?"

Speechless for a change, Verlin glared back at me and nodded. I found his response quite satisfying. He liked it when I talked tough, and I was happy to oblige.

"My phone rang at eleven forty-five . . ." I said, beginning a full accounting of the events that had led me here.

Throughout my long news-reporting career, I had never allowed anything, short of the occasional midnight rendezvous with Mr. Burt Reynolds, to pry me from my bed on a work night. But the call that night had blown my unwritten, time-honored rule all to hell.

"What?" I'd grunted into the receiver of my bedside Princess phone. I peeled open one eye and was nearly blinded by the four glowing orange numbers on my digital clock. "This better be good."

"This is better'n good," my caller said in a barely audible tone. Yet even at a whisper, the toothless lisp of town kook and freelance housekeeper Gertie Tyroo was unmistakable.

In the nine years I had been editor of my hometown newspaper, the *Elmwood Gazette*, Gertie had earned my trust a hundred times over as a confidential informant. What she had done with her life before that, I didn't know. Didn't ask. Didn't care. There was one thing, though, of which I was certain. She was a natural snoop.

"Gert," I said, my grogginess ebbing, "what is it?"

"Listen up," she said. "A few days ago, while I was cleaning one of my clients' houses, I found something I thought might be tied to that old Potts case. After going back today, I'm positive, and if—"

"Potts," I said, trying to make the connection. "You mean *Eugene* Potts?"

Eugene Potts was a local high school boy who went missing back in 1993.

"Of course, I mean Eugene Potts," she shot back. "So stop interrupting. I've got something new on that case, and if you want it, meet me at Bud's in fifteen minutes."

"Oh, for God's sake," I said, "can't you just tell me now?"

"If you think I'm going to talk about this on the phone, you've got rocks for brains." Her volume rose. "You know who's listening, don't you?"

I sighed. "No, but I'm sure you're going to tell me."

"For starters, the FBI 'n' the CIA—not to mention them boys down at NSA. They've all tapped my phone line. Maybe yours too."

Knowing Gertie as I did, I didn't even try to reason with her. I let it go. "Then come by the office tomorrow morning," I said. "There aren't any bugs there."

"That you know of," she said. "Besides, it won't work. I'm heading out tonight for my nephew's over in Noble City."

"Nephew?"

"So, unless you want me giving this information to the *Logan City Ledger*, meet me at Bud's in ten minutes."

"Ten? I thought you said 'fifteen.' "

"The clock's a-tickin'." And the line went dead.

Surely I could convince her that her tip could hold until morning. I called her right back, but all I got was a busy signal. I was not pleased. Eugene Potts had been missing for more than twenty years. I couldn't imagine what difference another eight hours would make. Nevertheless, having spent decades harvesting current events to spoon-feed to a news-hungry public, I wasn't about to risk getting scooped by the damned *Ledger*.

Every inch of my weary body resisted as I rolled out of my toasty bed, pulled on a flannel shirt and sweat pants over my pajamas, coiled my blonde mop into a tight bun, and slipped into my slicker. As an afterthought, I deposited my trusty can of mace into my coat pocket. Trekking into the cold, misty Midwestern night, I pretended I was off to meet Burt Reynolds. It was a trick that never failed to warm things up.

I drummed my fingernails on the coffee-stained countertop at Bud's Roadside Diner for forty minutes before my stack finally blew.

"Ye gods. What am I doing waiting around this filthy dump like some loser who's too dumb to realize she's been had?"

At the far end of the counter, Bud stopped his sweeping and flashed me a searing look.

"Sorry, Bud. I didn't mean that. It's not a filthy dump."

He grunted, "Whatever," over the cigarette balanced on his lower lip and went back to work. In reality, the place reeked of stale smoke, deep-fried fat, and Pine-Sol. It was a dump all right. But I hadn't meant to hurt Bud's feelings.

"It's just that it's almost midnight, for cripes sake, and I should be home in bed," I said.

Bud swapped his broom for a wet dishrag and started wiping

down the stainless-steel wall behind his grill. I resumed my finger drumming. After a couple of minutes, he threw the rag into the sink and peered at me over his reading glasses. "Crystal, if you're going to take up a stool, you'll have to order something."

My annoyance spiked, but I smiled sweetly. "I'll tell you what," I said. "Why don't you fix me a French vanilla latte with a fluffy whipped-cream froth and a nice chocolate-chip bagel?"

Bud sighed, and the inch-long ash that clung to his cigarette broke loose, tumbling down the front of his mustard-stained undershirt. At least I hoped it was mustard.

"Never mind. I don't want anything," I said. "I'm just here to meet someone."

"That someone better get here quick because in five minutes, I'm closed."

Dominating the wall over the diner's front door was a clock the size of a manhole cover advertising Big Rod's Root Beer. Its hands pushed toward twelve, nudging my irritation about Gertie's truancy toward genuine worry. Sure, she possessed odd traits, but tardiness was not in her nature.

Bud finished his setup for the breakfast rush—salt-and-pepper shakers filled, sugar bowls topped off, plates and coffee cups washed and stacked. Turning to me, he slid his glasses to the end of his nose and flashed another look.

"Go home, Crystal. You've been stood up."

He got no argument. I slipped off my stool and headed for the door. Stepping outside, I called over my shoulder to him, "G'night, Bud. It's been a gas."

Bud's "Eat Here, Get Gas" neon sign lit up a desolate stretch of Indiana State Road 280 five miles west of Elmwood. It lured unsuspecting travelers who were too tired, too hungry, or too darn trusting to drive on to the next greasy spoon. Little did they know the sign was more of a promise than an advertisement.

I climbed into Nellie, my trusty '72 Plymouth Duster that I'd bought brand-new right off the showroom floor decades ago, and revved up her engine. I tapped the bright-lights button with my left toe and drove the five miles back to town without passing a single westbound vehicle. As I approached the mouth of the curve leading to Elmwood, Nellie's headlights illuminated the city limits sign. I could have stayed on the highway and been home in less than a minute. Instead, I veered to the right and headed down the County Road 50 bypass.

I let Nellie idle at the curb in front of Gertie's house, while I cased the neighborhood from behind the wheel. Indiana weather is a bugger in early March, shifting from tepid to arctic in the span of a few hours. The frigid air felt like it had dropped ten degrees since Gertie phoned. I shivered and slid the heat-control lever to "high."

The wind ripped holes in the cloud cover, revealing sporadic glimpses of the twinkling, starlit universe. Down on planet Earth, I took another visual sweep up and down Hoover Street. Near as I could tell, it was lights out for all but one house— Gertie's—where a wee glow shone through the living-room drapes. I debated whether to go knock on her door or go home. If I disturbed her needlessly, she would punish me with one of her tongue-lashings, and frankly, I'd rather be waterboarded. But knowing I couldn't sleep until I was certain of her well-being, I pattered up to her hermetically sealed sun porch and tapped the screen door.

No answer. I tapped again. Still no answer. I tried the knob. Locked. Gertie's enclosed porch looked pretty well insulated and may have accounted for why she hadn't answered my knock.

I had followed the brick walkway to the side of the house, where I'd passed through the carport, on to an open patio, and up the steps to the open back door.

". . . so I entered through the back door," I told Verl, who had listened to my whole story with his arms crossed and a stern look on his face, "and surprised the intruder. We got into a little scuffle, and he bolted. Then I ran in here, and found Gertie unconscious."

"You have any idea with what she was attacked with?"

I pointed to the brick lying in front of the sofa. "I assume it came from her patio."

"You get a description of the unsub?" Verl asked, flaunting the police lingo he learned at a refresher course last fall at the Indiana Law Enforcement Academy in Plainfield.

I shook my head. "Afraid not." The lights were off and the unknown subject—or rather, the *unsub*—jumped me, threw me out the back door and skedaddled. As soon as I found Gertie, I called for an ambulance, performed a cursory investigation of the premises, and—"

"You did *what?*" Verl croaked again.

I ignored him and went on with my report. "—found some highly suspicious situations. In addition, I have a description of the escape vehicle. I will brief you on all of it. I haven't touched much, so you needn't worry about contamination of your crime scene, other than your fingerprints on the front door and the mud you tracked into the living room."

I turned my attention back to Darrell and Darlene, who by then had lifted Gertie onto a stretcher and were unlocking the wheels. "You two doing okay?"

"Yes, ma'am," said one of them, but don't ask me which one. I couldn't tell them apart. No one could. Rolling the stretcher past Verlin and out the front door to the waiting ambulance, the other twin called out over his—or her—shoulder, "We'll get Miss Tyroo to the ER stat. So don't you fret, ma'am."

They're such nice, well-mannered kids.

3

I DROVE TO ELMWOOD MEMORIAL HOSPITAL and took a seat in the otherwise unoccupied waiting room. I was eager for Verl's company but appreciated the solitude and the time to think.

Gertie's condition scared me. She was old. I had no idea what her chances for recovery would be.

Her work as a "domestic engineer," as she sometimes called it, afforded her the perfect excuse to nose around people's private business. Even better, her client list included some of Elmwood's most persnickety families. Gertie's job not only provided her a decent living, it occasionally handed her nuggets of inside information that were pure gold. The ones she passed on to me as news tips more often than not proved to be the mother lode. A reputable journalist was nowhere without trustworthy, anonymous tipsters, and I was fortunate to have Gertie Tyroo as mine. As a token of my appreciation, I comped her subscription to the *Gazette* and tipped the carrier to insert each day's edition into her mailbox. It may not sound like much, but Gertie wasn't the kind of woman who needed—or accepted—accolades for doing what she considered her civic duty. Gertie was a good egg, and I liked her despite her prickly personality.

I had last seen Gert about a month ago. At her request, we had met at the park's open-air shelter, even though it was the middle of February and well below freezing. When I arrived, she was seated stiffly on one of the benches with her green Hush Puppies planted squarely before her. Her leopard-print coat was cinched tightly around her scrawny body to ward off the frigid winter air. When she saw me, she scrunched up her wrinkled, putty-like face and cussed me up one side and down the other for being late.

Her tip involved the mayor's use of strong-arm tactics to persuade the city council to award demolition contracts to his brother-in-law without first opening them up for bids. When she finished giving me all the dirt she had, she draped a raggedy wool scarf over her wiry, colorless hair, and collected her cane and straw handbag.

"Don't you go telling nobody where you got this," she said, shaking a gnarled finger at me. "You do, and I'll be taking my business to that young editor *fella* over in Logan County. Understand?"

When I assured her that I did indeed understand, she smiled and stood. She took a few steps, stopped, and peered back at me over her slight dowager's hump. "Maybe one of these days I'll give you something that'll win you one of them *Poolitzers*," she said. Then she gave a wink and shuffled off to her car.

Everything she told me checked out with the city auditor, and the next day, the *Gazette* reported that the mayor's shenanigans had cost local taxpayers roughly a hundred thousand dollars. Even better, thanks to Gertie's fine detective work and my reporting, the county prosecutor launched an investigation, which he said could lead to charges and possibly arrests.

Every January, I've considered naming Gertie the *Gazette*'s citizen of the year for her public service. If I ever did, she would kill me.

• • • •

Verlin rolled into the waiting room shortly before three o'clock and flopped down beside me. I was grateful he had put his tough-guy persona to bed. He actually could be very sweet.

"Crys, hey," he said, gently squeezing my shoulder, "you okay?"

I told him I was fine but worried sick waiting for a status report on Gertie, and then I asked, "What took you?"

"I called in Chuck and Ernie to help me secure the premises with yellow tape," he said. "The last thing we need are looky-loos poking around before we collect the evidence to send to the state crime lab for analysis. Come morning, I'll send them back there to see what they can scrape up."

"In a criminal case like this," I said, "you might want to consider calling in the state police. You know, so they can lend a hand if the investigation gets to be too much for Tweedledumb and Tweedledumber."

"That's real funny, Crystal," Verl said flatly. "Did you make that up yourself? Let me ask you something else. How'd you get all that dirt on the back side of your britches?"

"What were you doing looking at my backside?"

Verl snorted. "I wasn't exactly looking, but a person'd have to be blind not to notice the filthy muck all over your big hind end."

"My big *what*?" My anger flared. "Excuse me? Isn't that a little like the pot calling the kettle—"

"Hello," came from a gentle voice from the doorway.

My head swiveled from Verl's snarky grin to a smallish, olive-skinned man crowned by a full head of tousled, rust-colored hair. He wore dark blue scrubs. A stethoscope was draped around his neck. Approaching us, he extended his right hand and said, "Are you here for Gertie Tyroo?"

I stood. Verlin followed my lead. "Yes, we are," I said.

"I am Doctor Shamus Bannerjee."

Returning my smile, he shook my hand, then Verl's. We introduced ourselves. His dark eyes sparkled, telegraphing kindness. I liked him.

"How's she doing?" I asked. "In case you didn't notice, Gertie's not big on being the center of attention, so I hope she didn't give you too much trouble."

"Not at all," the doctor said. "But, under better circumstances, I have no doubt that she can be quite a handful."

Verl and I joined him in polite laughter, but his smile faded quickly and he turned somber.

"At any rate," he said, "Miss Tyroo's cranium took a serious blow, and we have made her as comfortable as possible in ICU. Her vital signs are stable, but she has been heavily sedated to put her in what we call a medically induced coma. We do this procedure in instances of severe bilateral, subdural hematomas." As if reading my mind, he explained, "It's a fancy term for head trauma. We induce a coma to maximize the body's ability to draw from its own reserve of healing properties."

"How is she?" I asked, dreading Dr. Bannerjee's answer. "Is she going to be all right?"

He sighed and lowered his gaze to his bright orange Crocs. After a long moment, he shook his head and looked up at me. "At this point, I can't say. It's too early. The next seventy-two hours are going to be crucial."

"If . . . *when* Gertie wakes up, and I promise you she will," I said, not totally believing my own conviction, "will she be all right? Will she remember what happened?"

"Only time will tell," the doctor said. "Even if Miss Tyroo wakes from her coma, we have no way of predicting whether she will regain all her mental faculties. We have to wait and see."

"When can we visit her?" I asked.

"Let's give it a day or two," the doctor said. "I will instruct the staff to release updates about her condition whenever you call."

I felt assured Gertie was in excellent hands and thanked Dr. Bannerjee again as he exited the waiting room. Everything that could be done for her was being done—at least from a medical standpoint. I turned back to Verlin.

"Looks like you've got your job cut out for you," I said. "If you don't want the state involved, why don't you call in that private forensics team from Indianapolis—Have Gumshoes, Will Travel? You told me yourself that they've solved several cases for some of your cohorts here in central Indiana."

Without a blink, Verl said, "Look, Crystal, you and I both know you're itching to make this investigation your own."

"You and I also know you *need* me," I said. "I can get the local gossip. People talk to me. Combined, Chuck and Ernie's investigative skills aren't worth a bucket of spit."

"My boys are perfectly capable of handling this case," he shot back.

I huffed a humorless snicker. "A case of what?" I said. "Fleas? Measles? Amnesia?"

"You've got issues, lady," Verl said, "and it pains me that I have to remind you—*again*—that you are *not* a crime scene investigator. You're the editor of a tiny, hometown newspaper."

"Yeah," I said, "I'm the editor and a damned good one. I don't see the harm of me poking around while I work the story. So? What do you say?"

Verl shook his head and sighed. "Have you not been listening?" he said. "We don't need any civilian sleuths poking around, mucking things up. So thanks, but no thanks. I've got this one."

"All right," I said, raising my hands in mock surrender. "Leave it to your crack team." I paused for dramatic effect before adding the zinger. "Gertie's *your* friend, same as she is mine. I thought you might want to go the extra mile for her."

"The extra mile?" he said with disgust. "That's rich. Do you really think I wouldn't do everything within my power to find her attacker?"

"Sure you would," I said, patronizingly. "You investigate it, and I'll report it. Have your secretary, Elsie, feed me the daily updates, same as she does for all the papers."

"Fine," he said, "if things change, and we need your help, I'll let you know."

"Nuh-uh," I said, "you've made yourself perfectly clear. Chuck and Ernie are in. I'm out. No way I'm getting mixed up in your case. My days of playing Jessica Fletcher to your Amos Tupper are over. Kaput. *Fini*. Done."

4

I ARRIVED BACK HOME a little past 4:00 a.m. and flopped into bed. My alarm buzzed a whole three hours and thirty minutes later, and I dragged myself into the shower. By rote, I donned work clothes befitting an editor—an ankle-length, gray wool skirt, matching blazer and peach-colored shell—rouged my cheeks, brushed and finger-styled my hair, and downed my usual nutritious breakfast—a strong cup of joe, black, of course, and a Sara Lee blueberry muffin nuked to tongue-scorching perfection. Customarily, on workdays, I march through the *Gazette*'s front door at nine o'clock on the nose. But that morning, there was a stop I needed to make first.

Cruising past Gertie's house, I scanned the street in both directions, studying the vehicles parked along the curb. Most of the vehicles—modest economy cars, SUVs, vans, and, yes, a couple of pickup trucks, although small and dark—occupied driveways, leaving the street essentially deserted, except for a dark blue Crown Victoria parked curbside a couple doors north of Gertie's. Unlike the other cars, the Crown Vic was immaculate, and its glass was tinted an impenetrable, smoky gray. That could have meant nothing, but it was worth noting. I checked the windows of the surrounding houses. In light of what had happened to Gertie, I figured her neighbors would step up their vigilance. I half-expected Verlin and his A-team, Chuck and Ernie, to be there mopping up. But I saw no sign of life anywhere. I glanced at my watch. It was eight thirty. Verl and his boys might be off having breakfast, and they could return any minute. I had no time to dillydally.

I parked Nellie at the end of the block and hiked down the alley to Gertie's back door. As Verlin mentioned at the hospital, the house was wrapped in crime-scene tape. I imagined him racing in circles around the place two, three times, growing dizzy as he gleefully tied it up like a Christmas present. To further deter prowlers—like me, I suppose—he had strung extra layers of tape across the patio, securing it around the wrought-iron posts at either end. Undeterred, I ducked under the yellow streamers and shuffled up the steps to the door, onto which a sheet of plywood was nailed to conceal the broken window. I gave the doorknob a twist, but it was locked. Reaching into my purse, I grabbed my laminated press pass and slid it into the crack between the door and the jamb. I jiggled the card around as I pushed the door, and with little effort, the spring lock popped, and the door opened. I stepped into the utility room, where I tuned my ears for aberrant noise. The furnace kicked on, a clock ticked, and the refrigerator whirred. Otherwise, the house was quiet.

I flashed back to my encounter with Gertie's assailant. I'd been ambushed and knocked off-balance in that very spot, and my mace had flown from my grip. Based on the dynamics of the fight and the room's layout, I calculated the possible flight patterns.

A white Maytag washer and dryer took up most of the space, and beside them was a metal shelving unit which bore an assortment of cleaning products and supplies—sprays, solutions, powders, rags, sponges, and a bright pink feather duster that looked like it had seen better days. The room was out of plumb, the floor slanting downhill away from the house.

I dropped to my hands and knees and crawled to the supply cabinet. I inserted my hand into the narrow space below the bottom shelf and let my fingers do the walking. Surprisingly, what they first walked through felt like . . . dust balls? *Surely not*, I thought, *not here at housekeeper extraordinaire Gertie Tyroo's*. I doubled over for a look under the shelf and couldn't believe what I found hiding there: dust bunnies and dead bodies—petrified moths, flies, a cricket, and a couple of ladybugs. Beyond them was a small, metal cylinder. Eureka! It was my mace. I deposited the can in my coat pocket, stood, and pulled a pair of white cotton gloves from my handbag. Typically, they were reserved for my secret bedtime beauty regimen for which I've never revealed details, other than to say it involves petroleum jelly, a versatile product for which I have found many interesting uses.

I slipped the gloves on and proceeded to Gertie's kitchen: simple, dark wood cabinets above and below the counter, cracked brown-and-tan linoleum floor tiles arranged in a checkerboard pattern, and a chrome-and-red Formica dinette suite straight out of June and Ward Cleaver's TV Land home. I sniffed the air. It was filled with a musty perfume scent that I call "eau de old lady." The day I noticed "eau de old lady" wafting from my own pores would be the day I stripped naked and marinated in a tub of Febreze for as long as it took. Besides the old lady smell, I detected a combination of what I figured was a pine-scented cleaner and—did I dare even imagine?—Stetson men's cologne? It couldn't be, could it? Then again, Gertie was full of surprises.

Her words from the night before replayed in my head: "Listen up. A few days ago, while I was cleaning at one of my clients' houses, I found something I thought might be tied to that old Potts case, and after going back today, I'm positive." That sparked so many questions. Whose houses had she cleaned Monday? Of those, which one contained the clue to the boy's disappearance, and what exactly could that clue have been? I wondered if the linchpin to my questions rested in Gertie's appointment calendar.

Oddly, in the years I had known Gertie, this was only the second time I had been inside her home. As I had the night before, I felt I was treading on sacred ground. Nevertheless, I dove in, pawing through cabinets, drawers, closets, canisters, coffee cans, the cookie jar, and even the wastebasket, with all the stealth of a master cat burglar in search of priceless jewels. I uncovered no valuables, nor the calendar, anywhere in the kitchen, but I had a hunch the calendar did not occupy a logical place anyway. Knowing Gertie, she had stashed it somewhere unconventional—perhaps in the freezer, or sewn inside the sofa, or even somewhere as distasteful as the toilet tank. The only thing predictable about Gertie Tyroo was her unpredictability.

Finding only food in the freezer, I moved on to the living room. It was still a shambles and looked even worse in the daylight. The intruder had been looking for something, but I couldn't tell if he had found it.

I was fascinated by the eight floor-to-ceiling bookcases that lined the walls and lent the room the feel of a public library. I stepped carefully through the small mountain range of books that cluttered the floor, pausing here and there to read some of the covers. The predominant theme provided a glimpse into a fascinating, unexpected dimension of my old friend: she was a conspiracy-theory buff.

She had literally scores of books with titles ranging from *Apollo 11: The Hoax* to *The Mothman Prophecies* to *Sasquatch Walks Among Us*. Someday, after Gertie regained consciousness and was well out of danger, I would ask her about her odd obsession. Perhaps she could fill me in on Area 51 or explain what really happened to Amelia Earhart. Or better still, maybe she could tell me some stories of her own. As much fun as it would be to delve further into Gertie's reading material, I had a job to do. I wanted that appointment calendar.

I took two small steps to the sofa, where I went down on all fours, stretched out flat and probed its underbelly. *Ah-hah!* As I'd hoped, I found a tear in the lining. I plunged my hand through the opening and felt . . . springs, tightly coiled springs. Nothing else. *Nuts!* I'd been so certain I'd find Gertie's appointment calendar covertly stashed in an unlikely hiding place. Perhaps I'd have better luck in the toilet tank, but that notion went spiraling down the drain when the toilet flushed. *Oh, crap!* Someone was in the bathroom and apparently his or her business was done. My heart rate spiked. Was it Ernie? Was it Chuck? Had Gertie's assailant returned? I heard more water rush through pipes, followed by the creak of squeaky hinges and the flip of a light switch. Soft footsteps brushed across Gertie's flocked carpet. They headed my way.

5

THE CYLINDER OF MACE IN MY COAT POCKET again seemed woefully insufficient against the threat of actual peril. I pushed myself up on my knees and scanned the chaos around me for a potential weapon—a lamp, a vase, an ashtray—anything I could hurl at the approaching danger and inflict pain, or at least buy me enough time to sprint off to safety. The hallway was short; the footsteps were very near. I grabbed the hefty "A" volume of the Encyclopedia Britannica off the floor. Grasping it with both hands, I hunkered down, using the sofa for cover.

A pair of expensive-looking leather loafers swept before me, eliminating all of Elmwood's law enforcement officers as suspects. I'd never seen any of their feet adorned in anything but your basic, no-frills work shoes. In the same instant the trespasser was passing, I let him have it with all I had, walloping his left shin with the ten-pound tome and driving one of its corners into his kneecap. He shrieked like a frightened chimpanzee and keeled over, cupping his left knee in his hands as he went down. The look on his face as it slammed into the floor revealed shock and confusion. It told me that he knew he was toast. I scrambled to my feet and positioned my makeshift weapon over my right shoulder like a baseball bat.

"Who are you?" I demanded. "And what are you doing here?"

He glared at me. Dressed in neat tan slacks and a tailored navy-blue blazer over a white shirt and maroon tie, he didn't look anything like a burglar was supposed to. He actually looked sort of nice. In fact, he looked barely old enough to shave. The young man twisted his gangly body upward to a half-sitting, half-crouching pretzel pose. "Quigley," he said. "And, frankly, I'd like to ask you the same question."

I took several steps back, injecting several feet of breathing room between me and this Quigley fellow. Although I didn't have to answer his question, I did. "The name's Crystal Cropper. I'm Gertie's friend. Who are you?"

"A relative," he said.

"Ah, yes," I said, "you must be the nephew Gertie speaks of so frequently."

Quigley's mouth stretched into a satisfied grin. "Yes, that's right. She's my aunt."

"You her sister's kid, or her brother's?"

His answer was swift and easy. "Her brother's."

I jammed my right hand into my coat pocket. "Wrong answer. Gertie's an only child." I wrapped my fingers around my cylinder of mace and said, "Let's try it again—who are you?"

The young man's eyes shifted down to my pocket. Raising his hands, he said, "Ma'am, please don't shoot." His voice's timbre was flat and controlled. "I am going to reach into my inside breast pocket for my ID. It will prove who I am."

Actually, I hadn't intended to give the impression that I carried a weapon, but Quigley's assumption gave me welcome leverage and an unexpected sense of power. Which was fun. "Okay," I said, "but slowly."

He eased his right hand under his left lapel and extracted a black, wallet-sized folder, which he flipped open to display a badge and photo identification card.

I shook my head. "Look," I said, "my eyes are at least twice as old as you are. If you honestly expect me to read that thing, you're going to have to either enlarge it to movie-poster size or hand it to me."

He gave the wallet a gentle fling. I snatched it from the air and flipped it open. "That's better," I said. The ID bore the young man's mug shot and name. Assuming it was genuine, I was speaking with Special Agent Harold Quigley of the Indianapolis office of the Federal Bureau of . . . I stopped, did a double take, and squinted harder at the words. They still read "Federal Bureau of Investigation." I swear my heart did a somersault and my knees buckled. This young whippersnapper was with the FBI? My head grew light at the mere thought. If it were true, then Gertie's outrageous assertions that her phone line was tapped and her house was bugged might not have been so dotty after all.

"Looks good to me," I said, keeping my bewilderment to myself, and tossed the wallet back to him. "How'd you get in?"

"I've got a key to the front door. How'd *you* get in?"

"I've got a press pass. You packing?"

"Yes, ma'am."

"Show me."

Agent Quigley nibbled at the inside of his lower lip. His eyes darted about the room. He let a moment tick past before he spoke. "Ma'am, you show me yours, and I'll show you mine."

I couldn't help but smile. "Why don't you unfurl yourself

from that silly position and take a seat," I said, withdrawing my hand from my pocket and slipping off my white gloves. When Quigley stood, I was dismayed by how much he towered over me. He could have overtaken me easily. Instead, he obligingly moved toward the easy chair I motioned to. "Agent Quigley, we need to talk."

6

HAROLD QUIGLEY EASED ONTO THE BURGUNDY-COLORED ARMCHAIR, and I sank into the center of the matching sofa across from him. His torso erect, he rested his right ankle atop his left knee and jiggled his dangling foot like a cocktail shaker. Picking a speck of dark lint from the cuff of his slacks, he rolled it into a tiny ball and looked around. With the absence of an appropriate receptacle, he inserted the orb of lint into the pocket of his blazer. He caught me staring and blinked several times. "So?" he said, drawing out the syllable into what sounded like a question.

"Tell me something," I said. "You typically scream when a woman takes you by surprise?"

"No, ma'am, I don't," he said, his right foot abruptly inanimate. "And I'd appreciate it if you wouldn't mention what happened here to anyone."

I felt a smile coming on but reshaped it into a compassionate pout. After a moment, I stopped pouting and said, "Why don't you tell me why the FBI is interested in Gertie."

Quigley's response was immediate. "I can't do that."

"Why not?"

"That information is classified."

"Classified," I repeated, feeling a bit baffled but revealing none of it. However, there was one way to crack this nut, and I held the hammer. "Well, then, suit yourself. But it sure looks like I've got me one heck of an editorial going into tomorrow's paper."

I thought I detected a faint shudder course through Harold's body before he said, "Oh. You're *that* Crystal Cropper."

"There's more than one?"

He didn't answer. I leaned forward and stared hard at him, hoping I could further dislodge some of his crumbling agency brass. "So, are you going to tell me why a sweet old lady like Gertie Tyroo merits the attention of the FBI?"

"We're not investigating her," he said. "We're keeping an eye on her."

It was an intriguing notion, but it sounded like BS to me. I allowed a beat to pass and said, "Go on. Tell me what's so interesting about an eighty-year-old cleaning woman."

"Ma'am," Harold ran a finger under his white collar and stretched it forward. "I really can't divul—"

"Can't divulge why you're snooping around an elderly woman's bathroom?" I huffed a humorless little laugh to simulate contempt. "Surely you're not going to tell me the United States government has sent in its spies to steal a secret bathroom-cleanser formula."

"Of course not," the agent snapped. "It's far more complicated than that."

"Then you better *un*complicate it for me, or need I remind you I'll have me one heck of—"

"I know," Harold said. "One heck of an editorial for

tomorrow's paper."

"You bet your bippy," I said, imagining the fun I would have at my keyboard if this crazy situation were to escalate: "US security tightened Tuesday, the day after an alleged terrorist broke into the home of Gertie Tyroo, the country's most technologically savvy cleaning lady, and bashed in her skull. Although the FBI's not talking, the *Gazette* has learned that the attempted killer was after Tyroo's secret formula for ScrubbyBare, the missing compound essential for disinfecting nuclear warheads . . ."

"She's one of ours," Harold said in a near whisper.

I leaned forward. Surely I had misunderstood. "What did you say?"

"Gertie Tyroo is one of ours."

"You can't mean, 'one of ours' as in 'one of our secret agents?' " I said, feeling my demeanor of cool superiority thaw like a scoop of Ben & Jerry's Jamaican Me Crazy sorbet impaled on a broiling-hot rotisserie spit.

"One of our undercover agents?" Harold snorted a laugh. "Gertie Tyroo—a secret FBI agent?" He snorted again. And again. "Not quite."

"Well, then," I said, my impatience growing, "how do you know her?"

"She was a secretary," he said. "As in one who types letters, files reports, makes coffee for her superiors."

"A secretary?" That was actually harder for me to imagine than her being a secret agent.

"Yeah," he said with another snort, "for our Indianapolis office. About a hundred years ago. Before computers and way before Starbucks. All the agents loved her. They called her their *Aunt* Gertie, and she called them her nephews. Then she had some sort of accident. I can't say what it was, but it left her a little . . ." Harold grimaced. "Well, you know how she is. When she left, J. Edgar himself promised her that the bureau would always be there for her. The agents have been taking turns checking up on her ever since. It's part of our job description—the unwritten part. This is my week for Gertie detail, and that's all I know."

"Holy cow," I said, clutching my heart. "That may be the single most touching story I've ever heard."

I hadn't believed a word of it. I was confident I could squeeze the truth out of him, but I didn't have the time. The deadline for the day's paper was looming, and I needed to scoot. When I glanced at my wristwatch, my eye was drawn to the encyclopedia I'd used to bring down Quigley. It was lying on the floor exactly where I'd dropped it, but the impact had shaken lose a corner of a softbound booklet that had been tucked inside. I could read just a portion of the hidden book's title, "tment Calendar." I had to marvel at Gertie's cleverness for hiding her appointment calendar inside the encyclopedia's "A" volume. She was good. In my head, I danced a jig, but quickly realized the energy would be better spent figuring out a way to sneak Gertie's appointment book out of the house without raising Quigley's suspicion.

Maintaining my composure, I said, "I wish we could continue our little chat, but unfortunately I've got a deadline to meet."

Quigley offered a trite grin and stood. "Okay then, can I walk you to your car?" He seemed pretty eager.

"That's not necessary," I said, reaching into my jacket pockets and fishing around. "But would you check the kitchen counter for me? I think I left my car keys there."

Quigley strode into the kitchen, and I dove for the appointment calendar. Tucking it into the waistband of the back of my skirt, I sang out, "Oh, here they are." I plucked the keys from my handbag and dangled them from my raised hand. "Silly me. I had them all along."

I wasted no time in slipping past him and getting out of there. I was certain it wouldn't be my last encounter with the fidgety, young special agent. My only hope was that the next time, I would be ready for him.

• • • •

Five minutes later, I started Nellie's engine and rolled out of Gertie's neighborhood at an inconspicuous twenty miles per hour. I drove two blocks and turned onto Columbia Avenue and began to flip through the calendar's pages, many bearing Gertie's comments about various people she worked for. "Hoarder," "smells like sewer gas," "hides sex toys in freezer," "moldy toilet," "cheapskate," and on and on. I fanned the pages until I came to Monday, March 3—yesterday. She had made two notations: "Grady Markle, time to clean drawers," and "Baxters—K to confirm." Grady was a harmless old coot who had lived in Elmwood forever. Everybody knew him. Kathryn Baxter's presence in Elmwood was no less well-known than Grady's, although she deserved a far less endearing term than "harmless old coot." And that's when it hit me—someone living in my hometown, perhaps someone I was acquainted with, might be capable of cold-blooded murder.

7

"GOOD AFTERNOON, CRYSTAL." The biting salutation came from my twenty-one-year-old production assistant, Darcy Abbott, seated at her tidy desk. Her red-tipped fingers were flying across her computer keyboard, and she gestured to the wall clock with her chin. "Glad to see you could make it. For you to be draggin' in here almost an hour late, it must've been a humdinger of a party last night."

We both understood the caustic tone of our relationship was played purely for giggles. But this morning, I was in no mood for the sarcasm.

"What have we got for today's paper?" I grumbled, stopping momentarily to thumb through the mail. I hoped to find nothing that couldn't hold until after our noon deadline.

"First, you might want to look at these," Darcy said, slapping a stack of "While You Were Out" messages and printed copies of emails into my hand as the phone started to ring.

Elmwood, like most communities, was continually mired in a love-hate relationship with its newspaper. That was especially true for a paper like the *Gazette*, which operated on a shoestring with an absentee publisher and a regular staff of three. Besides me, the trio included advertising salesman Leo Byrne, who logged few in-house hours, conducting most of his busy work on his clients' home turf, and Darcy. Despite her appalling lack of common sense, she was a resourceful young woman who was not only adept at cranking out editorial copy, but also tracking circulation, keeping the books, fielding calls and emails, and designing pages like a Rembrandt apprentice. Most impressive, however, was her uncanny ability to stay out of my way while she simultaneously kept one step ahead. I was still holding out hope that her brains would one day catch up with her business skills.

Darcy answered the phone, and I read the messages, around a dozen of them. They all appeared to be from readers registering their approval or disapproval, depending on their political sway, of Monday's editorial calling for the resignation of the mayor, Richard "Don't-You-Dare-Call-Me-Dick" Head. My editorial added fuel to our front-page story exposing him as an underhanded, corrupt buffoon.

Thanks mainly to Gertie's tips and a few bold city employees willing to talk on the record, we reported that in the five years since Elmwood voters first elected him to the office, the mayor's questionable alliances and overspending had reaped him enough dirty money to buy a small island. Our story also revealed that the county prosecutor had recently launched an investigation, which was about to wrap, and an arrest warrant surely couldn't be far behind. Mayor Head was only in the first year of his second term, and his flagrant misuse of public funds—and worse, its trust—had plunged him into deep you-know-what. I felt there was no reason to drag the good citizens of Elmwood through an expensive trial, and so I used the editorial platform to demand his immediate resignation. But, judging from the phone messages, apparently not all the good people of Elmwood saw things my way. Many of them were demanding *my* resignation.

Darcy hung up the telephone, scratched out a message, laid it across my palm, and resumed her typing. The call was from another pissed-off reader.

"As for today's paper," Darcy said, "the school board decided last night to declare Friday 'Jack Baxter Day' and will suspend classes at two o'clock for an assembly in his honor."

"Make sure that gets on page one," I said, "and pull a file photo of Baxter to go with it. Any word yet on who the keynoter will be for his dinner Saturday night?"

Jack Baxter, Elmwood's long-retired, near-legendary high school football coach, would be inducted into the Indiana High School Football Coaches Hall of Fame at a big shindig Saturday night in the high school gymnasium. A late-morning parade would kick off the day's festivities, including a street fair and flea market, which the town hoped would attract several thousand visitors. Our chamber of commerce had teamed up with the hall of fame folks to organize the dinner. My friend and chamber director Shay Nichols promised it would be the event of the century. Oddly, though, the organizing committee had been so tight-lipped about the identity of the dinner's keynote speaker that even Shay could only speculate. She figured the speech would be delivered by no one more interesting than some football has-been or washed-up politician.

"I called Shay again," Darcy said, "but she insists the organizers still won't tell her."

"Well, they're clearly not rushing on my account," I said. "Who doesn't want to write a fifty-inch preview story at the last minute? It's only four nights away." I knew I was whining. But darn it, writers didn't just whip these gems up out of thin air. "Aside from that, is there anything I need to know?"

Darcy stopped typing and made eye contact with me. "There are a couple things. Mayor Head called twice, screaming about yesterday's story and editorial. I'm paraphrasing, but he would appreciate hearing from you at your earliest convenience."

The muscles in my shoulders tightened. The call was not unexpected. "What's the other thing?" I asked.

"There was an incident last night involving an attack on an elderly woman in her home. It was that batty cleaning woman you see all over town."

"You don't say?" I said nonchalantly. "Gertie Tyroo?"

"Yes, and from the sound of it, she was hurt pretty bad. Somebody broke in and turned the house upside down looking for something—probably money—and when Miss Tyroo surprised the guy, he shot her, pistol-whipped her senseless, and stabbed her twenty-seven times."

The rumor mill in this town seemed to be cranked up to its maximum today. "Oh my," I said, raising my brows to exhibit a sense of horror, "that's awful."

"Uh-huh, but wait 'til you hear this. Even though she about bled to death, when the ambulance got there, she cussed out the Minnear twins and tried to chase them away."

"Are you serious?"

"Yep. And once they got her to the hospital, she ran up and down the hall screaming like her hair was on fire. So the doctors had to put her in a medically induced coma before they could treat her."

"Who told you all this?" I said.

"My neighbor works in housekeeping at the hospital, and she

heard it from one of the cooks."

"Talk about reliable sources," I said, my sarcasm eluding Darcy. "Good job."

"Thanks. I called the sheriff's office and asked them to fax over the report. Soon as it comes in, I'll contact a few more sources and write it up."

"That's not necessary, Darcy." I moved past her desk and headed for my office. "I'll take care of it."

"Okay," Darcy said, "I'm almost done with the page-one layout. I'll save a spot. You want that story above the fold or below?"

"Neither," I said, shimmying out of my coat and looping it over a hook on the cloak rack. Out of deference to my good friend's privacy, I would sit on the details of Gertie's story. At least for a little while. "Just list it with the police blotter news as an unlawful entry."

"But, Crys—"

"Just bring me that fax when it comes in," I said. "Please. And see what clips we have on file concerning the old Potts case."

"The old *whats* case?"

"A seventeen-year-old boy named Eugene Potts," I said. "He left home one morning back in 1993 and was never heard from again."

8

I STEPPED INTO MY OFFICE, my modest little sanctuary, which I had perhaps over-decorated with cherished photos and other reminders of my achievements, adventures, and former alliances. I closed the door and eased into my executive desk chair, my one extravagance. I scanned my desk and groaned. It was a shameful mess, cluttered with stack upon stack of paper work, most of it untouched for months and possibly longer.

I unlocked my left bottom drawer, where I kept my confidential records, and slid it open. All the tips Gertie Tyroo had supplied me were filed in a manila folder I'd cleverly labeled "GT on the QT."

Leafing through the pages, I was reminded how valuable an asset Gertie had become to me over my years with the *Gazette*. Remarkably, every claim she made concerning trusted Elmwood leaders' unorthodox behavior had panned out. Although a good portion of it wasn't actually illegal and thus not fitting fodder for full-fledged public vetting by the *Gazette*, I had been able to develop a good number of her tips into major stories. A few even resulted in prosecution of the guilty party and restitution for the town. Such victories were a source of pride for a hometown girl, one who found she still needed to prove herself, even so late in life.

I'd always been a late bloomer and didn't become a journalist until I was well into my thirties. I'd gotten myself into a bit of trouble during my senior year of high school. The situation was temporary, about nine months, but the timing made it impossible for me to make a natural progression to college. I didn't care anyway. Back then, women weren't encouraged to continue their education since there were plenty of men looking for a wife or a secretary—code words, in my estimation, for "nursemaid" and "arm candy." With college off the table, I weighed my options and moved to Southern California, where I dove into a Hollywood movie studio typing pool. I splashed around for about a dozen years, going nowhere, before I decided to try my hand at newspapering. That's when I found my niche as a crime beat reporter. Chasing down stories became my life, leaving no time for socializing and certainly no time for men. But that was okay. My work and my identity were inseparable, and I loved it. Unfortunately, as an only child, I was compelled to return to Elmwood in the mid 2000s to care for my aging parents. Mom passed first, and Dad followed her a few months later. Coincidentally, when he died, the *Gazette* was looking to hire an editor. It was a good fit. And it still was, even nine years later. Despite having reached the age where most people traded their career for a rocking chair, I was better than ever and still going strong.

About two months after I stepped into the editor's slot, Gertie phoned to alert me about the town's treasurer who, she claimed, was cooking the books and pocketing thousands of local tax dollars. With my *Gazette* tenure in its infancy, I was not in a good position to start shaking trees for bad apples. But I did it anyway. Surprisingly, with little effort, I convinced a state auditor to come in and sniff around. Turned out, Gertie was spot-on, and the *Gazette's* stories under my byline resulted in the treasurer's firing and her subsequent sabbatical at the Indiana Women's Prison.

Fortified by that success, Gertie fed me tidbits of intelligence on a fairly regular basis, maybe every two or three months, outing more perpetrators of costly or morally corrupt injustices against the community.

The crimes, scams, and schemes the *Gazette* unveiled over the years, thanks to Gertie, read almost like a season of *Law and Order*, and as I thumbed through my notes, I was reminded of some of our peachiest page-one disclosures. Like the time we garnered a bit of national prominence over our coverage of Ned Friendly, the Elmwood doctor who scammed his weight-loss patients with pricey injections of what turned out to be frog urine. After the state stripped him of his license to practice medicine, he moved on to New York, where he became the personal physician to an aging, overweight rock star, who made international headlines when she mysteriously croaked in her sleep.

Although less titillating, the *Gazette* scored beaucoup points with readers when it reported that a former city councilman's brother—Elmwood's animal control officer—routinely picked up dogs, even the tagged ones, and sold them to an out-of-state pharmaceutical company for experimentation. Readers praised us when we outed despicable practices by local businesses, like the used-car dealer caught turning back the odometers on his inventory, and the all-you-can-eat buffet that recycled its garbage back on the serving table. The public service the paper provided our community built trust with our readers and bolstered my pride in journalism. I believed the purpose of any newspaper was to be the public's watchdog, to keep an eye on its officials—elected, appointed, and salaried—to keep them in line, accountable, and beholden to their electorate. Nowhere were the effects of that purpose more gratifying and more appreciated than at the grassroots level.

Whenever I asked Gertie how on earth she stumbled upon her tasty morsels of inside poop, she would say that it was none of my beeswax. She was conscientious, she had never been wrong, and that was good enough for me. In return, I protected her by keeping my lips sealed and my files locked. Obviously, if Gertie's name had leaked out as the source behind these explosive exposés, any of the subjects could have had it in for her. But call me naïve. I could not imagine any of them being capable of murder.

The instant I reinserted my "GT on the QT" file into its slot in the drawer, my phone rang. Its sudden, abrasive peal ripped through my concentration like a serrated utility knife, spurring me to jump three inches in my chair. I yanked the receiver off the cradle and huffed a blistering "What?" into the mouthpiece.

"I hope you've got yourself a good security system because I'm fixin' to bust your bubble."

Oh, joy. It was the mayor, and as a bonus, he was yelling.

"Oh, hi . . . *Dick*," I said, confident that addressing him with the detested four-letter nickname would make his blood boil. "How lovely of you to call."

There was a pause. I swear I could hear his pulse pounding. Then he snarled, "Listen, you old biddy—"

Old biddy? Gee, that really hurt. It hurt so much, I almost forgot the pain in my butt from last night.

"—you been nothing but trouble to this town since you took over that rag, but by the time I'm done with you . . . darlin' . . .

you're gonna wish you never came back. In fact, you're gonna wish you was never borned."

"Goodness, *Dick*, that almost sounds like a threat." I was starting to enjoy myself. Baiting oafs was a sport at which I excelled. "You're not threatening me, are you . . . *Dick*?"

"Let me put it this way . . . witch . . . you better watch your back."

And then the line went still.

"Dick?" I said. "Dick?" But the connection was dead. And it sounded like if I didn't take Mayor Dick Head's threat seriously, I might be dead too. Sooner than I'd expected.

9

DARCY TOSSED A BULGING FOLDER ON MY DESK. It was labeled "Whitfield and Potts, 1993" and contained clips of Lance Whitfield, a seventeen-year-old quarterback who died of heatstroke during football practice, and his classmate, Eugene Potts, who vanished shortly after.

"I hope this is it," Darcy said. "I had to dig through a bunch of boxes in the basement, and I don't intend to go back. It's nasty down there—silverfish and spider webs. Gross."

"Thanks," I told her. "This looks like what I need."

"What's up with this anyway?" she asked, ever one to nose around in places she had no business.

"Oh, not much." I dumped out the clips and spread them across my desk. "I thought we might do a retrospective. You know, rehash the cases and see if there's anything new." I flashed Darcy my warmest smile. "Don't forget to watch for the fax from the sheriff's office."

Darcy nodded and pulled the door shut behind her as she exited. The moment the latch clicked, I dove into the stories, separating them into two piles—one for Whitfield, one for Potts.

When that was done, I sorted each stack chronologically.

Back in '93, when the double tragedy took place, I was a hard-working reporter for the *Daily News of Los Angeles*. Though my father had been religious about keeping me up to date on local news, I was absorbed in building my career. Back then, the goings-on in my hometown were of little interest to me. But sitting there in my office some twenty years later, my interest was piqued. I leafed through the old clips, reading them with fresh eyes, looking for unanswered questions and inconsistencies in the reporting.

The first *Gazette* article, dated Saturday, August 7, 1993, had been that day's top story beneath a five-column banner headline that read, "EHS Quarterback Collapses During Practice, Later Dies." Accompanying the story was a mug shot of a smiling, tousle-haired young man sporting thick, black, non-reflective streaks under each eye. The photo was captioned simply, "Whitfield."

The story read:

Elmwood High School quarterback Lance Whitfield, 17, died Friday night at Elmwood Memorial Hospital. His death occurred just eight hours after he collapsed during football practice at the school.

At the boy's bedside were his parents, Frank and Tammy Whitfield, and Coach Jack Baxter. Whitfield never regained consciousness.

An ambulance was called to the school at 2:10 p.m., according to the Sheriff's emergency dispatch records. Medic Rob Greenwich said that when he arrived, he found Whitfield lying on his back on the ground. The boy was unresponsive, and his vital signs were unstable, he said.

"We recognized the severity of the situation and didn't spend much time at the scene," Greenwich said. "I worked on him en route to the hospital and did get a pulse, but it was pretty weak."

Baxter told Elm County Deputy Sheriff Verlin Wallace that after a short break, Whitfield had walked onto the football field, where he fell to the ground without warning and began to convulse.

"At the time Whitfield collapsed, the team had been practicing for roughly an hour in full uniform," Wallace said, "complete with pads and headgear."

However, because the afternoon temperature had exceeded ninety degrees, the boys were reminded to watch for signs of overheating and given frequent water breaks, he added. At press time Friday night, Elm County Coroner Ed McBain was uncertain to what extent the heat was a factor in Whitfield's death. That likely would be determined following an autopsy and toxicology study by the state, he said.

The Gazette's repeated attempts to reach Baxter for comment were unsuccessful.

"The coach is very, very upset," Wallace said. "This is a very tight-knit community, and I would hope the Gazette might show some compassion and restraint in its effort to sell newspapers."

I sneered at that last remark. No small-town paper writes about tragedies in hopes of selling more papers. Rather, it is particularly sensitive to tragedies involving local citizens. Verlin had mellowed over the years, but he was a bit of a blowhard back then.

I shuffled through several more of the clips chronicling the Whitfield story as it developed over the next several days. Most were predictable: the obituary, reactions of classmates, reactions of neighbors, faculty, school officials, and city officials, followed by sidebars listing warning signs of heatstroke and other problems associated with overheating. Among the more interesting stories was the August 11 report on the autopsy results.

"Heatstroke Caused Student's Death, but Drug a Factor," the headline read. It was followed by the story.

A report from the Indiana Medical Examiner's Office confirms that a significant amount of the drug pseudoephedrine was present in Lance Whitfield's body and contributed to his August 6 heatstroke death. The 17-year-old boy collapsed during afternoon football practice at Elmwood High School, where he was a senior.

The story continued, pointing out that pseudoephedrine was a common ingredient in several popular over-the-counter decongestants, according to Ned Friendly.

"Well, well," I muttered under my breath, "if it isn't our old frog-urine diet doctor again." Interesting that the reporter had used Friendly the quack as an expert source to explain how the decongestant could have hastened Whitfield's death by causing his body to rapidly dehydrate.

The drug inhibits the ability to sweat and increases the heart rate, Friendly said. It's been known in the medical community for a long time that, under the right conditions, pseudoephedrine can spell disaster, as it did for the Whitfield boy. Unfortunately, that information has been slow to reach consumers.

Funny, I thought. The same could have been said about Friendly.

The next clips described Whitfield's funeral on Thursday, August 12, held in the high school gymnasium rather than Markle's Mortuary, which was too small to accommodate the unprecedented number of mourners. The last clip focused on Elmwood's sterling gridiron season that year. How the community could even think of continuing its football program after losing a player in the manner it did was beyond me. But it had, and the team had gone on to capture the '93 state championship, dedicating the victory to the memory of their fallen quarterback. How very noble.

10

MY DESK PHONE—one of those old-fashioned jobs that didn't tell time, snap a picture, play Beethoven's Fifth, send or receive text messages, calculate my income taxes, take my temperature, measure my cholesterol, or display the Dow Jones average—rang. Regretting that I hadn't asked Darcy to hold my calls, I grabbed the receiver and snapped, "What?"

"Hey, pal, if this is a bad time, I can call back." It was one of my best buddies, Auggie Stillwater, the county's longest-serving superior court judge, an elected position she had held since 1991. Auggie had an uncanny gift for reading my moods based on the most insignificant piece of evidence.

"Don't you dare," I said. "What's shaking?"

"Hey, I just heard about Gert. Is she going to be okay?"

"Too soon to tell," I said. "We need to give her at least a couple days. How'd you find out?"

Auggie chuckled softly. "This is Elmwood. 'Nuff said?"

" 'Nuff said," I conceded.

"So who'd our illustrious sheriff assign to the case?"

"I told him to call in the forensics specialists from Indy," I said. "But I think he's sticking with the local crew. I might poke around and see what I can dig up myself."

Auggie sighed. "You don't need to get mixed up in solving crimes. I know you think of yourself as the female Philip Marlowe reincarnate, but—"

"*Stop,*" I said. "I'm not getting mixed up in anything, just doing my due diligence as Elmwood's leading news source. Who's got time for crime busting when there's a daily paper to run? So kindly get off my back and tend to your own business. Go release a couple drug dealers back onto the street."

I waited an agonizingly long moment for a response, but from Auggie's end of the connection came only silence.

"Okay," I said, "I'm sorry. That last dig was completely unnecessary."

"Kiddo," she said, "I know you, and I know you want to help. Gert's a keeper, and a lot of people care about her. But there are plenty who care about you, too. You need to watch out for Crystal and let Verlin handle the lawbreakers. It's why we pay him the big bucks."

Auggie had a heart of pure gold, and I understood her concern was genuine. However, someone had tried to kill Gertie, and I couldn't let that kind of behavior slide.

"Thanks, Auggie. I'll remember that."

"Cool beans." I could hear the smile in her tone. "You know I'm right."

"You're the judge," I said. "Thanks for the call. And the two cents."

"Hey," she said, her tone lifting, "I'll see you tonight."

I banged my forehead with the butt of my hand. Tonight! I'd forgotten it was Tuesday, my bowling night with the girls. "Who're we up against?"

"The Queen Pins," she answered with a grunt.

"Don't worry," I said. "We'll slaughter 'em."

"Slow and painfully," she said. There was that smile again. "See you later, and keep your nose clean."

I returned to the stack of clips and unfolded the first one in the Potts pile. Dated Saturday, August 14, it reported that Eugene Potts had gone missing Thursday, the day of the Whitfield boy's funeral, and the police were looking for him in earnest.

The story read:

Police are seeking information concerning the whereabouts of 17-year-old Eugene Potts of Elmwood.

"No one has seen Eugene Potts since around noon Thursday," Elm County Deputy Sheriff Verlin Wallace told the Gazette. *"The boy's parents are totally at a loss as to his whereabouts."*

The boy's parents, Ray and Noni Potts, as well as school officials and friends, were unable to provide any clues as to where Potts might be.

The Elmwood community is still stunned from the August 6 death of 17-year-old Elmwood High School quarterback Lance Whitfield, who died a few hours after collapsing on the football field during practice. An autopsy revealed the death was due to an excess of the over-the-counter decongestant, Mucxyphed.

Potts is manager of the football team and witnessed Whitfield's collapse, and officials are contemplating whether Potts's disappearance is connected to the Whitfield death.

"We haven't yet determined whether there's a connection," Wallace said, "but there is no denying the sad coincidence."

Coincidence indeed. If there was one thing I'd learned, it was this: if something sinister could be easily dismissed as a coincidence, then it probably wasn't one.

Subsequent articles provided no new information, only a

rehash of the boy's initial disappearance and baseless speculation.

"Law enforcement officers are clueless," said Ray Potts, Eugene's father, in the *Gazette*'s August 6, 2003, anniversary piece. "They still think our boy is guilty of murder, and all his mother and I know is, we want him back. Please, if anybody has any information about Eugene, let us know."

It was another heartbreaking tragedy, which, for me, sparked two very crucial unanswered questions: What happened to the boy? And what had Gertie stumbled upon that may have provided the answer?

I gathered the newspaper clips into a neat stack, and as I stuffed them back into the file folder, an inch-long centipede slithered out and tore across my desk. I thought of Gertie's warning the night before about my office being bugged. It almost made me laugh. Plucking a tissue from the box on my credenza, I gently captured the critter inside one of the wads. I crossed the room, slid open the window, and released my new hundred-legged friend to the great outdoors. While I stood there, I looked out past the *Gazette*'s back door, just twenty-six steps from the back entrance to the sheriff's office. Verlin's patrol car, as well as Chuck and Ernie's, were parked in their assigned stalls next to the building. I knew I ought to pay my pal a visit, but for the moment, he was right where I wanted him. He would keep.

Most pressing was my grumbling stomach. It reminded me that I'd been running on a lone blueberry muffin for nearly five hours. In an attempt to appease my hunger, I folded a stick of gum in my mouth and began to chomp. Lunch would have to wait. First there was an old geezer I wanted to grill.

11

GRADY "MIRACLE" MARKLE OPENED HIS FRONT DOOR and stared at me blankly through the screen. "Yes?"

"Hi, Grady."

"Whatever you're selling, I'm not buying," he said and started to shut the door.

"Grady, wait!" I called out. "It's me, Crystal Cropper."

He stopped and squinted at me with one eye. I could almost hear the wheels humming in his head as he connected the dots. "Oh, for heaven's sake," he said, brows arching. He unlatched the screen door and pushed it open. "Why didn't you say so? Come in, come in."

Despite suffering from the obvious mental and physical maladies that come with advanced age, Grady was still a handsome bugger. I always thought that with his symmetrically balanced face, thick white hair, and strong cleft chin, he was a dead ringer for a latter-day Cary Grant.

I thanked him and entered his modest, ranch-style home. Its tidy but simple interior was cheered up considerably by bright sunlight that spilled through a big bay window facing the street.

The furnishings looked well worn but of a superior quality that suggested a time when service-oriented stores delivered their goods in one piece, rather than expecting customers to cart their purchases away in boxes to assemble themselves. *For Love and Life* blared from a giant, flat-screen television set, its volume set so high I was forced to raise my own. "How're you doing?"

"Not too bad." Grady also spoke louder. "How 'bout yourself?"

"I'm good," I said, nearly shouting. "Do you have a couple minutes? I need to talk to you about something."

"Beg pardon?"

I pointed to a chair. "You'd. Better. Sit. Down."

Grady nodded and, gripping the handles of his walker, shuffled across the nubby beige carpet toward his recliner. I couldn't help but notice the miniature footballs attached to each of the walker's front feet to enhance its handling.

"Cute," I said, pointing to the football gliders. "Nice touch."

"Beg pardon?" Grady said.

"The footballs," I hollered. "Nice." I gave him a thumbs up.

He raised his chin at me and smiled broadly. I doubt he understood what I'd said, but I let it go at that. The years had not been kind to him. In his heyday, he was one of the town's luminaries, a distinction that originated during the championship game of the 1953 state high school football playoffs. Grady, then a senior, had scored four running touchdowns for EHS during the game, in addition to completing four successful touchdown passes. Elmwood beat Newfield Central 56-30 and won the title, something it had not done in the preceding twenty-five years. Because of Grady's monumental achievement playing that final game of his EHS gridiron career, townsfolk affectionately honored him with the "Miracle" moniker, which he carried his entire life. After a long, successful career as an undertaker, he retired about five years back and turned Markle Mortuary over to his only offspring—son Glenn and grandson Bobby. After that, Grady's health deteriorated quickly. Now, with his frail body ravaged by rheumatoid arthritis, congestive heart failure, osteoporosis, and God knows what else, it seemed like a miracle he was still breathing.

Flopping into his chair, he picked up the TV remote control and muted the set's volume. "What can I do for you, Crystal? I hope you're not here about that damned parade on Saturday. You hear about that?"

I nodded.

"I can't figure to save my soul why they would ask an old goat like me to be the grand marshal. You'd think they'd want somebody everybody knows."

"What are you talking about?" I said with a theatrical flinch. "That's exactly what they did. Besides, you're not just well known. You're a living legend, and that makes you the perfect grand marshal."

Grady rolled his eyes. "What can I do for you?"

"I need to ask you a couple questions about Jack Baxter. It's for the feature story I'm writing about him. Is that okay?"

"Fine with me," he said with a shrug. "Have a seat."

I perched myself on the edge of his sofa. I didn't need to interview Grady for the story, but doing so provided good cover for the real reason I was there. After we chitchatted several minutes about Baxter's contributions to the city of Elmwood and to its football history, I moved on to my actual purpose. "I'm also working on a story about Gertie Tyroo," I said.

Grady's smile wilted. "Gertie? Why? Is something the matter?"

I didn't quite know how to break the news to him. As I searched for the right words, Grady probed, "She's not dead, is she?"

"Oh, no, no, no, no," I said with categorical assurance, surprised he would jump so quickly to such a radical conclusion. "No. She's not dead. However . . ." I hesitated for a second. I was unsure of Grady's relationship with Gertie and less certain how he would react. But no one lives in a town the size of Elmwood without feeling a kinship to a fellow citizen. Softening my tone, I continued, ". . . someone broke into her house last night and gave her what for. They hurt her pretty bad."

Grady shuddered. "That's terrible," he said, glowering through his tinted glasses at an invisible spot on the floor. For the next several seconds, he worked his jaw forward and back, forward and back, tightening and untightening. When he looked back at me, he asked, "They know who done it?"

Frankly, I was a little bothered that he hadn't instead asked about Gertie's condition. "Not that I'm aware of," I said. My physical altercation with the unknown suspect obviously wasn't anything Grady needed to know.

"Do you mind if I ask you some questions?"

"Mind?" he said, almost sounding defensive. "Is there some reason I should mind?"

"Not that I know of."

"Then ask away."

"Okay," I said. I flipped open my slim reporter's note pad and uncapped a ballpoint pen. "When was the last time you saw her?"

"Yesterday. I've had a standing appointment with the woman for as long as I can remember—noon, the first Monday of every month she shows up to clean the house for me."

"Did you two have a chance to talk?"

"Oh, sure, a little, mainly while we had our lunch. It's her habit to bring a bite to eat, usually peanut butter and jelly. Sometimes I heat up a can of soup to share, and we'll sit at the kitchen table and chat a spell."

"What'd you two chat about yesterday?"

Grady stroked the dent in his chin with his bony, twisted fingers. "Well, let's see. It seems to me she was pitching a fit about something. She pitches a fit pert near every time she comes by."

"What was it about yesterday?"

"Well, see, she'd gotten herself all worked up about the banquet for Jack Baxter."

"What in particular was her gripe?"

"Just the hubbub it was creating," he said. "She didn't like all them big-city folk flocking in and taking over."

It made sense. Maybe that's what had prompted her to want to get away for a few days. "Did she mention she might go visit a nephew in Noble City?"

Grady rubbed his chin again. "Can't say that she did. I didn't know she had a nephew. Matter of fact, I didn't know she had any family at all."

"Besides the Baxter banquet, did she mention being bothered by anything unusual?"

Grady looked at me over the top of his glasses. "Unusual how? Gertie finds something 'unusual' in a lot of things."

"I know she does, Grady, but did she happen to say whether she suspected anything unseemly going on around town, or if she felt like she was in any sort of danger?"

Frowning, Grady pursed his lips and quickly answered, "Nope."

So far, my little interrogation had been far less fruitful than

I'd hoped. Did I dare ask him about Eugene Potts and risk leaking a possible motive in her attack? I thought about it for a second, then, against my better judgment said, "Do you remember a young man who went missing back twenty-one years ago? A boy named Eugene—"

"Potts," Grady said, "the Potts kid. Boy, if that wasn't a screwed-up deal."

"What do you mean, 'screwed-up deal'?"

"Him taking off after what happened to the Whitfield boy. He broke two mothers' hearts, that's what he done. I took care of the Whitfield boy's final arrangements, and I never seen such grief. My, oh my. And what a funeral it was. We expected a big number to turn out for it, which is why we had it in the high school gymnasium instead of at the funeral home. I thank the good Lord we did."

"Lot of people showed up?"

"Oh, yeah," Grady said. "Must have been a thousand. Most were just kids all tore up about losing their friend. The death of a young person is always hardest on kids, you know. It makes them realize death is so goddamned . . ." he paused, narrowing his eyes, ". . . permanent. It's so goddamned permanent. Then on top of it, to have the Potts boy run off without getting what he deserved—it was more than most people around here could handle."

"What do you mean? What did he deserve?"

"After he went missing, they found an empty box of Mucxyphed in his locker. You know, that same stuff that killed that boy."

"You think Eugene Potts is responsible for Lance Whitfield's death?"

"I sure do, and I ain't the only one. 'Specially when he takes off before anyone can ask him about it. Looks pretty guilty to me."

"Did you and Gertie ever talk about what you thought happened to Eugene Potts?"

"Nuh-uh." Grady shook his head. "But you know Gertie. I wouldn't be surprised if she thought he'd been abducted by visitors from outer space. That woman sees a conspiracy in everything. One time, she was positive she was being watched by Russian spies. She said they had bugged her phone, had hidden cameras all through her house, and sent the KGB to follow her. I told her to stop taking herself so damned serious, and you know what she told me?"

"I can't imagine."

"She told me she was a secret agent, and I told her she was a flat-out nut. She laughed in my face. She's a pip, that old gal, but God love her. She can sure clean house."

The route I intended to take Grady had swerved way off course, so I decided to try a more direct line of questions. "Did Gertie tell you where she would be heading when she finished up here?"

"If she did, I don't remember."

"What time did she leave?"

"Oh, I'd say it was around three o'clock," he said, squinting toward the ceiling. "Yes, I remember. That bald-headed fella's talk show was just coming on. He always starts at three."

I jotted down "Gertie at Grady's, noon to three" on my pad. Grady watched me. When I stopped, he said, "One more thing."

I looked at him. A beat passed. "What is it, Grady?"

"Gertie's a fine gal," he said.

"I know she is." I stood, shoving my pad and pen into my handbag.

"I don't know what I'll do if we lose her," he said. "Do you think she'll be back on her feet in time to clean my house next month?"

"We can hope so," I said, reaching for the knob on the front door, "but I doubt it."

"Say," he said, "if you hear of anyone looking for house-work, I'd be much obliged if you'd pass my telephone number along to them."

So much for kinship.

• • • •

I had just started up my car when the Markle Mortuary hearse pulled up beside me. Its driver was Glenn Markle, Grady's look-alike son and my choice for that year's most venerable honor, the *Gazette*'s Citizen of the Year. We'd announced him as the winner in a front-page feature story in early February, followed by a chamber of commerce dinner at which I'd presented him with a handsome gold clock for his mantel and a framed copy of the article. He had seemed genuinely humbled.

He lowered his passenger-side window and said, "Hey, Crystal, Grady been giving you a hard time? He's always conniving to get beautiful women into his den. What was his excuse this time?"

I felt myself blush, although blushing in this situation was totally irrational. Glenn was easily twenty years my junior. On the other hand, finding an eligible man who is also handsome and intelligent within a hundred miles of Elmwood is a rarity that I suppose is more than enough to make any female with a pulse blush. More than simply good-looking and single—divorced in this case—Glenn was one of our community's most upstanding members, contributing a great deal of his time, energy, and money to many local youth organizations, like Little League and Kids for Christ.

"Grady doesn't need an excuse to get me into his den," I chirped. "I enter willingly."

Glenn laughed too. "If only I'd inherited half his charm instead of his business," he said. "But hey, seriously, what's up? Is everything okay?"

"Everything's fine. I stopped by to get a comment from him about Saturday's parade."

"He sure is excited about being grand marshal," Glenn said. "And I'm excited for him."

There was an awkward silence. "Well, I'd better be getting along," I said. "You're probably wanting my parking space."

"Naw," he said, "I was just passing by on my way to Hart County to talk to the family of an old gal named Violet Hornsby about arrangements for her burial here in Elmwood. Know her?"

"I sure don't," I said.

"Me neither, but her family said she requested Markle Mortuary, and I never turn down anybody's last request."

"Or their first one either, I bet."

"That we don't," he said. "You take care. I'll probably see you Saturday, if not sooner."

"If not sooner."

And he drove away.

12

NOT ONLY WAS I FAMISHED, I was AWOL. Normally at 2:45 on a weekday afternoon, I would have been at the office making sure that the day's paper was being delivered. But heck, Darcy could handle it, and I was only a couple blocks from Kathryn and Jack Baxter's neighborhood. Might as well check off another box on my to-do list.

Theirs was arguably the nicest home in town—English Tudor style, built on a sprawling three-acre lot on a hill that rose at the end of a quiet street lined with towering, mature trees. I tootled up the Baxter's steep, private drive and parked Nellie in the bow of the U, a few footsteps from their front door.

I pressed the doorbell and was quickly greeted by a soft-spoken, diminutive young woman, who couldn't have weighed more than ninety pounds soaking wet. Her features were rodent-like—sharp and small. Drab, short brown hair framed her wedge-shaped face, which looked to be in the twenty-five to thirty-year range and totally devoid of cosmetic enhancement. She wore a form-fitting pink uniform that buttoned up the front from its mid-calf hemline to its Peter Pan collar. No jewelry adorned this unspectacular presentation, except for a modest gold ball affixed to each earlobe. Perhaps it was her flawlessly plain-Jane guise that made her eyewear—blood-red horn-rims with thick, round, oversized lenses—seem so arbitrary.

I handed her one of my business cards and explained that I had been in the neighborhood anyway and thought I'd see if Kathryn might be available for a brief interview for the profile I was writing about Coach. The mousy young woman led me to what she called the "sitting room," a spacious alcove off the main corridor shadowed by the second floor. Until that moment, I had no idea there were local people pretentious enough to own a sitting room. But the Baxters, Elmwood's equivalent of royalty, were no ordinary local people. In a sense, in the same way Santa Barbara, California, had coddled its Reagans, Elmwood coddled its Baxters.

"I'll inform Mrs. Baxter that she has a visitor," the woman said, reciting her script without disturbing her deadpan countenance. "Please make yourself comfortable."

I thanked her and carefully settled into the brocade-upholstered seat of a fragile-looking dining chair, which, for all I knew, could have been salvaged from the seventeenth century. To me, it—like everything in the little room—looked old. And expensive. Indeed, the digs were impressive, particularly for an old sports jock.

Jack Baxter had coached the high school football team for fifteen years, beginning in the '70s, and took the school to the state finals not once, not twice, but eleven times. His teams had won an unprecedented five state championship titles, claiming its last in 1993, one year after his first wife, Ginny, contracted breast cancer. Her death just three months later brought an outpouring of sympathy from the community. But just nine months after Ginny's death, he married Kathryn, a much-younger, high-strung snob he imported from Paducah, Kentucky.

While Coach and his new bride vacationed during their first Thanksgiving holiday, he became the victim of a debilitating stroke. The stroke stripped him of his mobility and his ability to communicate, but his celebrity status remained healthy, teetering on that reserved for legends. Even after all these years, he was still the yardstick by which all the state's high school coaches were measured. He had won accolades from Indiana governors, had been featured in a nationally televised documentary about high school athletics, and was the namesake for a dozen scholarships. Despite all of that, his health had forced him out of the limelight of his former prominence. Few people had seen him over the past few years, and those who did were required to first penetrate Kathryn's protective shield.

From the vantage of my assigned chair, I studied a pair of landscape paintings that hung over a red velveteen loveseat. Behind them, the walls were covered in red paper with black-and-gold velvet flocking. As I took it all in, I wondered what the price tag was to furnish a room like this. Probably more than I spent to furnish my entire house. But more puzzling, why would anyone want to?

A good ten minutes passed before the waifish woman who led me to the appropriately named "sitting room" returned. "Mrs. Baxter is in bed with a migraine and cannot be disturbed," she said. She gestured toward the front entrance, which I found mildly annoying, but I took the cue and followed her. We were just steps from the door, when my attention was drawn to a small, bright pink item lying on the marble floor. It was a feather. I had noticed a pink feather duster at Gertie's that very morning. If my suspicions panned out, the feather might be useful in Gertie's case, if only I could get it without arousing suspicion from the young woman.

In an attempt to mask my true purpose, I affected an exaggerated gasp, then another and then, just in time, extracted my hankie from my coat pocket to stifle a nasty, counterfeit sneeze. I blew my nose with extra gusto into the cloth square, but, oops, clumsy me, it slipped from my fingers and fell to the floor, lighting of all places, atop the pink feather. With little chance that Miss Mouse would offer to retrieve the sullied snot-rag, I stooped and snatched up both it and the feather it concealed and stuffed them into my pocket.

"Thank you for your assistance," I said. "Please ask Mrs. Baxter to give me a call as soon as she feels better. My story about Mr. Baxter won't be complete without a few quotes from his wife."

"Of course," the rodent said.

I was about to proceed out the door, when I got an idea. "Say," I said, "I was wondering if you could tell me something."

Her beady eyes widened.

"I can't help but wonder how on earth you keep a big house like this looking so perfect. The floors, the windows, the furniture—everything shines. It looks like one of those showplaces you see featured in *Better Homes and Gardens*. I live in a one-bedroom bungalow, and to tell the truth, keeping it up is almost too much for me. I commend you if you do all this yourself."

I passed the cheese ball to the rodent, figuratively speaking, and was delighted she took the bait so readily.

"I am Mr. Baxter's nurse," she said. "I might do a little cooking and help with a few chores, but his well-being is my primary responsibility."

"Oh, I see," I said, pretending to mull over a fascinating

revelation. "Mrs. Baxter does all the housework herself."

The rodent girl grinned, revealing mirthless amusement and a set of front teeth the size of Montana. "Mrs. Baxter doesn't clean," she said. "She hires a woman."

"Miss Muridae," snapped an omniscient, female-sounding voice, its point of origin not immediately identifiable.

My mousy companion wriggled her nose and tilted back her head. I followed her gaze to the upstairs landing, where Coach's wife, Kathryn, stood looking down on us. I had to admit she cut a striking figure, if it had been a 1980s episode of *Dynasty* and she were Alexis Carrington. She wore a boxy-shouldered, slinky, floor-length white dressing gown, trimmed with white fur at the neck and wrists. Her long, dark hair was styled in a crisp page-boy, and her face was painted in what I would call theatrical makeup. As was always so predictable about Kathryn, she demonstrated her overestimation of her self-importance with an exaggerated air of regal authority.

"Randa, have you forgotten?" Kathryn said, intoning a con-flicted message of both coercion and congeniality. "It's time for Mr. Baxter's afternoon snack."

I detected a glaze of anger harden on Randa's face, but she recovered quickly and scampered away.

"Hello, Crystal, lovely to see you again," Kathryn cooed.

Lovely indeed. Our last face-to-face encounter had occurred a few months before when she showed up at my office to pro-test my decision to list her speeding ticket in the paper's public record column. She threatened to sue me if I printed it, which I did with enormous pleasure and without fear of retribution, thanks to our constitutionally guaranteed freedom of the press.

"Lovely to see you too, Kathryn," I purred.

"Didn't my girl give you my message, Sweet Cakes?"

Clearly she was not going to descend from her haughty post, and her patronizing tone made me want to slap that phony smile off her plastic face.

"What message is that, Sugar Plum?"

Kathryn grinned tautly. It appeared as if she'd had one too many facelifts. She stretched her mouth into a smug smile, and I worried the added strain on her anchored jowls might cause her face to rip. It didn't. But the mental picture made me shudder.

"I'm afraid one of my killer migraines is coming on, Pumpkin, and I regret that I can't do your little interview now. I know you understand."

"Of course, Muffin," I volleyed, wondering how she had suckered me into this idiotic name-game. "Why don't I check back with you tomorrow?"

Displaying a real flare for the dramatic, Kathryn laid the back of her hand across her forehead and expelled a deep sigh. "Thank you, Peaches. You're an absolute doll."

I started to step over the threshold again but stopped. Casting a different tack, I said, "What time did your girl say Gertie Tyroo finished cleaning here yesterday?"

Abandoning her hospitable hostess affectation, Kathryn's demeanor stiffened and she hurled a wrecking ball response. "Gertie Tyroo has never been in this house—not as a servant and certainly not as a guest." She cocked her eyebrow and looked down her perfect, rhinoplastied nose at me. For an instant, I thought I saw it growing.

"I don't want to sound insensitive," she said, "but if that woman would mind her own business, she wouldn't end up a victim dumped at death's doorstep. And I know you know what I mean. Now, good day, Miss Cropper."

Like a stretched rubber band suddenly released, her lips

snapped together. Her eyes radiated bone-chilling vindictiveness. Frankly, it sort of hurt my feelings. Oh, well, I'd recover. Besides, I'd gleaned far more information than I'd hoped for.

"Yes, good day . . ." I sang out as I searched the produce and bakery aisles of my mind for yet another tasty confection to defile . . . Sour-Prune Puff? . . . Snicker-Doodie? . . . Deviled Nutcake? But in that instance, I did the name-calling under my breath. I cut Kathryn my best cubic-zirconia smile and said, "How about I come back tomorrow for that interview? Say 10:00 a.m.?"

"Let's say eleven," she said, "if it's absolutely necessary."

"Perfect," I gushed, then gave her a little wave and let myself out into the cool, fresh afternoon air.

My stomach was rumbling. Dishing out all those food-related terms of *un*dearment had left me famished. But not for long.

13

"WELCOME TO MR. HAPPY BURGER," said the giant, garish clown face mounted beside the drive-through menu at my favorite fast burger joint. The voice belonged to Rusty, the pimply-faced manager, who couldn't have been more than a day out of adolescence. "Go ahead and order whenever you're ready."

I chirped my usual request into the clown's cavernous smile, where the microphone was hidden. "I'll have a double hamburger with extra onions, medium fries, and a large vanilla shake, please."

"You want cheese on that burger, sir?" came from the clown.

"No, thank you."

"Can I get you some fries with that cheeseburger, sir?"

"Yes, I want fries, but I don't want cheese."

"Okay. That'll be a double cheeseburger, cheese fries, and a medium chocolate shake. Please drive forward."

"No," I shouted into the gaping, red-rimmed mouth, "I don't want cheese. I want a plain, double hamburger with extra onions, medium fries—plain with no cheese—and a large vanilla—not chocolate—milkshake."

"Sir, there's no need to shout. I can't hear you when you do that. Please repeat your order. And please speak clearly."

My patience was wearing as thin as the lining of my growling stomach. I garnered all the composure I could muster and repeated my order, enunciating each syllable. "I want a plain double hamburger with extra onions, medium french fries, and a large vanilla shake."

"Just . . . *CREECHREECHREECH.*"

I quashed the urge to swear and responded crisply to the speaker's static squawk. "What?"

"Sir, I said, just . . . *CREECHREECHREECH.*"

It was a sign. I should not have been there. I had absolutely no business tempting the cholesterol gods with that sort of reckless abandon. I'd missed my lunch, and it was well past three o'clock. I was ravenous. My blood-sugar level had about hit the skids. I floored the gas pedal, and Nellie lurched forward, her tires squealing. She rounded the corner of the building, and I brought her to an abrupt stop at the pick-up window. Rusty was not amused, and neither was I.

"Oh, it's *you*," he said. "Why didn't you say so? Just a minute."

Three minutes later, he handed me a large vanilla shake and a white paper sack containing a double hamburger smothered in onions and an order of medium fries. In return, I handed him exact change—six dollars and thirty cents. To my surprise, he gave me back the thirty cents, explaining I'd forgotten about my five percent senior-citizen discount. Senior-citizen discount, indeed. Had my dignity been for sale, which it wasn't, it would cost considerably more than a measly five percent chopped off the price of a lousy fast-food meal. Shaking my finger at Rusty, I spurned his pity and informed him that my age was none of his concern. Then I threw the coins back at him and got the heck out Mr. Happy Burgerland.

When I got back to the *Gazette*, Darcy was gone for the day, but she'd left a message: "Call Verlin ASAP, and an FBI guy was here looking for you." *Great*, I thought. The note ended with, "See you at Rosie's," a reference to our Tuesday night bowling.

Yes, I certainly intended to give Verl a call, but first things first. I scarfed down my burger in as few bites as my mouth would allow, gobbled up a handful of fries, and was in the midst of washing it all down with a long slurp of my icy, thick shake when my phone jangled. "Aww, cwap," I grunted, my words muffled by my mouthful of half-chewed fries. I swished what I could of them into my cheeks and answered on the third ring. "Ha-wo."

"Is this Crystal Cropper?" my female caller said.

"Yesh i' ish," I spluttered. "How ca' I he'p you?"

"Miss Cropper, this is Randa Muridae, Jack Baxter's nurse. We just met."

"Uff coursh," I said. I was more than moderately surprised to hear from her, especially so soon. The possibilities intrigued me. I forced the half-chewed foodstuffs down my throat in hopes of restoring intelligible elocution and managed, "Please, call me Crystal."

"Thank you," she said. "And you can call me Randa. Do you have a moment?"

"Of course, Randa. What can I do for you?"

"I have some information that may be of help to you and Miss Tyroo, but I don't want my name associated with it in any manner. If I tell you, can you promise you won't mention where it came from?"

"Absolutely. You have my solemn word," I said, followed by

several seconds of dead silence. I didn't push. As a former crime beat reporter, I'd learned that sources often need to play their narrative out in their head before dedicating it to spoken words.

"All right," she said, "here's the deal. Mrs. Baxter sent me out fifteen minutes ago to buy a case of adult diapers for her husband, so I've got to make this quick."

"I'm all ears."

"I heard what happened to that sweet Miss Tyroo last night, and so I think you should know that when Mrs. Baxter told you Miss Tyroo had never been to the house, she was lying. Miss Tyroo was there yesterday. She arrived at three o'clock sharp to clean and didn't finish until dinnertime."

"No kidding," I said, twirling the pink feather that I'd plucked off the Baxter's floor. I thought if I proceeded cautiously, perhaps I could learn something useful. I was particularly eager to find out how Kathryn, and now Randa, had learned of Gertie's mishap. "Has Mrs. Baxter been out of the house today?"

"No," Randa said. "She hadn't even ventured from her bedroom until you saw her."

"Has she received any guests?"

"Only you."

"Any phone calls?"

"Look," she said.

I just hated it when people began their answer with "Look." It was a game-changer that informants used. Even when the interview had gone swimmingly, "Look" signaled to me that, all at once, my source had realized that she'd spoken too freely, and the interview was basically over. From that point on, whatever information followed was censored.

I struck back swiftly. "Look," I said, "I know how hard this is for you. I can only imagine how much courage it took you to pick up the phone, but I assure you, you're doing the right thing. Gertie Tyroo is in trouble, and what you saw and heard may help her." Pressing on, I pushed my luck. "Did Mrs. Baxter say anything to you after I left?"

Randa gave a huff. "Well, yes. She said plenty."

"What did she say?"

"Actually, I'm too much of a lady to repeat it."

"Then just give me the gist."

"The gist is, I'll be looking for a new job if I ever let you in again."

"Sounds like Mrs. Baxter can be a tad difficult."

"You don't know the half of it," she said.

"What's the other half?"

"Why, *Mr.* Baxter," she said. "He's so out of it that sometimes I wonder if there's anyone in there at all."

Out of it? Jack Baxter had been a recluse for some twenty years since he'd suffered a debilitating brain hemorrhage, but I always assumed he was merely homebound. But totally incapacitated? I made a note. Surely Randa was exaggerating. If Coach was in such a bad condition, what would drive Kathryn to expose him to all the attention that went with his impending hall of fame induction? How well could he hold up under the glare of a spotlight?

"What about phone calls?" I said. "Did anyone call Mrs. Baxter before I got there?"

"Yes, there was one. But look, I've got to go."

"Wait!" I said. "Who called? Why did Kathryn lie about Gertie?"

"I've really got to go. I'll call you later." *Click.*

14

I HOPED RANDA WASN'T IN TROUBLE. She'd obviously placed herself in jeopardy to give me some information. I scrolled through the caller ID on the phone and retrieved the number Randa had called from. I started to call her back but wrote it down instead and then scribbled out some notes about our conversation. I would check on my young informant's welfare the next day.

I hurriedly chomped downed my remaining fries and sucked up the rest of the milkshake. I was about to punch in Verlin's number, when the phone rang again.

"Crystal Cropper speaking," I said into the receiver.

"I should have you arrested." It was Verlin. What a coincidence.

"Good afternoon to you, too," I said.

"I distinctly remember telling you last night not to go sticking your nose into the Tyroo investigation, and I thought we had an understanding. You said it yourself: *I* investigate; *you* report. But first thing this morning, just as big as you please, there you go, busting in."

"Sheriff, I did not *bust* in." I always addressed him by his job title when he started to tick me off.

"A couple of my boys saw you sneaking in through the back door, so I don't know what else you'd call it but 'busting in.'"

I knew he was bluffing. If any of his "boys" had seen me, they—and he—would've been buzzing all over me like flies in a barnyard. "Okay, thanks for calling," I said in the tone I re-served for the crackpots who phoned the office to complain. "Gotta run now."

I started to hang up on him but didn't when I heard his wee, disembodied voice barking through the receiver, "Crystal, don't you hang up on me. I need to talk to you. You might be in trouble. . . . Crystal?"

Curious, I returned the receiver to my ear and said, "Trouble?"

"Yeah, an FBI agent came to see me. A young guy looking into the Tyroo case."

"Oh, really?"

"Yeah, he said he wanted to stop by your office to talk to you. Matter of fact, he ought to be moseying into your building right about now. So if you don't want to dig yourself in deeper, you'll talk to him."

I looked at the closed door. My Xray vision was temporarily on the fritz, so I couldn't confirm Verl's prediction. But one thing I did know was that the old boy would surely rupture him-self if I didn't hose him down. And fast. I gently laid the receiver on my desk and tiptoed toward my office door. Even after I stepped out the back door and into the alley, I could still hear his yammering wafting from the phone.

• • • •

"If you're smart, you'll tell him everything you know about the woman, and then butt out. One thing I know for sure is you don't need the FBI breathing down your throat. And *you* in pa'ticular don't need to be raising any FBI agent's eyebrows. You read me on this? Butt. Out. A word to the wise is suffi—Crystal? . . . Crystal! God dang it. Where'd she go?"

"I swear, if I were a snake . . . ," I said calmly to the back of Verl's head.

Verlin spun his swivel desk chair halfway around, still pressing his telephone receiver to his ear. When he realized I was standing in his office doorway, he slammed down the phone and jumped to his feet. Masking his embarrassment as anger, he growled, "Nice one, Crystal. I suppose you think that's funny."

I did, but I dashed the urge to laugh and opted for a deeper dig. "Not especially," I said in the quasi-aloof tone I knew drove him crazy. "Pathetic, perhaps, but not funny."

Verlin's blue eyes constricted into two, pink-rimmed ball bearings. "What do you want?"

"You got about fifteen minutes?"

"No, but don't let that stop you."

"Good," I said, thinking I was about to divulge helpful information to Verlin, my dear friend, rather than to Verlin, the pompous-ass sheriff, "because I want to tell you what I found at Gertie's this morn—"

"Crystal!" Verlin snapped.

The harshness in his tone stung like a slap in the face. My defenses locked into "Ready" mode.

"Crystal," he repeated, "dang nabbit, read my lips: Gertie's. Case. Is. Off. Limits. To. You."

He paused. His nostrils flared and he snorted like Ferdinand the Bull. I considered reminding him that before his investigation was over, he would end up begging for my help, as he always did. Instead, I said nothing. He went on, and his tone softened to condescension.

"I knowed last night, that *irregardless* of my orders, nothing could keep you from snooping around this case. And see? I know you better'n you know yourself. And, heck fire, norm'ly I'd be all for you helping out. But good God, woman, we're talking attempted murder. We don't know who we're dealing with or how dangerous this thing will get. Besides that, today the FBI comes around and tells me this is *their* case. Why they're interested in a one-horse-town nutcase like Gertie Tyroo, I have no clue, and the agent ain't about to spill no beans. All he's saying is, it's *their* case now, and I'm to assist only when invited to."

Verlin paused again. Narrowing his eyes and puffing out his chest, he added, "And that goes for well-intended, busybody civilians. *Capiche?*"

Anger surged through my veins, but I held my tongue. If Sheriff Verlin Wallace wanted to believe he could restrict the free press by telling it to butt out, let him think it. More than that, his little lecture told me at long last where I stood with him. Apparently, I was dispensable. But he was in for a rude awakening.

"*Capiche?*" he repeated with a bit more bite.

"Hey, not a problem," I said. "I told you last night I wasn't going to get myself mixed up with your criminal investigation."

"Then what, pray tell, were you doing busting into Gertie's this morning?"

"I told you before, I wasn't busting in. I went back only to find the can of mace I dropped there last night."

"Did you find it?"

"I did."

"Then will you give me your word that you won't interfere with Special Agent Quigley's investigation?"

I had a word for him all right, and not a very nice one. Instead, I drew an invisible X across my chest with my right hand and said, "Cross my heart," while I hid my left hand behind my back and crossed my fingers.

"Good," Verlin said, "now that we've reached an understanding, I can assure Agent Quigley that I've reined you in, so charging you with breaking and entering won't be necessary."

I felt my blood pressure ramp up again. Rein me in and charge me with breaking and entering? I would have expected better from a man who claimed to be my friend. "Answer me this then," I said. "How could some FBI suit possibly know all the ins and outs of this town like we do? What makes you think he's the best man for this job? Charge me, indeed."

"Oh, for corn sake, Crys. If he'd wanted to arrest you, he would have done it on the spot at Gertie's."

"No, he wouldn't. And you want to know why he wouldn't? Because even though I was armed with nothing but a book, I took him down."

Verl shook his head and glanced at his wristwatch. "Crystal, I'm sorry, but I've got to meet with some state police bigwig in five minutes. He wants to put two or three of his men on security detail at the Baxter banquet Saturday night, and I plan to talk him out of it. All I need are more out-of-town jokers traipsing around here, sticking their schnozzolas into my business. You and I can finish this conversation some other time."

"Bull pucky. I'm not leaving until I know exactly what Quigley told you to get me declared *persona non grata.*"

Verl shot back, "Oh, all right, if you *must* know, he said that in light of your meddling at the crime scene today, as well as last night, if I don't keep you off this case, he will consider *you* the leading suspect."

At that moment, Verlin Wallace's status as "beloved best friend" toppled to "back-stabbing weasel." I wanted to strangle him, but my head told me my numerous obligations afforded me too little time for the hassle. Instead, I got out of there fast. And, no, I did not let the door slam my backside.

15

"EXCUSE ME," I SAID to the nurse seated outside the hospital's intensive care unit. "I'd like to sit with Gertie Tyroo for a few minutes, if it's all right."

The nurse was a heavyset, middle-aged woman I'd never seen before, but the badge pinned above her left breast read "Becky." Nurse Becky looked up at me, stretched her valentine-shaped lips into a supercilious smile and said, "Are you a relative?"

"I'm her sister."

"Yes, of course you are," she said. "I see the family resemblance."

Resemblance? This, coming from a professional who was expected to use her eyes, ears, and mind to save people's lives, worried me greatly. Gertie was barely five feet tall, compared to my almost six. Gertie was built like a pear; I like a stick of celery. Gertie was of Mediterranean ancestry, while my gene pool had sprung from Scandinavia.

"Actually," I said, "we're stepsisters."

"That's all right, Hon. You go on in. She's in the first room on the left. Hospital policy allows you ten minutes every two hours."

I plodded down the corridor with apprehension, the rubber soles of my loafers defiling the unsettling stillness with each squeak against the waxed, institutional-beige tile floor. The walls also were beige, but framed prints of floral still lifes, apparently someone's idea of art, provided a focal point every few feet. It was dinnertime, and the scent of Salisbury steak and disinfectant hung heavy in the air. Once inside Gertie's dimly lit cubicle, I approached her on tiptoes, although I didn't know why. The Elmwood high school marching band could have performed "Hail the Conquering Hero," and she wouldn't have known. If only she would have though, I'd have moved heaven and earth to get all fifty-four of its members packed into the tiny room.

"Hi, Gertie," I cooed, feeling somewhat self-conscious. I'd never tried to converse with someone in a coma before. I patted her arm. "The doctor tells me you're doing just fine, and he expects you to be up and around in no time."

Such BS. She would have blown a fuse if she'd heard my drivel. But what do you say to an unconscious eighty-year-old suffering with a near-fatal concussion? The truth?

The truth was, she didn't look so good. Her head was all wrapped up in white gauze. Contrasting her ashen complexion were the blue-black bruises that underscored two puffy slits that bore little resemblance to eyelids. A heart monitor beeped its monotone harmony, and a machine that looked like a fancy VCR flickered alternating pea-sized lights of red, green, and yellow. I couldn't tell whether she was ebbing or flowing, coming or going, or simply proceeding with caution.

"Gert, for someone who shuns the spotlight, you sure are making a spectacle of yourself."

My heart was breaking for her, and I was being eaten up with guilt. Quite possibly the undercover work she had been doing for me had prompted the attack. I stroked her hollow cheek and was ambushed by a gush of emotion. I swallowed to push back the knot that formed in my throat just as something wet broke loose from my left eye and dripped onto my cheek. I wiped it away with the back of my hand and shook off the sentimentality. Sappiness was not my typical MO.

"Excuse me," came from Nurse Becky, poised just outside the door. I turned toward her, and she pointed to her wristwatch. "It's time. You're going to have to let Miss Tyroo get her rest."

"Yes," I said, "look at her. Poor woman. Obviously, running all those laps around the hospital gym has left her exhausted. And me too. Do you have somewhere I also could stretch out?"

Nurse Becky didn't smile. Maybe I was being a bit too acrid.

"Sorry," I said. "I'm a little edgy."

"Of course you are, dear. That's perfectly understandable."

"Has there been any improvement?" I asked. "Does Dr. Bannerjee have any idea when she might wake up?"

"Her vitals are strong," Nurse Becky said. "All I can tell you is that she'll come back to us when she's ready."

I bit my lower lip and nodded. The knot at the base of my throat expanded. It felt like it was on fire. I released a deep breath and said, "May I have just a moment longer?"

Nurse Becky looked at me over the top of her glasses and raised an eyebrow. "Hospital rules are hospital rules," she said. "But shoot—what good are rules if you can't break them now and then? Take all the time you want. I'll be at the nurses' station if you need anything."

Seeing my friend in that helpless condition renewed my sense of responsibility. I was livid over Verl's threat to pull the plug on my involvement in the case. Verl's pathetic deference to Quigley only bolstered my determination. The very thing Agent Quigley told Verlin he must do was the very thing I wouldn't allow. Tracking down Gertie's attacker was too important to leave in the hands of an uncaring federal agent. He didn't even know Gertie, and no one told Crystal Cropper what she could and could not do. Not then, not ever, and I would not be deterred from my quest. I would, however, proceed with a bit more caution—keep a watch over my shoulder, pare down my profile, brush up on my self-defense tactics, let Verlin think everything was A-okay. There was no use in shaking the ol' coconut tree unnecessarily.

I leaned over the bed and gently gripped Gertie's bony shoulders. "Gertie Tyroo, you're not done yet," I said, looking straight into her barely recognizable face. "Not by a long shot. So come on, friend. Pull it together. I need you. Elmwood needs you, and I promise you this: no matter what direction you ultimately decide to take, I will be there to personally make sure whoever did this to you is caught and that he—or she—gets what's coming."

16

I HURRIED ACROSS THE HOSPITAL PARKING LOT. Despite the late afternoon air's ice-cold chill, Nellie's engine started without complaint. Heading east on Main Street, I marveled at the enormity of the glowing orange ball sinking into the Elmwood skyline. It would be dark soon, not the most ideal time to make a cold-call visit. But then again, I've never been known for my warmth.

"Crystal?" said Noni Potts, greeting me with a polite smile through the glass storm door. She pushed it open and propped it in place with her left toe. "What a surprise." Folding her arms across her flat bosom, she said, "What can I do for you?"

Originally, my intent was to tell Noni and Ray Potts that I needed information for a retrospective I was writing about the 1993 misfortune that claimed Lance Whitfield and their son, Eugene. However, when I looked into Noni's eyes, I realized I couldn't lie to her.

"I was needing to speak with you and Ray. Is he around?"

She peered over her shoulder into the house's dim interior. "Ray," she shouted, "can you c'mere?"

I wasn't close with Ray and Noni, but we were no strangers. Over the years, she and I had exchanged cordialities, but nothing more significant than pausing in the grocery store to complain about the price of bread or stopping along Main Street to comment on the weather. She was a slim, petite woman around my age and basically unspectacular. She had been blessed with an oval-shaped face, its smallish features symmetrically balanced. But she kept herself plain, refraining from makeup and flattering hairdos, instead slicking back her graying locks and shaping them into something that resembled a breadstick secured horizontally at the base of her skull. She carried over the country bumpkin theme to her wardrobe, outfitting herself in shirtwaist dresses cut from drab cotton prints. The ensemble was never complete without a pair of opaque support stockings and sturdy brown wedgies.

"Sorry for just popping in," I said. "I hope this isn't a bad time."

"No," she said, turning to look at Ray lumbering up to her side. He grasped a long-handled fork in one hand and wore an oven mitt on the other. Covering his pale denim work shirt and jeans was a bibbed black apron upon which "Kiss the Cook" had been stamped in bold pink letters. He'd been retired as the county's highway foreman for several years, and it was good to see he had since gotten in touch with his softer, feminine side.

"Hey, Crystal." Looking down at Noni, whom he dwarfed by at least a foot, he said, "What's the matter? Why don't you invite her in?"

Noni flashed me a weak smile. "Would you like to come in?"

"Why, yes, thank you," I said, fully aware that I had interrupted their dinner preparation. "But I can come back later if this is inconvenient."

83

"No, it's fine," Ray said, motioning me inside with his mitted paw. "I'm barbecuing some porkburgers out back. You'd be welcome to join us. They're real tasty."

I begged off, fibbing that I was still full from my late lunch. At Ray's invitation, I seated myself on one end of the living room couch. Noni sat on the other, while he remained standing, poised to dash out the back door, I supposed, whenever the urge to flip a porkburger moved him.

Compounding my guilt over the purpose of my unannounced visit, a large studio portrait of Eugene hung on the wall opposite us. Redheaded and freckle-faced, baring a smile that stretched from one oversized ear to the other, he looked like a wholesome, happy kid who would have made any parent proud.

"I apologize for bothering you this way," I said, pushing on despite my growing discomfort at the prospect of dredging up the worst heartache these nice people had ever endured, "but I've got to talk with you about Eugene."

Their smiles hardened, and the room temperature plummeted.

"Please, let me explain," I said quickly, deciding at that moment to switch tacks and give it to them straight. "Can I ask you to keep this between us?"

"Sure, I guess so," Ray said. "What is it?"

"Gertie Tyroo woke me up last night to tell me she'd figured out what happened to Eugene."

"What?" Noni gasped, her posture stiffening. "That nutty old woman called you about my boy? She called me a couple weeks ago asking questions. What'd she want from you?"

"I don't know. She refused to discuss it on the phone. We agreed to meet at Bud's, and she never showed up."

"You think she was she making one of them crank calls?"

Ray said.

"No," I said, "it was not a crank call. Right after we spoke, someone attacked her and left her for dead. She's in intensive care right now, and she might not make it."

"Oh, my," Noni said.

"Oh, my, is right," I said. "I think Gertie stumbled on to some key information about your son's disappearance, and that's what almost got her killed. I'm hoping the two of you can help me sort it all out. But I need you to keep this visit and Gertie's . . . let's call it a 'mishap' . . . confidential for now." I glanced at Ray, then Noni. "Okay?"

Neither answered. Neither moved. They reminded me of characters out of an old *Twilight Zone* episode, where a small town's entire population had been placed in suspended animation, stopped dead in their tracks, just like that. I looked again at my hosts—his eyes fixed on his wife, and hers on him. Lacking mind-reading skills, I assumed they were mulling over my request. But after several seconds of the silent treatment, I pulled my purse straps over my shoulder and started to stand.

"Just sit yourself back down there," Ray said. "Where you think you're going?" Without waiting for an answer, he forged on. "You said whoever it was that tried to kill Gertie might be connected to Eugene's disappearance?"

"That's my take," I said.

"If that's so, seems like it'd be to our benefit to help you out," Ray said. He looked down at Noni. "You agree with that, Mother?" Without waiting for his wife's answer, Ray said to me, "What is it you want to know?"

"For starters," I said, "can you tell me what happened the day Lance Whitfield collapsed during practice?"

"We all know what happened," Noni said, "and all that

matters now is two boys are gone, and neither of them would have been anywhere near the football field that day if not for Jack Baxter's selfish arrogance."

"The man's a finkin' SOB, excuse my French," Ray piped in.

"Ray," scolded Noni, "you know I don't like you using the 'F' word."

Noni was correct that everybody knew the story. Much of what happened that day was public knowledge. What wasn't so easily obtainable was Eugene's part in it.

"It must have almost killed you to lose your son and to get no closure," I said to Ray.

"There's not a day goes by that his mother and I don't . . ." Ray's voice cracked. He clenched his trembling lips and looked to Noni.

"That we don't hope and pray this will be the day he comes home to us," Noni said, gazing up at her son's portrait.

"When was the last time you spoke with your son?" I asked.

"Around 10:00 p.m., Wednesday, August 11, 1993," Ray said. If retelling the story stirred more of his anguish, he kept it in check. "He kissed us good-night before he went to bed, and the next morning, when we woke up, he was gone. He didn't say a word, didn't leave a note, not a clue, not a hint, nothing out of place, nothing missing. Nothing but him. He was just . . ." Ray swiped the air once with his oven mitt. ". . . gone."

"Did he have a car?" I asked.

"Nope, he didn't drive," Ray said. "He had a bicycle."

"Did anyone see him?"

"Oh, yeah, people seen him," Ray said. "Charlie McGinnis seen him riding through the park around nine o'clock that morning. Kent Wilson, the school's custodian back then, noticed Eugene wandering around the football field sometime later, maybe ten or ten thirty. Grace Bushman said she saw a boy who looked like Eugene pedaling his bike up County Road 350 East toward the Whitfield farm just before noon.

"And that was like Eugene to face a problem square on," Ray continued. "Wouldn't have surprised me if he was headed out to talk with Lance's folks."

"I take it he never made it to the Whitfields'," I said.

"No, he didn't," said Noni. "At least, that's the story Frank and Tammy Whitfield told."

"Now, Mother," said Ray.

"What about his bike?" I asked. "Was that recovered?"

Ray shook his head. "Naw."

"The police came by later that day. What did they tell you?"

"At first," Ray said, "they claimed they just wanted to clear up the confusion about how Lance got that cold medication. But when we told them Eugene was unaccounted for, they accused him of supplying Lance with the medicine and us of lying to protect him. They said Eugene obviously was guilty because innocent people don't run off."

"And you're certain Eugene didn't give the medicine to Whitfield?"

"Damn it, Crystal," Noni sputtered, overt anger bristling in her voice. She slapped a hand across the blasphemous expletive's portal and rolled her moist eyes toward her husband. He flashed her a disapproving look, and she diverted her gaze to the gold carpet as her flushing cheeks betrayed her humiliation.

"I'll tell you what makes us so sure," Ray said. "Eugene was allergic to pseudoephedrine. He had a bout with it when he was twelve years old. It made him sick as a dog, and the doctor made him wear one of them medical alert necklaces. I tell you, Eugene never had that stuff in his possession."

87

"Couldn't you have proven that?"

"Of course we could," Ray snapped. "And we tried. We told the authorities, and all they had to do was call Eugene's doctor, which they didn't do. They were so all-fired certain that Eugene was guilty, they told us that him being allergic didn't matter. They brushed us off like dirt. Guess the truth was too much of an inconvenience."

Ray paused. He shifted his gaze to his feet and huffed out a small breath. "Look," he said, glancing up at me, "we were out of our minds with worry about finding our boy. We thought we'd get it all settled after we got him home. Surely you know how we felt."

I nodded, although, actually, I didn't know how they felt. I had avoided parenthood and never raised a child. But it didn't take much effort for me to imagine how it felt to lose the most precious person in your life.

Ray went on. "I knew . . . *know* my boy well enough to be positive he didn't give Lance that poison. But with all my heart, I believe Eugene knew who did."

"Did you ask him?"

Ray glared daggers at me.

"All right, I get your point," I said. "Why wouldn't he tell you?"

"We've asked ourselves that a million times," he said. "We assume he was protecting someone."

"Who?"

"Well, now," Ray said, "that's the million-dollar mystery, isn't it?"

I let that rhetorical question resonate for a moment. Then I asked the obvious. "Jack Baxter, did he offer you any explanation, any consolation?"

"Shoot no," Noni said. "That man was so full of himself, he didn't know one iota about relating to simple folk like us."

"Did the police ever come up with any leads for you about what might have happened to Eugene?" I asked, even though I was sure of the answer. But a change of direction in the conversation was in order.

"Naw," said Ray, "even the private detective couldn't come up with anything."

"Private detective?" The notion of a freelancer had never occurred to me.

"Uh-huh," Ray said, "a guy by the name of Nolan Sparks from down around Earlville."

"Who footed his bill?"

"We did," said Ray, gesturing toward Noni. "The local boys weren't doing us any good."

"Did he come up with anything the police hadn't?" I asked.

Noni shook her head. "Not really. He spent a month checking into people's backgrounds, talking to people, and going over reports. But he came up with zip. He said that until he could put a pattern together, he couldn't help us."

"How much did Sparks set you back financially?" I asked.

"Everything we had saved—about $5,000," Ray answered.

I glanced at my wristwatch and was surprised that it was nearly seven o'clock already. Time flies when you're having fun, so I couldn't explain why it had passed so swiftly during my visit with Noni and Ray. I expressed my thanks for their generous hospitality as I stood up and inched toward the front door. Stopping at the threshold, I asked the question that had gnawed at my insides since our conversation had turned to their son.

"Noni, you mentioned that Gertie had contacted you about two weeks ago."

She frowned and looked to Ray. "That's what she said," he answered.

"Do you remember the gist of the conversation?" I said to Noni.

"Sure we do," Ray said. "She wanted to know something about Eugene, but I still don't know what business it was of hers."

"Specifically, what was she looking for?" I said.

"She asked if we had ever found Eugene's medical alert pendant," Ray said. "Noni told her pert near what I told you. But there was one thing about that call that's still got me scratching my head."

"What's that?" I said.

"How'd she know about it?" Ray said. "Like I told you before, after we mentioned it to the police, they never publicized it."

That was an excellent question and one that deserved unhurried time to mull over. For the moment, I had one last question for Ray and Noni.

"Do you ever blame Jack Baxter for what happened to Lance and Eugene?"

They both nodded, but it was Noni who gave a voice to their answer: "Every single day."

17

I HURRIED THROUGH THE PLATE-GLASS FRONT DOORS of Rosie's
Bowl-a-Drome, a noisy, smoke-filled leviathan, where members
of Elmwood's sedentary working class assembled to challenge
one another to a friendly, or sometimes not, game of bowling.

My team—the Holy Rollers, sponsored by Friends First
Presbyterian Church—was the defending champion of the
Tuesday night Gutter Chicks League. We had enjoyed a healthy
lead for most of the season, but lately our overconfidence had
made us sloppy. To our chagrin, the league's least ladylike, most
despised, bloodthirstiest team, the Queen Pins, had advanced to
within three points of our lead. The match that night pitted us
against the Queens, and both teams knew the battle would not
be pretty.

I quickly spotted my teammates warming up on lanes seven
and eight. Three of them were among Elmwood's most impressive achievers: Shay Nichols, CEO of the Elmwood Chamber of
Commerce, Richelle Evers, pastor of Friends First Presbyterian,
and Auggie Stillwater, the judge. Darcy, whom we recruited not
for her bowling skills but for her youth, rounded out the squad.

Throwing Darcy's age—twenty-one—into the mix, kept our team members' average in the double nickels range. Vain? Of course. But, hey, vanity is a woman's prerogative.

Lugging my regulation, sixteen-pound ball at my side, I claimed one of the seats behind lane seven and peeled off my jacket. Under it, I, like the other Holy Rollers, wore a black-and-turquoise team shirt on which my name had been embroidered on the cross above the breast pocket and the team's name across the back.

"Hey, Crystal, glad to see you could squeeze us into your busy social schedule," the Queen Pins' team captain, Wanda Silverberry, cackled with a phlegm, guttural laugh, which promptly mutated into a coughing fit that sounded like two hogs mating.

I ignored her and went about stuffing my size 9 tootsies into my bowling shoes. As I bent to tie the laces, I felt a hand on my back. I looked up. It was Darcy's.

"Where were you?" she said. "I was trying to find you all afternoon."

"What's up?"

"Some guy from the FBI stopped in to see you."

"You're kidding," I said, dropping my jaw to feign surprise.

"What's that about?" Darcy said.

I shrugged a shoulder. "What'd you tell him?"

"What do you think? The guy's a federal agent. I told him he could catch you here."

I scanned the faces in the crowd, and indeed she had. Here came Quigley sauntering through the lobby. I was sure he hadn't yet seen me.

"Good work, Darcy," I said, lying with forced spunk. I would deal with her later. "He's the grandkid of an old friend.

Haven't seen him since he was in diapers." Whatever he wanted, I thought it best to keep Darcy out of it. I needed to quickly separate myself from her and get to Quigley before he got to me. "I'll be right back, dear."

I bolted and ducked into the crowd. Carving a giant arc through the alley, I cut him off at the ball rack.

"You didn't tell me you were a sports fan," I said to Quigley's back.

Turning in my direction, he conducted a visual sweep of the smoke-filled house. I'd taken him by surprise, but he gave no indication. "You didn't tell me you were an athlete," he said, shouting over a thunderous crackle of exploding pins on alley four.

"Only when it's no more taxing than knocking down ten sticks with an oversized billiard ball," I said. Dialing back the thermostat on my tone about twenty degrees, I added, "What are you doing here, Quigley? Checking to make sure the sheriff reined me in?"

Quigley shifted his gaze to something over my left shoulder, avoiding direct eye contact. "I won't apologize for that," he said. "It was the right call at the time." He paused, cleared his throat, looked me in the eyes, and continued. "However, I have since realized that I could use your help fleshing out some leads on this investigation."

Interesting, I thought. *He could use my help.* I was touched. Deeply. He didn't deserve it, but I could be persuaded to give the kid a hand. But he was going to have to work for it.

He pulled a roll of antacids from somewhere under his coat and inserted one into his mouth. "I've talked to about a dozen people, and not a single one knows a thing about Gertie Tyroo. Is this woman an apparition, or am I being jerked around?"

"Look at it this way," I said. "You missed the pocket, and now you're left with the seven-ten split."

A beat passed. "You're definitely jerking me around," he said.

"No," I said, "I'm giving you some free coaching. The seven-ten split is a near-impossible spare to pick up. You overshot your mark, and now you've got to take a different approach."

"Look," he said, "could we cut the double-talk? Are you willing to help me get these people to talk to me or not?"

From lane eight, Darcy called out, "Crystal, you're up."

I acknowledged her with a nod, then I stared hard at Quigley. "You realize, don't you, that you're asking me to remove a lot of deadwood that's of no benefit to me?"

His lips parted but they passed only air.

"Let me sleep on it," I told him. "Give me a shout tomorrow." I took a few steps toward my assigned lane and stopped. I needed to clarify something Quigley had said. He was already halfway to the exit, when I looked back at him and called out, "Hey."

He stopped and turned.

"She's no apparition," I shouted.

He gave a chin wave and headed on toward the front door. He and I definitely bowled in different leagues, but who could say? Perhaps someday, someone with the right motive will teach him to put some spin on his balls, and he might actually improve his game.

Wanda Silverberry yelled my name again. She stood on the approach to lane seven, sipping from a can of Red Bull and puffing on a brown cigarette. She'd rolled up her blouse's cap sleeves, maximizing the girth of her massive biceps that duplicated her enormous, sculpted calves around which stretched the cuffs of her polka-dotted capris. She puffed up her flat chest like a Kevlar shield, while her four teammates stood safely behind her, their designated bully.

"What's wrong, Hon?" she whined with mock concern. "You're not stalling are you? 'Cause if you are, you're just diddlin' with the *unevitable*."

Wanda, bless her heart, was not known for her acute mastery of the English language.

"You know it, doncha, that the Holy Rollers is about to get themselves *crucifried?*"

Even during our days at Elmwood High, Wanda had thrived on attention, and she'd gotten it in any manner available to her. Because of her limited intellectual resources, she utilized her God-given gifts—then a svelte, soft body that was indisputably feminine—to pursue the nonacademic tactics guaranteed to get her noticed and branded as defiant and easy. Those pursuits finally got her expelled. Back in the 1960s, when a high school girl wound up pregnant, she was obliged to abort her education. If she didn't do it willingly, the school did it for her. The idea that a teacher could overcome the classroom disruption caused by a knocked-up teen was simply inconceivable. At least that had been the school board's claim. And that was why Wanda, all knocked up with nowhere to go, was kicked out of school at the age of sixteen. Personally, I never held that against her and would have reached out to her had my own circumstances been somewhat different.

I had to hand it to Wanda, though. She never tried to hide her shame by running away. She stayed put in Elmwood, had her baby, and raised her daughter alone. The fact that her daughter grew up and married Mayor Head is what I found so deliciously intriguing.

No, in answer to Wanda, I did not believe my team was about to be *crucifried*, and I could have told her so in the same mean way she had put it to me. However, being editor of the local paper compelled me to maintain a certain professionalism. Thus, I would record my comeback to her challenge in the amiable column.

I breezed past her, avoiding eye contact, and focused on lane eight. I stepped up to the approach and ground my heels into the hardwood floor, exactly five boards right of the alley's center, and hoisted my Black Beauty ball squarely under my pointed chin.

I carried a 170 average, and I planned to do a little showing off. Concentrating on the ten pins facing me like ready soldiers at the end of the lane, I cheeped to Wanda, "Keep your eye on the dancing ball."

I shifted into automatic pilot and launched my perfected four-step approach toward the foul line. I slid my right foot forward, and in synchronous harmony with my footwork, cast my delivery, pushing my ball onward to initiate its arcing swing at the end of my right arm. I continued my ritual, rendering my second, third, and fourth steps in perfect rhythm with the pendular sweep of my arm. I planted my left foot well in front of me to bear the bulk of my weight, and then dipped and stretched for the pins as I swung my right arm high behind me and then forward. Reaching the frontal apex of the arch, I released my ball precisely where I wanted it, over the second arrow. The momentum of the swing propelled the ball along its imaginary groove, about six inches from the lane's right edge, to a point about two-thirds the length of the alley where, my ball suddenly and quite inexplicably hooked to the right and plopped into the gutter.

96

The Queens went nuts, slapping high fives while they whooped and cheered like twelve-year-olds at a Justin Bieber concert. Good sportsmanship was not their strong suit. To my consternation, it wasn't the Holy Rollers' strong suit either.

"Excuse me," yapped a raspy-voiced female from the vicinity of the scorekeepers' desk. It was the Queens' Marge Winger, a Keith Richards carbon copy who looked like she'd crawled out of a hole. "Seems to me you girls might want to forfeit, and we can all sit this one out in the bar."

"Shut up, Marge," came from Darcy. "We're not forfeiting anything. Matter of fact, before the night's over, you guys'll wished you'd been the ones to forfeit 'cause we're gonna stomp your sorry keisters to smithereens."

"Yeah," I piped in, caught up in the moment, "if anyone's getting nailed to a cross tonight, it'll be the Queens, and my girls have the hammers to do it. After tonight, you Queens will finally get to wear your crowns . . . a crown of thorns, that is."

Darcy and I shared a fist bump, while Wanda looked at me like she'd swallowed a mouthful of vinegar. I smiled back sweetly and joined my teammates for a group smug.

"Oh, yeah?" jeered Wanda, barging through her teammates huddled next to Marge. "You wanna lay some folding cash on it?"

"Yeah," came a brilliant reply from Darcy.

"Okay, little missy," hissed Wanda, "how much?"

"Now, now," I said, elbowing my way between Wanda and Darcy in an attempt to run interference.

But before I could extinguish the escalating fracas, Darcy croaked, "A hundred dollars a game too rich for you?" I wanted to clobber her.

Without hesitation, Wanda grinned like a hungry hyena that

had pinned her prey in a corner. "A *hunderd* a game?" Cocking her head and arching her furry brows, she surveyed the other four Queens. After each nodded approval, she cooed to Darcy, "Honey child, bring it on."

18

"REMIND ME IN THE MORNING TO FIRE YOU," I said to Darcy. I had held my tongue about her locking the team into a high-stakes bet until the five of us gathered at Bud's to wallow in our humiliating crucifixion and divvy up the cost of our shame. "I mean it, Darcy. I am using every shred of my self-control not to lunge across this table and wring your neck."

It made no sense. My teammates and I carried higher averages than the members of the Queens. Our collective team average was twenty-five pins per game better than theirs. We were smarter, we were spryer, we were nicer, and doggone it, people liked us better. Still, we'd lost all three games. Why? Because no one could have predicted Wanda Silverberry, whose previous personal best was 192, would roll a perfect game—twelve strikes in a row—and set not only her own new record high but an alley record for the highest individual game, as well as the highest team game ever bowled there during a women's league. It was a feat that even the Holy Rollers couldn't compensate for.

Despite my disparagement, I refused to elevate the Queen's

satisfaction by acting like a sore loser. To fortify my illusion of good sportsmanship, I had put on a show of nonchalance while I wrote a check for the full amount of our loss—three hundred dollars—and presented it to Wanda with the sweetest grin and most sincere-sounding "Congratulations" I could muster. I was fit to be tied.

"I've got an idea," Darcy smarted back. "Why don't you just wring my neck tonight? That way you'll have your top story for tomorrow's *Gazette*."

"Great idea," I said, reaching for her with both of my eager hands.

Shay, seated to my left, gently pushed my arms down. The gesture was typical of Shay, a classy, caring woman. Tall, shapely and auburn-haired, she was easily the most attractive of my single, overachieving, over-the-hill gal pals and greatly enjoyed flaunting her womanly attributes. Despite her fussiness, any time a downtrodden underdog needed a hand, she could be counted on to batten down her push-up bra and pull more than her weight to help. She'd do the same for the community. She was always right there, its toughest champion, defending its rights, looking out for its interest. In the dozen years she had headed the local chamber of commerce, no new business had hung its shingle in Elmwood without a nod from Shay Nichols.

"You can't do that," the eternally level-headed CEO reminded me. "You kill her, you go to jail. Who'd be left to put out the paper?"

"What can I get you ladies?" came from Bud from behind the counter where he stood, filling salt-and-pepper shakers. "The usual?"

I looked around the table. "The usual?"

Four heads nodded.

"Four decafs and a diet cola," I said to Bud.

"Kiddo," Auggie said to Shay, "if Crys kills Darcy, she has nothing to worry about. It's called 'justifiable homicide,' and in my court she walks."

"Oh, for Pete's sake," Darcy said. "I don't see what the big deal is. Between us we lost three hundred dollars. Split five ways, that's a mere . . ." Darcy tore a napkin from the dispenser and scribbled down some figures. "Oh," she said in a small voice. "Sixty dollars apiece?"

Now, I wouldn't have said the girl couldn't add, subtract, multiply, and divide, but it was true that for any sum over ten, she required pen and paper. "That's right," I affirmed.

"Oh, well, so what?" Darcy said perkily. "What's sixty dollars? Big hairy deal."

"Big hairy deal?" blustered Pastor Richelle. "We're talking hard-earned cash here. Do you have any idea what my outreach ministry could do with sixty dollars? Or what it would mean to a single mother scrimping to care for her kids, or a senior citizen living on a fixed income?"

"Speaking of senior citizens," Shay said, "what's the deal with Wanda Silverberry? She'd better lay off the body building before she's mistaken for Arnold Schwarzenegger."

"If you ask me, the woman's on steroids," Auggie said.

"Steroids?" Oddly, Darcy, Richelle, Shay, and I repeated the word in unison.

"How could that be?" Richelle said. "Steroids are illegal. Where would she get them around here?"

"Lots of places," Auggie said. "Internet, dealers, a friend of a friend. Or if you're really lucky, you know a shady doctor who's happy to supply them. For a price."

"But this is Elmwood," Shay said, raising an eyebrow at

Auggie. "You dabble in illegal substances here, you have Verlin Wallace to contend with."

"You have to contend with Verlin Wallace regardless of what you dabble in," I said.

"Who gets the diet drink?" asked Bud, standing over me. I pointed to Darcy, and he set the glass in front of me and walked away.

"Thanks, Bud," I said, pushing the cola across the table.

"Oh, hey, not to change this fascinating subject," Richelle said, changing the subject, "but I was at the hospital this afternoon praying with one of the patients and discovered Gertie Tyroo in the ICU. She didn't look good at all. I couldn't get the nurse to tell me a thing. Any of you heard?"

"I haven't," Shay said, shaking her head.

My eyes met Auggie's. She shook her head. I did the same. I dearly wanted to share the details of Gertie's assault with my friends. They, like me, cared deeply for Gertie and recognized the depth to her character, even though it eluded most others in Elmwood. But I just couldn't say anything yet.

"Somebody broke into her house last night and attacked her," Darcy chirped brightly.

Crap, I thought. I'd forgotten about Darcy's *mis*informant. "Now, Darcy," I said calmly in an attempt to neutralize the narrative I feared was coming, "as you know, nothing official's been released."

Ignoring me, Darcy continued. "The poor thing put up quite a fight before the guy shot her, pistol-whipped her senseless, and stabbed her twenty-seven times."

Shay and Richelle—and even Auggie—recoiled, their eyes bulging, their jaws dropping.

"Darcy," I snapped, wishing like hell I had a sock and some

duct tape, "that's baseless rumor and simply not true."

"It's not rumor, Crystal," Darcy insisted. "As I told you, I got it from my next-door neighbor who works at the hospital." Shifting her focus back to the other girls, she resumed her Münchausen-esque tale. "The wound to Gertie's head was so severe that before the doctors could treat her, they had to put her into a medical coma, and—"

"Darcy," I said, flashing her a dirty look, "why don't you let me order you one of Bud's bodacious, double bacon burgers to go with that diet pop? My treat."

"No thanks," Darcy said with a shudder. "Those are gross. Besides, I don't eat red meat, remember? Say," she said without coming up for air, "where's that FBI agent from anyway?"

"What FBI agent?" Shay said.

Things were deteriorating fast. I tried to kick Darcy under the table. But I missed, kicking Shay instead, as Darcy, apparently oblivious to my displeasure, blathered on.

"What FBI agent?" Richelle said.

"He's a hottie," Darcy said. "How long's he here for? Is he single? Is he on Gertie's case?"

"What FBI agent?" Auggie said.

One by one, I made eye contact with Shay, Richelle, and Auggie and shook my head. Looking back at Darcy, I gritted my teeth and slowly recited, "He's the grandson of an old friend, remember? I don't know where he's from. He's just passing through. And I didn't ask for his marital status."

"You need any cream?" Bud grumbled as he set the four cups of coffee in the center of the table.

"I don't," Shay said, "but hey, I would love a cinnamon stick."

"Oh, yes, that would be delightful," Richelle said.

"Cinnamon sticks?" Bud scratched his three-day-old five o'clock shadow. "Can't say I have any sticks, but I've got cinnamon in the can," he said. "Why don't I go get it for you girls, and you can just stick it up your—"

"Bud," I interjected, "it's fine. We're good. Thank you."

Our eyeballs locked for a long moment. "You're most welcome," he said, breaking the staredown with mawkish sweetness as he sauntered back to the kitchen.

"Crys, is this true that somebody attacked Gertie in her house?" asked Richelle.

"Yes," I admitted, "but Verl wants to keep a lid on it for a couple days while he investigates. And that's all I know."

"Really?" Richelle said.

I nodded.

"How's she doing?" asked Shay.

"It's just too soon to say," I said. "Before I left the house this evening, I called my source at the hospital for an update on her condition. And you know Gertie," I said, walking the thin line of veracity and bull in an effort to avoid revealing too much of the truth. "She's a fighter, and she's holding her own." I had merely regurgitated the rhetoric I'd heard that afternoon from the ICU nurse. It disgusted me that I was supposed to be a wordsmith, but for once, I didn't know what to say. "The truth is . . . the way I see it . . . I just don't know. I just don't know . . ."

"She's in God's hands," Richelle said, coating my impotence with her cleric's perspective, "and we have to trust that whatever the outcome, it's His will, and He'll take care of her."

"Crystal's right about Gertie being a fighter," Shay said, "so let's not give her the short shrift. We need to pool our positive vibes for her and keep them flowing."

A wrinkle creased Richelle's brow, and her head bobbled slowly. "The woman's heart is pure gold. Anytime my congregation holds a fund-raiser for someone facing a personal crisis, Gertie's always right there to offer a helping hand—usually money."

That was news to me. I never knew she had money to give.

"She always gives anonymously," Richelle said, "and what she's able to give is liable to surprise you."

"Exactly how surprised would we be?" I asked.

Richelle took off her glasses and rubbed her eyes. After a long moment, she said, "As Gertie's pastor, I shouldn't be telling you this, but in this case, I think God would make an exception."

"Absolutely," I said, "she wants you to tell us."

"Well," Richelle started, "remember last fall when Jake Obermeyer's tractor tipped over on him and crushed his legs?" Richelle paused; all heads nodded. "Okay, then you know that after he was out of work for about three months, the church hosted a silent auction to raise money for him and Sara and their five kids. You knew they had two more on the way, too, didn't you? Twins."

I shrugged. I didn't typically keep track of who in town was expecting what.

Richelle went on. "Peterson's Home Electronics Store donated a sixty-inch TV worth about six hundred dollars, and we opened up the bidding."

Richelle stopped her story to sip from her coffee, made a face, and pushed the cup away. "After all the bids were in," she said, "I sorted through them and was more than delighted that the top one was twelve hundred dollars. I was about to announce the winner when Gertie eased up to me real quiet-like and slipped me a wad of cash. 'This ought to better anybody's bid,' she told me. I counted what she'd given me and almost fainted. It was twenty-five hundred-dollar bills.

"I invited her to join me at the pulpit while I announced her as the winner, and she jumped down my throat, threatened to quit the church if I even hinted she'd given a cent. And then, when I said I had to at least inform Peterson's Electronics so they could deliver the TV set to her, she went off again, telling me, 'What in tarnation would I do with a contraption like that? Just give it to Jake.' And that's what I did, and, until now, nobody but Gertie and I knew what she had done."

"Twenty-five hundred dollars . . . wow," Auggie said to no one in particular. "Where do you suppose Gertie came up with that kind of money?"

"Well," I said, "I haven't a clue, but the woman does work hard."

"Yeah, but cleaning houses?" Darcy said. "Looks like I'm in the wrong profession."

"Looks like we all are," Shay said.

"I'll pray for her, and," looking at me, Richelle added, "I suggest the rest of you do the same."

"Cool beans," Auggie said. "I'm sure Gertie will appreciate that."

"It's all we can do," Richelle said.

Changing the subject yet again, I held up the bowling score sheet and said, "But who, pray tell, will take care of *this*?"

"Here's my share," Auggie said, tossing me three twenty-dollar bills.

"And here's mine," said Richelle, placing a small stack of cash on the table as she flashed a frown Darcy's way.

"Hon, I'll have to write you a check," Shay said. "You'll take a check won't you?"

"Sure," I said, "as long as you have proper ID."

As the four of us snorted laughter, Darcy remained somber, pawing through her purse.

"What's the matter?" I asked her.

"I'm really sorry I got us into this tonight," she said, her eyes wide. "But Crystal, there's something I have to ask you."

"What's that, dear?"

"Can I borrow sixty dollars?"

"Darcy," I said.

"Hmmm?"

"Come morning, remind me of something."

"Remind you of what?"

"To fire you."

19

MY TEAMMATES AND I were the last of the diehards still hanging out at the diner when, at half past eleven, we settled up with Bud and reconvened outside. The previous night's rain had washed away the remaining stubborn packs of February's big snow, leaving the diner's gravel-covered parking lot mushy beneath our feet. Although a winter chill still permeated the air, spring's imminent arrival fostered my own cavalier indifference to the cold, which I demonstrated by refusing to zip up my goose-down-lined jacket.

We lamented one last round of woe over our bowling defeat and followed with a pledge to wreak revenge on the Queens at the next opportunity. We said our goodbyes and piled into our vehicles. I lagged behind, watching the girls drive eastbound on State Road 280 toward town until the last flicker of their taillights had been absorbed by the darkness. Aside from the low hum of Bud's "Eat Here, Get Gas" neon sign and the soft patter of my footsteps, the atmosphere was eerily still. I was eager to get home and dug into my purse for my keys. Not finding them, I riffled through my pockets.

"Aw, damn it," I grumbled, at once remembering I'd left them on the counter next to Bud's cash register. I spun around toward the entrance and screamed, my nerves completely undone by the backlit, black silhouette of a man standing before me.

"Glad to know I can still make a woman swoon," he said. It was Bud.

Embarrassed, I sputtered a four-letter expletive.

"Forget something?" he said, dangling my key ring from his index finger. "Or were you just laying the groundwork for an excuse to come back for another dose of my charms?"

"Busted." I snatched my keys. "What woman wouldn't want more of your sexual magnetism?"

Bud scratched his stubbled chin and gave me a wink. For an instant, I could almost imagine him as a virile young man, long before the years of hard living had taken their toll.

"You watch yourself out here on the road," he said.

I was touched. He almost sounded like he cared.

"You watch yourself, too," I said.

Aside from Bud, there was not another soul within miles. My uneasiness had manifested as a case of heebie-jeebies lodged in my solar plexus, pushing me to pick up my pace to a near-jog as I returned to Nellie.

I inserted the key into the ignition and gave it a twist. Her engine purred. I cranked up the heater, tuned the radio to a Beethoven symphony and eased onto the two-lane road headed for home.

Once a busy thoroughfare between Elmwood and Indianapolis, State Road 280 had been downgraded to secondary-road status a few years back, after Indiana decided to build a superhighway around that stretch. While the uninterrupted bypass may have shaved a few minutes off of commuters' drive time, it also diverted traffic away from all the little mom-and-pop businesses that had thrived there. Most shuttered due to lost revenue, while a few, like Bud's, hung on by a thread.

As I accelerated to a comfortable fifty miles per hour, I tapped the bright-lights button with my left toe and began a vigilant lookout for deer. They were prevalent along this road, especially between dusk and dawn. Straight ahead, my high beams revealed only the barren highway, but from a good distance behind me, a pair of headlights pierced the night like two tiny pinpricks.

I started a mental list of my tasks for the next day: call the hospital for Gertie's status, have Darcy pick up an updated incident report from the sheriff's office, write a brief article about Gertie for page two. I still firmly believed that sensationalizing Gertie's attack would serve neither her nor the community. I hoped my new friend Quigley would stop by early, as he had promised, so I could get him out of my way. I needed to get back into Gertie's house. Had it not been anatomically impossible, I would have kicked myself for not raking through all her rooms for clues when I'd been there the first time, which seemed like days ago.

From the radio, the orchestra's wood section trilled a solemn largo, which matched my mood and carried my thoughts to Kathryn Baxter. Her haughty-but-nice attitude earlier in the day left a nasty taste. Clearly, I hadn't been welcome in her home, but why not? She barely knew me, and even people who knew me well seemed to think I was okay. Why had she lied to me about Gertie being there the day before?

I glanced at the rearview mirror. The vehicle behind me had gained ground. I figured it was a pickup truck. Its headlights shone like lighthouse beacons. It was my observation that men who drove big pickups typically embraced an innate cowboy mentality that spurred them to prove their manhood by riding the tail of every motorist darkening their path. It was a weak attempt at intimidation and even more pathetic after nightfall, when they could use their blinding headlights to intensify the assault.

My thoughts turned to Randa Muridae. I wondered what prompted her to call to tell me Gertie had indeed visited the Baxters on Monday. What else did Randa know, and why had she ended our call so abruptly? Should I fold and tell Verlin about it?

Ah, yes. Verlin. My best friend. We'd parted that afternoon on a rather bitter note. But my jets had since cooled, and knowing Verlin as I did, I was certain his had too. I would call him in the morning to patch things up and tell him about my concern for Randa.

And then there were the Pottses. What a sad pair. Not only had they endured the loss of their only child, they felt the system had tainted their son's memory by branding him as an alleged killer. But if, as the Pottses insisted, their boy was innocent, why hadn't he spoken out to defend himself? Was he simply guilty as suspected, or had he been protecting someone? Of course, the elephant in the room was the uncertainty over the boy's fate. It was illuminating to me that the Pottses still harbored so much anger for Jack Baxter.

I had my work cut out for me, but first I would go home and get horizontal in my bed. While I had long since dismissed the notion of beauty sleep as myth, I still found that the functionality of my brain greatly improved when I gave it at least seven blissful hours in solitary lock-down. My eyes, too, would benefit from a long rest. But at that moment, they were being blinded by the bright lights of the pickup truck that had all but attached itself to my back bumper.

"What the hell?" I yelled. I tapped my brake as a signal for the jerk to back off. To my relief, he did, stretching the distance between his front end and my rear to about one car length. We progressed that way for perhaps a tenth of a mile before he started to narrow the gap again. There was no traffic in the westbound lane, so I expected him to pass. But he didn't. He just rode my tail. And rode it. And rode it.

"Okay, so you want to play games," I snarled and pressed the gas pedal until my speed reached sixty. Still, the monster truck kept pace like it was tethered to my poor Nellie with a two-foot rope.

Since arrogant blockheads couldn't be dealt with like nice people with brains, I let up on the gas and eased my speed to fifty. I'd traveled about two miles since leaving Bud's, which, at that rate, meant I'd cross the city limits in about three and a half minutes. I told myself to ignore the imbecile breathing down my trunk and remain calm. Once I entered town, if he was still tail-gating, I would simply lead him to the sheriff's office. Surely, he would be happy to stop and introduce himself to one of the deputies.

I adjusted my rearview mirror so the beam of his headlights would shine onto the ceiling, rather than in my eyes, and hunkered down for the remainder of my trip. My anxiety diminished a little after the driver finally moved to the westbound lane, where, I assumed, he would pass me.

When I was a kid, my parents used to take me to the state fair, and I'd get a huge thrill out of driving the bumper cars, where rules dictated that drivers ram each other's cars with their well-padded bumpers. Aside from mild shake-ups, no one got hurt, and it was great fun. To the contrary, getting rammed by a carnivorous, predatory pickup speeding down a desolate two-lane highway at midnight wasn't as funny as it might sound.

For a fleeting moment, when the trucker banged his right front bumper into Nellie's left-side rear, it seemed as if I'd hit a patch of ice. The impact slid my car forward like a walnut hurled by a slingshot. Before my head registered what actually happened, I had already shifted into autopilot. I held on tight to the steering wheel and maintained control. Somehow I kept Nellie on the road, rather than let her spin head over tail through the darkness and end up like a helpless, capsized water bug.

I didn't know if the lunatic behind me was drunk or stoned or just stupid. It didn't matter. I knew what I had to do. I hammered the accelerator to the floor. The needle on Nellie's speed gauge inched to the right, from sixty to seventy and on to eighty. Moving further ahead of the pickup truck, Nellie shimmied from the excessive speed. And so did I. Until then, I never dreamed that my modest, antique sedan could still exceed sixty. But there she was, zooming down the highway like a rocket, leaving the souped-up phallic symbol to eat her dust.

"Good girl," I shouted, patting Nellie's dashboard.

Soaring at eighty, I maintained a safe distance between the truck and me. It seemed he had accepted his place behind me, and I started to doubt the ramming had actually occurred.

But then, the truck bolted forward and smashed into me a second time. The strike was solid. My car scudded forward and my head snapped back. The padded headrest saved me from whiplash and preserved my control. I'd come within a mile of town, where new homes lined both sides of the road. I was desperate to keep Nellie from veering off the shoulder and into someone's living room. Fighting the urge to brake, I strangled the steering wheel and accelerated. Had it been necessary, I would have pushed Nellie's speed to the end of her gauge—one hundred thirty miles per hour.

Probably even that wouldn't have been fast enough. The truck gained on me again, seemingly without effort, riding my tail, blinding me with his headlamps, illuminating Nellie's interior like Times Square on New Year's Eve. I knew he could see me, and I flashed him the finger. I almost laughed, but my attention shifted ahead to two tiny, orange-colored reflectors hovering some five feet above the centerline. I needed no more than a half-second to realize the orange dots weren't reflectors. They were eyes, the eyes of one very unfortunate deer. Without the intercession of a miracle, I was going to hit it.

20

I WILL ALWAYS THANK MY LUCKY STARS for the split in the road at the bend of the curve, my exact location when I spotted the deer. At that point, County Road 50, a narrow, gravel road, veered gently southeastward, while the highway forged to the north and then east into town. I pounded the knob to kill the headlights and wrenched the steering wheel hard to the right. I whipped down the side road at the last possible moment, faking out the truck, which sped onward into the bow of the curve. My reporter's curiosity compelled me to glance back in time to see the pickup start its slide across the asphalt, shifting angles, weaving side to side, and then sideswipe a mailbox, missing the deer by less than a foot.

Unable to tear my eyes from the action on the state highway, I sped down the county road without looking where I was headed, until my left front tire plunged into a pothole. It was a veritable abyss that, upon impact, ripped a spine-splintering jolt through Nellie and pitched her off the road and into the field. I mashed the brake pedal with both feet and wrestled the steering wheel to the right to keep from hitting a tree. I quickly brought

Nellie to a stop behind a small wooded area that provided a modicum of cover, and killed her engine. I rolled down the window and gulped in a lungful of the cool air until I thought my chest would burst. When I exhaled, my anxiety started to deflate, but my anger was running pretty high, directed almost as much at myself as it was at the crazy goon in the truck. If not for my damned addiction to danger, I'd have been almost home. But there I was, a sitting duck a couple hundred feet from this jacked-up weasel, and all I could do was hope that whoever he was, he had been too involved with his own near-disaster to notice mine.

A narrow opening in the trees provided me a straight-line view of the highway where the truck had come to rest. My eyes were glued there. Several seconds passed, and I began to wonder if the driver was injured. I hoped not, because my Good Samaritan gene was temporarily out of service. More time passed with no sign of movement, and I was about to call the sheriff's office to report the accident, when the truck's driver-side door creaked open. I slapped my hand over my mouth to stifle an unexpected yelp as an indistinguishable figure climbed out. The stranger glanced up and down the road, then swaggered across in my direction, displacing the din of silence with clacks of leather upon the pavement. The driver reached the road's shoulder and stopped. My cell phone was in my purse, but I dared not even breathe, let alone move. After an interminably agonizing moment, a hand-held floodlight suddenly flashed on. The beam swept the landscape, washing everything in its path with harsh, white light.

The probing, bright beam illuminated the wooded area that shielded me, and I foolishly ducked. My precarious situation caused my mind screen to flicker back to another classic woman-in-peril movie, where the defenseless heroine breaks all the light bulbs and takes cover behind a curtain, while the deranged killer pursues her with an ax. My plot took a different turn when a large, white-tailed deer, perhaps the one that just narrowly avoided death, sauntered up to my car door and snorted. With the roving flashlight sweeping the undergrowth all around me, the last thing I needed was a magnet. "Shoo," I whispered, flapping my hands at it. The deer looked at me, snorted again, and moseyed on, its hooves snapping the underbrush with each step. The light's ray instantly reversed course and landed on the deer. The startled animal wanted no part of it and fled, sprinting across the open field toward the safety of a nearby woods. The light stayed on it for a short distance and then went dark. The clack of boot heels returned, and a few seconds later, the pickup's door slammed, and the truck roared away toward town, giving me an unobstructed view of its taillights: the left one red, the right one orange.

21

CALLING THE AUTHORITIES COULD WAIT. I rushed home and eased Nellie into the garage. My nerves were shot, my emotions shredded, but I could cope by transferring my angst over my close call with the stranger to the battering my car had suffered. I examined the damage, and my heart sank.

Nellie's left rear end was a mess. Except for a few broken shards of red-colored glass poking upward like tiny stalagmites, the taillight was gone. A sizeable portion of her smooth, shiny bumper was crinkled like a wadded-up gum wrapper, the left corner of her fender was smushed into her trunk, and the front wheels were undoubtedly out of alignment, thanks to the massive crater I plowed her into. I had hoped for a mercurochrome and Band-Aid cure, but proper healing would require the services of my car doctor, Clip Parker, a veritable genius in the automotive world. I would stop by his shop on my way to the office in the morning.

The moment I set foot in the house, I called Verlin at home. I knew he was already sawing logs, but I didn't care. The highway chase had me spooked. No matter how much he and I got under each other's skin, when the going got rough, he was there for me, and I was there for him. This particular call for comfort and reassurance exemplified our relationship perfectly. When I told Verl that a homicidal trucker had tried to run me off the highway, he called me a paranoid schizoid, and I called him an obtuse old fart.

"Dang nabbit, Crystal. This is getting to be an every-night thing. What is it with you that you can't let a man get a good night's rest?"

"Fine then," I snapped, "don't worry about it. If this fiend breaks in and murders me in my sleep, at least you'll be well rested in the morning when you start the criminal investigation—that is, if you can still remember how to conduct one."

The bickering continued back and forth for a few more jabs, until he finally relented, promising to assign a deputy to keep an eye on my house until dawn. That suited me fine. A few minutes later, I peeked out my front window. Parked across the street was Verlin himself. I owed him one again. With a little coaxing, I got him inside and fixed him a warm, comfy spot on my couch. When he was all tucked in, I crawled into my bed, too tired to even brush my teeth. Drained as I was, I barely slept. The harrowing race down State Road 280 replayed in my head on a continuous loop as I thrashed about for most of the night. The time or two I actually dozed off, I wore myself ragged running in slow motion, trying to keep from being gobbled up by the ravenous, four-wheeled tyrannosaurus nipping at my heels.

I had always found relaxation difficult after someone tried to kill me. I toyed with the notion that I was a random victim, but that didn't add up. Considering the red and orange taillights, just like the ones on the getaway truck at Gertie's, I had to think the ambush was intentional—either for what Gertie knew, or for what someone thought she knew and passed on to me.

Finally around 4:00 a.m., from sheer exhaustion, I conked out. But with the first glimmer of daybreak, I awoke. Three hours of shut-eye two nights in a row would have to do. I threw on my sexy, hot pink terrycloth bathrobe and warmed up a couple blueberry muffins and brewed a pot of coffee. I hoped Verl wouldn't insist on bacon and eggs. I was fresh out of microwaveable frozen breakfast entrées.

Shortly past dawn, Verlin and I sat at my kitchen table finishing our second cup of coffee. I was giving him an earful.

"One more time," he said, "tell me what you were doing at Bud's in the middle of the night, not once, but twice this week?"

I'd forgotten that the man's permanent bad mood started the moment he woke up.

"I was there with the team," I said, "Shay, Richelle, Auggie, and Darcy. Not that it's any business of yours."

"When you come crying to me for help, that's exactly what it is," he said. "You make it my business."

"Well then, excuse me," I said. "I must have misunderstood what a sheriff's job entails." I stood. "Sorry for the inconvenience. Now if you don't mind, I've got things to do."

And did I ever. My to-do list was growing like spring grass. As I scooted past Verl, he grasped my wrist.

"You know what I mean," he said. "Now sit down, and let's figure this out."

I sat.

"You say the truck that chased you last night was the same one that sped past Gertie's?"

"I can't be certain," I said. "It was dark, but the taillights definitely looked the same—oblong, one red, one orange."

Verl nodded. He pondered my ceiling for a long moment.

"Okay, you're calling in sick today. I'll get the boys to go beat some bushes."

"No," I said, "I'm not calling in sick. Someone's up to no good, and I'm not hiding in my house waiting for him to strike again."

Verl's eyes narrowed and glared at me. "Crystal . . ."

I admit—in a sweet sort of way, he was kind of scary.

22

CLIP PARKER STUDIED NELLIE'S BATTERED BACK END, running a permanently grease-stained hand across her crumpled bumper and broken body parts.

Clip was one of the few men I knew worthy of my complete trust. At age thirty, he already had built a reputation as a genius at fixing cars. He was also honest, respectful, and personable, and would make someone a fine husband once he learned to fawn over women the way he did cars.

I followed Clip around the parking lot outside his East Oak Street body shop, where I'd brought my poor Nellie for a diagnosis and treatment. He examined her wounds for several minutes, then pushed back his Cincinnati Reds baseball cap and snatched the pencil cradled behind his right ear. As he scribbled marks all over the form secured to his clipboard, I asked, "Can you fix her?"

"Oh sure," he said, punching buttons on his miniature calculator with the pencil's eraser.

"How much is it going to cost?"

"Depends," he said, making eye contact for the first time

since I'd first pulled in.

"On?"

"On whether I can rustle up some parts from the scrap yard in Logan Point."

"When will you know?"

"T'morrow maybe. Maybe Friday. If not, I'll have to start making some calls. It could take several days. Finding parts for these old girls is really gettin' hard. Gettin' more expensive too. If Nellie was my car, I believe I'd let her die a nice, peaceful death and get me some new wheels."

Horrified by the suggestion, I held up both hands, signaling him to stop. "No way, Clip. I love that car."

"I know you do, Miss Cropper, but now's a real good time to buy new, say a four-cylinder that gets forty, fifty miles to the gallon."

"No thanks."

"Up to you. I can fix her, but I'll need a few days to locate parts and work up a quote. Then I'll need at least a week to do the work."

Almost two weeks without transportation was definitely not going to work for me. "What am I supposed to do in the meantime? Do you have a loaner?"

Clip pulled off his cap and beat it once against his thigh, knocking loose a puff of dust that dispersed into the morning air.

"No," he said, "but I'll tell you what. I'll rent you my 'Vette for really cheap. I've been bogged down here, and she needs to be driven."

For an instant, the offer kind of took my breath away, but then I thought, *Why not? It might be fun.* While Clip and I were inside filling out paper work, I asked him to keep an eye open for a pickup truck with a smashed-up front end and mismatched taillights. Clip was such a good boy. He didn't ask questions, didn't balk, didn't say "boo." Just, "Sure thing, Miss Cropper."

• • • •

The potent engine of Clip's sexy, midnight-blue Corvette purred. As I tootled along through town at a brisk thirty miles per hour, five over the speed limit, I fed a mouthful of dust to everything I left in my wake—Elmwood School Bus Number Three, Garret Conner's souped-up golf cart, and numerous children on bicycles. I passed them all like they were nailed to the ground. Turning onto Main Street, I spun the omnivorous machine into the *Gazette*'s parking lot and whipped it into my reserved spot. I strutted into the office, fancying myself some overly endowed beauty pageant contestant flaunting her wares in a teeny bikini and spike heels.

"My vision for the future is freedom, world peace, and an endless supply of Botox for all mankind," I said to a puzzled Darcy as I stopped at her desk. "What's going on? Any calls?"

Darcy wagged her handful of pink message slips. "It's only nine o'clock, and already I've taken about a hundred calls."

"Anything important?"

Darcy shrugged and began thumbing through the notes. "Let's see," she sighed. "There were three complaints that we've printed nothing about a crazed killer supposedly loose in Elmwood, two callers wanted to know who was lined up as keynote speaker at Coach's banquet, and one said she dreamed Coach would get a surprise visit from . . ." Darcy hesitated. "I think she said, 'Prince Londarbi.'"

"Vince Lombardi?" I said.

"Whatever."

"Vince Lombardi was a big-time NFL coach," I explained. "Been dead about forty years."

"Ooo-kay," Darcy said with an eye roll. Her appreciation for sports apparently mirrored my own. "Another caller said she worked at the Indianapolis Ritz-Carlton and swore that some old movie star named Birk Wrengold reserved a room for Saturday night and a limo to Elmwood."

"Birk Wrengold?"

"That's what the woman said," Darcy answered.

The name didn't ring a bell. "Who else called?"

"Two people asked for Saturday's parade route, Millicent Fendergrass phoned to say her cat, Boots, was missing, Kathryn Baxter wanted to reconfirm your eleven o'clock interview with her, and eight concerned citizens wanted to know how long the sheriff had been shacking up with the newspaper editor."

"Boots went missing again?" I said. "Millicent's poor, little puddytat must be a hundred years old. What'd you tell her?"

"That we'd run a brief," Darcy said, her lips stretching into a rapturous grin. "You're changing the subject, aren't you? What's this about the sheriff and the editor?" She winked.

"Darcy, please," I said, "mind your own beeswax." Although, if she wanted to think her boss was sleeping around, that was her problem. "Do we have a top story for today's paper?"

"Oh, all right," she said, tossing the message slips onto her desk blotter. "Be that way. Yes, we have a top story. Mary from the prosecutor's office called. Louie's about to wrap his investigation of the mayor."

"Is he filing charges?" I said.

"She wasn't sure."

"I'll get you that story in about thirty minutes," I said. "Let's both stay on top of it. If Dick Head is charged, that's one story we do not want to sacrifice to another paper. Anything else?"

Darcy skimmed the scribbles on her note pad. "Yes," she said. "The high school wants us to cover its Jack Baxter Day program Friday afternoon."

"You take that," I said. "It'll make a good feature for Saturday's paper."

"Gee, thanks, boss. I feel just like Lois Lane."

"Don't be snide, dear," I said. "Lois didn't get the Kryptonite beat until she perfected her craft by reporting chicken-noodle news, just like the rest of us."

Darcy had so much to learn about the art of newspapering, but at least she was organized. And she typed.

"I'd also like you to write a parade preview," I said, "with a sidebar about the grand marshal, Grady Markle, and a map of the route."

"Are you serious?" she whined. "We need a map? The parade starts on the west end of Main Street and stops at the east end of Main Street."

"I know, dear," I said, "but not all our readers are as clever as you. They like visuals."

Darcy sighed. "You're the boss."

"Yes, I am," I said, stepping into my office. "We finally have something we can agree on."

I tossed my sweater cape over the back of the armchair, seated myself at my desk, and pushed up my sleeves. It was only Wednesday, but already this was the week from hell. And I feared things were only going to get worse. Where to begin?

Coach's induction into the state's high school football hall of fame and all the peripheral events were becoming the biggest story for the town in the ten years since I joined the *Gazette*. Upwards of five hundred people were expected to attend

Saturday night's banquet in the high school gym. All of this, and I hadn't even started to research my feature story recounting Baxter's life and professional achievements. And as two of our readers had already pointed out, we had an attempted murderer in our midst, not to mention the hullabaloo with the mayor.

Gertie's condition had stabilized overnight, according to the hospital spokesman I talked with prior to leaving home this morning. However—heaven forbid—should she die, it would be the paper's responsibility to flesh out the details and report them.

But first things first. If the prosecutor's secretary was right about Louie's investigation of Dick Head, he could issue a press release any minute. It would be helpful to know what was cooking, so I called Louie. I decided to bypass his office staff and punched in his cell phone number. He answered on the first ring, which probably meant he'd forgotten about giving me his private number.

"Louie," I said, "it's Crystal. How's your investigation into Richard Head coming along? Can you give me a status report?"

I heard his teeth gnashing. "Actually," Louie said, "no."

I accepted that. I have always appreciated a direct response.

"When will you alert the media about your findings?"

"Soon," he said.

"How soon?"

"As soon as I'm confident all avenues have been explored."

What the hell did that mean? I asked, "Specifically what avenues are you exploring?"

"Look," Louie said none too sweetly, "it means when I'm done, I'll make an announcement, and the *Gazette* will be among the first to know. Now, if you don't mind, I've got court in twenty minutes."

And he was gone. He'd cut me loose like I was a kite in an electrical storm.

23

I PHONED VERL AT HIS OFFICE. His secretary pushed me right through. "Hey," I said, "it's me."

"Hey, 'me,' don't expect this 'me' to be doing anymore sleepovers. You would not believe the razzing I've been taking. Apparently, half the town cruised past your house between midnight and seven this morning and noticed my car. What's wrong with people? Their minds are in the gutter."

"Oh, stop it," I said. "So what if you're busted?"

"So what?" Verl said. "A man's got to uphold his reputation."

"There, there," I said. "Don't worry. If your reputation is indeed irreparably stained, you can just tell everyone you're gay."

There was a long, pregnant pause. It was followed by, "What do you want?"

"I just got off the horn with Louie Sommers," I said. "He's keeping his lips sealed about the mayor. What do you know about it?"

"Not a lot. Just that Louie is close to filing charges."

"How close?"

"It could be today. Could be two weeks. I just don't know."

"You'll let me know when you find out?"

"Oh, I suppose so," Verl said, mumbling. "Spend one night with a woman, and she thinks she owns you."

"You got that right," I said. "I don't share my blueberry muffins with just any guy."

I hung up and checked my wristwatch. I had almost ninety minutes before my appointment with Kathryn. That gave me ample time to write my story about the mayor and conduct my first interview for my profile on Coach. I walked my fingers through my Rolodex looking for Sherm Hollingsworth's number. Hollingsworth had been a defensive lineman for EHS back in the late '80s and early '90s and went on to the NFL, playing for the Carolina Panthers. I expected him to be among the dignitaries for Coach's banquet, but his name wasn't listed in the hall of fame publicity fliers. I thought it odd, but perhaps his name had been omitted in error. However, if he actually was taking a pass, that might be a story, too—an even better one.

I tried his number, but after four or five rings, a recorded voice picked up and invited me to leave a detailed message. I did as instructed, stressing the urgency of my deadline. I had no more than finished, when Darcy stuck her head in my office and, speaking in a voice like a little girl, cooed, "Yoo-hoo, Crystal? Excuse me. There's somebody here I think you'll want to talk to."

Annoyed, I asked her who it was.

She answered, "Special Agent Quigley." Excitement fringed her tone.

Nuts. I'd forgotten about brushing him off last night at the bowling alley with an invitation to stop by. I was still in no mood for chumming it up with the agent, but it would be the perfect opportunity to find out what he knew and get him off my back in one fell swoop. "Fine," I said, "send him in."

Quigley immediately stepped into view, my doorway framing his tall, gangly body. "Miss Cropper," he said, "thanks for making time for me."

"Sure." I motioned him in. "Why not?" I could see the hem of Darcy's skirt swaying outside the door. "Thank you, Darcy," I said. "Oh, I almost forgot. Could you call the Whitfields and see if Frank and Tammy are available this afternoon or tomorrow for an interview? Tell them I'm gathering information for a profile I'm writing about Coach. Then, if it's not too much trouble, you might want to get back to typing up today's public records."

I heard her sigh. Soft footsteps followed. Quigley seated himself in the chair on the other side of my desk. "What is it you were trying to tell me last night at Rosie's?" I said. "Something about Gertie being an apparition?"

"Yes," he said. "Yesterday, I must have talked to ten people, trying to get a handle on what was going on with her, and not a single one of them would tell me a thing."

"What is it you're looking for, Quigley? I thought you knew her."

"Yes, I am acquainted with her, but I have no idea how the woman spends her time. What do *you* think happened to her? Why was an attempt made on her life?"

"One thing's certain," I said. "It wasn't for her money. When I found her, she was still clutching her purse. The wallet and several bills inside it were still intact. For me to tell you what happened to her, I can only speculate. I think you can understand that."

"Of course I can," he said, "but go ahead—speculate. What do you think happened?"

"It's only a guess, but I figure during her daily travels, she stumbled onto something connected to a twenty-one-year-old, unsolved missing-person case. If you ask me, even if what she found wasn't solid enough to close the book, it was enough to make somebody uncomfortable to the point of trying to shut her up."

"I don't know," he said. "An old cleaning lady figuring out a twenty-one-year-old case? Sounds like a stretch."

"A stretch my patoot," I said. "It's not like she's a complete novice at criminal investigation. You told me yourself that she was one of the FBI's most cherished secretaries. In my book, anyone with a close alliance to law enforcement—even a secretary—can learn to be a good detective." *Even a newspaper editor*, I thought. "Wouldn't you agree?"

Quigley's eyelids fluttered. "Sure," he said, "why not a secretary?"

"Exactly," I said. "So why not an old cleaning lady?"

"If you don't mind," he said, "what can you tell me about the case?"

"The Potts case?"

He gave a one-shouldered shrug. "The missing person case she was onto, what do you know?"

I hesitated, but not for long. What the heck? With so much hinging on the Potts case, help from the FBI couldn't hurt.

"There's plenty I can tell you," I said. I pulled the two manila folders off the stack of paper on my desk and handed them to Quigley. "It's all here, and it's all public record."

I was heartened that Quigley had lifted his ban on my involvement in Gertie's case. He was finally treating me as a worthy ally. I was almost flattered. Such trust could be useful as I forged onward with my investigation. On the other hand, if my plans for him panned out, his expertise could be even more beneficial. Before he left my office with the files, he asked me to keep him apprised of Gertie's condition.

With Quigley off my to-do list, I could give the mayor's pending charges the attention they deserved. Turning back to my keyboard, I pounded out that day's top story.

"Probe of Mayor's Part in No-Bid Contracts Nears End," the headline read. The copy followed:

The investigation into Elmwood Mayor Richard Head's alleged cronyism involving several no-bid contracts is nearing completion, Elm County Prosecutor Louis Sommers told the Gazette *this morning.*

Although Sommers would give no specifics as to when he expects to wrap up the probe, he did confirm that completion will be "soon."

"As soon as I'm confident all avenues have been explored," he said.

When asked for specifics, Sommers said, "Look, it means when I'm done I'll make an announcement, and the Gazette *will be among the first to know."*

The investigation was prompted by allegations of an elected city official, who has asked to remain unnamed while the investigation is pending. According to the unnamed source, Head has awarded contracts for four county projects to relatives and friends since he took office five years ago. Those projects include upgrading the infrastructure for the Dewer Field subdivision where Head resides, construction of a new, mile-long road leading from Dewer Field to the Elm County Golf Course, razing and renovation of the executive offices in the city building, and installing a wrought-iron fence around the perimeter of Pleasant View Gardens Cemetery. To date, a Freedom of Information Act Request, filed by the Gazette *in hopes of confirming the allegations, has not been answered by the mayor's office.*

Combined, those projects have cost the city more than $10 million, according to City Auditor Cara Beckwith.

If Sommers' investigation results in charges against Head, a warrant could be issued for Head's arrest, in compliance with Indiana criminal law.

I picked up the phone and tapped in the number for Head's office. It was no surprise that no one answered. I left a message: "This is Crystal Cropper. We've got a story running today about the prosecutor's investigation into Mayor Head's alleged improprieties with the city's money. Please have him call me by ten forty-five this morning if he wishes to make a statement for the story. Thank you."

I turned back to my computer, and finished my story:

A call to the mayor's office requesting his reaction to the investigation was not returned.

24

IT WAS ELEVEN O'CLOCK ON THE NOSE when I rang the Baxters' doorbell. I was both surprised and disappointed that it wasn't Randa who answered. After our phone conversation the day before, I had questions for her, plus I wanted to know why she had ended the call so abruptly.

"My kudos to you, dear," Kathryn said patronizingly as she swung open the door. "You're right on time. Punctuation is a virtue we girls must constantly nurture. Wouldn't you agree?"

Yes, I thought smugly, *punctuation is definitely important, particularly for us girls who write for a living*. In fact, back in my premenopausal days, one missed period could literally ruin my life.

Kathryn looked ghastly. Her dark eyes bulged, particularly her left one, which, despite a heavy, flesh-toned concealer, was rimmed by what appeared to be remnants of a bruise. It looked like a lid lift gone wrong. During my time in Hollywood, I'd encountered thousands of Kathryn Baxters—pathetic, aging women whose attempt to recapture their youthful verve had failed and left them wearing an expression of perpetual astonishment. For our meeting, Kathryn had swept her black hair into a poofy ponytail, which emphasized the obvious—that her heavily made-up face had been surgically stretched back and nailed down. The domino effect lent her chemically fattened lips a permanent, puffy, sardonic grin. In Kathryn's defense, her face wasn't totally repulsive. Something about it reminded me of the goldfish I'd cherished as a child.

"Absolutely," I said, referring to her punctuation remark. For my own amusement, I added. "We girls have to keep all our t's dotted and our i's crossed."

She smiled—I think—and nodded, although I doubted she'd caught my little pun.

Stepping aside, she invited me in and led me to the formal living room, an echo-filled chamber with a high, beamed ceiling, fireplace, and exquisite furnishings. She pointed to one of two burgundy-colored, velveteen wingback chairs grouped with a white sofa and glass-topped coffee table. I obediently settled into the chair, while she perched in the center of the sofa and crossed her legs. Her tailored, tweed, above-the-knee tube skirt showed them off, while a low-cut lime green blouse made it difficult to ignore her bulging cleavage, the kind which can be bought, if that was the way you wanted to invest your life savings.

"Thank you for agreeing to the interview," I said.

"Not a problem," Kathryn said, her tone pleasant but brittle. She gestured toward a flower-patterned teapot placed on the coffee table alongside two matching cups and saucers, a honey-pot, and two spoons. "I hope you like chamomile tea," she said. "I prepared it myself and find it quite refreshing. Don't you?"

I didn't. I hated tea. I've decided that hot-beverage drinkers fall into two categories: those with tea personalities, cerebral and proper; and those with coffee personalities, the risk-takers and the avant-garde. I, falling into the latter class, preferred a robust, fly-by-the-seat bite to my beverage as I did to everything else in my life. But considering the circumstances that day, I told Kathryn, "Why, yes, I do. I've found nothing charges my battery quite like a cup of chamomile."

As she poured the wan beverage from the dainty pot into the dainty cups, I opened my note pad and uncapped my pen. She smiled demurely and set one of the steaming cups of brew and its saucer on my side of the table, while I made a note in my cryptic shorthand that only I could read: *Heavy makeup cannot conceal subcutaneous phoniness.*

"Well now," she said, "I'm afraid I can give you only twenty minutes, and then I must prepare for another appointment. I'm sure you understand that there's still much to be done for this weekend."

"Of course," I said, "which makes me curious about whether your husband's nursemaid—Randa, I believe is her name—is working today."

"Even hired help get a day off," Kathryn said, drizzling a teaspoon of honey into her cup.

"Ah," I said, "even hired help. Of course. And your husband? Where is he?"

Kathryn stirred her tea and laid the spoon on the table. "Jack's asleep in his room." Her tone turned suddenly icy. "Why do you ask?"

"I was hoping to speak with him, too."

Kathryn frowned. "Surely you know that my husband is not well. He spends most of his time in bed and receives few visitors."

Yes, I hear he's little more than a vegetable, I wanted to say, but didn't. Instead, I asked, "But what about the banquet Saturday?

If he's not well, how will he attend?"

"We're hopeful," she said. "We're optimistic that Jack will be up for the demands of a public appearance, that he'll be alert and able to communicate. If he is, and I do stress 'if,' he will need all the rest he can get between now and then. So, dear, while I do appreciate your concern for him, must I remind you that my time today is rather limited? Whatever questions you need to ask for your article, I suggest you get to them without any further delay."

"Of course," I replied, gritting my teeth. I considered asking her who had called to warn her of my visit yesterday, but I changed my mind. It was too early to tip my hand. "Let's start with how you and Mr. Baxter met."

"Hmmm," she sighed, "how we met." She folded her arms across her bosom and pursed her lips. Her focus drifted upward. A beat passed before she embarked on her story. It sounded to me like a recitation. "After Ginny, Jack's first wife, passed away, he was understandably distraught."

"Distraught," I echoed while I made the notation onto my pad.

Kathryn looked at me with a forced grin. "Several months later, in the spring," she said, "he made a trip to French Lick. You're familiar with that lovely Southern Indiana resort, aren't you, dear?"

I took the question as rhetorical and did not respond. She went on.

"He planned to stay a week at the St. Claire Hotel down there, soaking up the sun, playing tennis and golf, and, in general, pampering himself. Fortuitously, I was there at the same time for the exact same purpose. I had lost my husband the previous autumn too. I must admit, when Jack and I met, it was love at first sight, and he proposed on our first date. Talk about a whirlwind courtship." Kathryn tittered. I could only guess she was feigning virtue. A moment went by and she resumed her storytelling. "Two months later, in June, we were married. We had a lovely little wedding right here in Elmwood in the chapel of Main Street Methodist Church."

"That would have been in June of '93?" I said.

"Yes, that's right."

I made another cryptic note: *Remarried six months after Ginny's death—a few weeks before Whitfield dies and Potts disappears.* "So, did you know what you were getting into when you said 'I do'?" I asked. "Did you have any idea you were marrying a Hoosier legend?"

Kathryn giggled into her teacup as she slurped up her first sip. "Yes and no," she said, replacing the cup onto its saucer. "I knew as soon as I met him that he was someone very special, but to tell you the truth, it wasn't until he brought me home with him that I realized how much he meant to this community. Why, it's been more than twenty years since he coached football here, and still, people act like it was yesterday that he—"

And that's when she turned on the spigots. Her eyes turned dewy, and her voice cracked. "Forgive me," she said, stopping to withdraw the hankie stashed between her boobs. She blew her nose into the embroidered cloth and continued. "It's just that Jack is such a wonderful, giving man. He means everything to me. The few months we had together before his—" She paused, biting her fist to stifle a tiny gasp. "—his stroke," she went on weakly, "surpassed anything even the most moonstruck romantic could imagine."

Whether the tears were genuine or crocodile, I felt slightly embarrassed for her. And since I lacked the innate skill to comfort a sobbing woman, I didn't try to.

"I wasn't living in Elmwood when your husband suffered his stroke," I said. "So, I hope you don't mind my asking what happened?"

It didn't make sense to me. Baxter had been a strapping man—six foot two, muscular, healthy, athletic. I heard there'd been nothing in his medical history to suggest he was a candidate for a debilitating illness. But apparently, it had been a stroke, the pressure building inside his head for years, preparing to erupt.

"They called it a massive cerebral hemorrhage," Kathryn said, twisting the hankie around her left forefinger to mop up the rivulets of mascara streaming down her face. "But it wasn't as if he was asking for it." She sighed deeply. "Not that anyone does, but what I mean is, for a man of sixty, he was in fantastic shape. Hell, he was in fantastic shape for a man of forty, the picture of health."

I softened my tone. "Were you with him when it happened?"

She raised her handkerchief to her mouth and nodded. Her eyes closed, and a beat passed before she took in a deep breath through her mouth and answered. "Are you going to use this for your article?"

"Well, his illness is an important part of his life story, isn't it?" I said.

"Yes, I suppose it is," she said. "We'd gone to Palm Springs for the long Thanksgiving weekend. We had planned a romantic getaway. It was a trying time for us. One of the boys on that year's team had died, and Jack was struggling to deal with it. There were days when—"

"Excuse me," I said, "but didn't two boys die?"

Her placid smile flattened. "No. Another boy, who was responsible for the other boy's death, ran away. He was never caught."

"Oh," I said, playing dumb. "I thought he'd been cleared of any wrongdoing."

"Actually, he wasn't, but I don't see what any of that has to do with a story about Jack." Kathryn made a show of looking at her diamond-studded wristwatch. "But you reporters are good at sensationalizing the minutiae, so you can write a story that'll sell more papers."

"Is that what you think I'm doing?" I said, relaxing my jaw to convey astonishment. "I'm merely asking questions to get to the heart of the story. The way a man of Jack's caliber reacts to the untimely death of not one but two students a few days apart will paint a powerful picture of what's in his soul."

"Perhaps," Kathryn said, uncrossing her legs and standing, "but our time is up."

"You haven't given me anything," I protested.

"Too bad," she said. "Make something up. That's what you would do anyway. But I warn you, if it's libelous, you'll hear from my attorney."

I took the cue and let myself out, feeling Kathryn's spidery eyes burn into my back all the way to the door.

Kathryn's behavior was not surprising. I only hoped she hadn't poisoned me with that awful chamomile tea. The interview wasn't very productive, but it wasn't a complete waste of my time either. I learned two things: the woman was insanely protective of her husband, and Randa was absent.

25

I SAT IDLING in Clip's Corvette at the bottom of the driveway, while I debated whether to stay awhile longer and play detective or go back to the office. During the interview, Kathryn had stressed her need to prepare for her next appointment, and I was curious about who she was meeting. I decided to stay.

I mulled over my brief interview with Kathryn. She obviously thought it was fine that Jack had jumped into the relationship soon after his first wife's death. But in good marriages, it's not all that uncommon for surviving spouses to dive right back in and tie the knot with replacement partners to recapture their familiar lifestyle. And face it—twenty years ago, Kathryn had been attractive and young. At some point, Jack's male ego fired up the ol' libido. If she had indeed hustled Jack, she had done it with his permission. And look how it had paid off for her. She had the best of both worlds. Jack was out of the picture for all intents and purposes, but he still provided her a cushy lifestyle and prestige as his wife. Exactly what ailed him and what kept him alive were two more of the many questions that ate at me. I hoped the arrival of her next appointment would provide a clue.

The Baxter house was perched at the top of a hill on a cul-de-sac. The traffic, both motorized and pedestrian, was light. I eased the car into the street and proceeded to the first intersection, where I made a right turn into a quiet residential neighborhood and parked along the curb. With the 'Vette out of Kathryn's view, I hoofed it back up the street and ducked behind a very large evergreen tree about fifty feet from the Baxters' driveway. Without the aid of a rope and pickax, I climbed the steep, heavily wooded hill that doubled as a barricade to the Baxter house, supplying them with full privacy that few homes could claim. By the time I reached the top, my pantyhose were streaked with runs, and my crepe-soled wedgies were caked with mud. Nevertheless, I was delighted to find myself in the side yard with a straight-line view of the front entrance. At least a dozen stately trees stood between me and the house to provide cover, alleviating my worry about being spotted. Although the questionable wisdom of spying on the Baxters gave me pause, I had to admit that it had been a long time since I'd engaged in covert surveillance. It felt good to be at it again.

I had hoped I wouldn't have to wait long for Kathryn's appointment to arrive, and to my relief, within a couple minutes, a silver sedan zipped up the Baxters' driveway and stopped in front of the house. I slunk behind a huge tree trunk and watched a well-built man wearing a brown bomber jacket and tight jeans climb out and swagger up the stoop. His golden-blond hair was streaked with gray and looked a skosh on the long side for Elmwood, but well groomed. He wore an earring in his left earlobe, another novelty for Elmwood. The instant he gave the door a knuckle tap, Kathryn greeted him with an open-mouthed kiss that I swear lasted longer than the Spanish Inquisition.

"I'm sure you understand that there's still much to be done for this weekend," she had told me during our interview. Much to be done for this weekend my ass. I've ridden the merry-go-round often enough to know when the horsey is going up and when it is going down. I hadn't the slightest idea who the man was, but one thing I did know—he wouldn't be anonymous for long.

The smart thing to do would be to go back to the office now. I'd far exceeded my original expectations, and lord knew I had plenty of work piling up on my desk. Yet, that work would still be there no matter when I got around to it, while the opportunity to gather new information that might help identify Gertie's assailant would be fleeting. After Kathryn and her eleven-thirty appointment retreated indoors, for what my dirty mind could only imagine, I threw my diminishing good sense to the wind and crept forward, scurrying from one tree on to the next, gaining ground with each advance. I felt ridiculous, like Wile E. Coyote in a Road Runner cartoon.

Reaching the house, I pressed my back against the brick exterior and sidestepped my way to the front, where I peeked around the corner at the car. I committed both the rental company sticker and the license plate number to memory and inched my way back to the first of four ground-floor windows.

I sneaked a look through the first. Inside was an unoccupied room outfitted with a desk, a credenza, and a bookcase, obviously an office or den. I scooted to the second window and peeked into another darkened room. Furnished with a couch, a couple of upholstered chairs, a side table, and a TV set, it looked like a typical family room. The curtain was drawn on the next window, so I eased on down to the fourth and last one, careful to avoid the bird feeder dangling from an eight-foot-tall pole planted to the left of the window. Inside, Kathryn was yelling.

Her diatribe was muffled, but I caught snippets of words—"bumbling idiot," "brain-dead gomer," and "miserable bastard" among them. She was definitely berating someone, and I feared that someone was Coach. Even at the risk of getting caught, I had to see what was going on. If this was a case of elder abuse, I needed to know so I could intervene. I scrunched down and peered in over the window's ledge.

It was Coach all right. He was seated in a wheelchair and covered chest to knees with what appeared to be vomit. He faced the window, and standing before him, with her back to me, was Kathryn, screaming like a wild animal. Coach gave no sign of comprehension, except for one unsettling curiosity. His eyes were locked directly on mine.

A breath caught in my throat. I couldn't tell if he could actually see me or was even aware of what was going on. I wondered if he shared my fear that his wife's rant would escalate to more than a verbal assault. I felt I had to do something, if only provide a distraction that might serve as a reset to the volatile scene I was witnessing.

Without giving much forethought, I rose to my full height and folded my right hand into a fist. My plan was to bang on the window and bolt, like a kid pulling a prank. I knew it was a piss-poor plan, but I had neither the resources nor the time to confer with a strategist. It was a United States Secretary of Defense who once said, "You go to war with the army you have." That's what I intended to do.

My arm was in a full throttle, forward momentum, my knuckles a millimeter from the glass, when Kathryn's friend entered the room. I pulled the punch and dropped to the ground, unintentionally bringing down the bird feeder pole with my left hip. The resounding clatter was my cue to burn rubber, or in that case, crepe.

26

ALONE IN MY OFFICE, less than a half an hour later, I was scarfing down a nutritious lunch of ramen noodles and sorting through a new stack of "While You Were Out" slips from Darcy. Among them was an 11:30 a.m. message from Verl marked "Urgent! Call ASAP!!!" and a confirmation from Frank Whitfield about our 3:30 appointment. There also was a threat from the mayor promising "heads would roll," which I thought an amusing pun, if I ran one more lie about him. I pitched his message into the trash can.

I picked up the phone, intending to call Verl, but on second thought, phoned the hospital for an update on Gertie. She wasn't any better, the nurse said, but she wasn't any worse either, which I took as a tick for the plus column. I then looked up the number of the Indianapolis-based Capitol City Rent-a-Car, the name on the automobile driven by Kathryn Baxter's visitor. I punched in the number, and an operator answered. I identified myself as the manager of Thrifty-Mart and explained that the key to one of the rental company's cars had been turned in to lost and found. I said I needed to confirm the driver's name before I gave the key to the man claiming it. The operator put me on hold and a minute later, a customer service agent came on the line and divulged that the car had been rented to a Mr. Brad Pitt of Hollywood, California. I rolled my eyes, thanked her, and hung up.

Before I returned Verl's call, there was one last detail I needed to attend to. I picked up the receiver again and tapped in Randa Muridae's number. The connection rang three times before a gravelly voice grumbled, "Hello?"

"What the hell?" I said. I knew that gravelly voice. "Verl?"

"Hell, yes," he said. "What took you? I've been waiting an hour to hear from you. I left messages at the office and on your cell phone. You might want to get over here. There's something I think you'll want to see."

I was confused. How the hell had I reached Verl? I thought I had called Randa. "What're you talking about? Where are you?"

"Didn't Elsie tell you? I'm over here at Herk Williams's duplex. He's been out of town since Monday and came home today to a real mess. There's water everywhere. Looks like the goddamned levee broke."

"Whoa," I said, "hold on a cotton-pickin' minute. I've been a little busy lately. So unless there's a good reason I ought to give a rat's rear about Herk Williams's drainage problem, I'm hanging up."

"Crystal," he barked, "zip your lip, and I'll tell you."

"Fine," I said, "tell me."

"Thank you," he said. "From the looks of things, we have us a crime scene, and I suspect you'll—"

"Crime scene?" I said. "Herk drowned?"

"I'm serious, Crystal. Shut. Up." A few bristling seconds of silence passed between us, then he said, "Herk came home this morning and found his apartment soaked with water leaking from the ceiling. He rushed upstairs to check on his tenant. She wasn't there, but apparently she had plugged up her bathtub drain and left the water running for hours."

"And this concerns me how?" I said, making certain my voice telegraphed my annoyance that he still hadn't gotten to the point.

"His tenant is a woman by the name of Muridae."

"Muridae?" I repeated. "*Randa* Muridae?"

"Yeah. The woman you mentioned last night, which is why I thought you might be interested."

"Hell, yes, I'm interested. She's the Baxters' housekeeper."

"Well, I certainly hope she's safe," Verl said.

"What?" A serrated jolt of fear ripped through me. One thing Randa had said to me the day before echoed in my head: *Mrs. Baxter watches me like a hawk.* "What happened to her?"

"I can't really say. She's—"

"She's what? . . . Shot? Stabbed? Strangled?" I shouted into the phone.

"I'm trying to tell you," Verlin shouted back. "I don't know. She's not here."

"Not there? I don't understand. If she's not there, why the hell would you call it a crime scene?"

"The dead bolt is busted," he said. "When Herk got up here, he found the front door standing open. Granted, this could'a been the work of vandals, but there may have been foul play."

"I'll be right there." I started to hang up, but remembering Verl's tendency to muck things up, I added, "Don't touch a thing."

27

I GAVE MY LONG, SKINNY LEGS ANOTHER WORKOUT and race-walked the half mile from my office to the duplex at Sixth and Oak. The moment my foot sank into Randa's soggy carpet, I was besieged by Verl's blustering histrionics. "I'm the sheriff here, and if I want to touch things, by God I'm gonna touch things."

I ignored him and made a visual sweep of the tiny, two-room apartment. Its centerpiece was a gray-and-pink love seat pushed against the north wall. Beside it was a nondescript dining table, accompanied by two matching chairs. On the west wall was a small, upholstered rocker, red with gold threads, and a desk, one of those cheap, assemble-it-yourself models. A pair of dollar-store-quality prints adorned the wall over the couch, and a sun-burst clock dominated the opposite wall. Except for the entire place being waterlogged, nothing appeared amiss.

"What happened?" I said, turning to Verl.

"It's too early to know, but since there's no sign of the Muridae woman, I'm inclined to think she was abducted."

Wading through the combination living room/bedroom

toward the bathroom, I said, "What makes you say that?"

Verl pointed to the black-and-brown tweed coat hanging on the coat rack. "Would you leave the house without your coat in this weather?"

"It's doubtful," I said, eyeing the bathtub, filled to the rim with water, and the bathrobe and towel draped across the closed toilet seat lid. "Especially not if I was dressed for a bath."

I reversed my rudder and sloshed toward the kitchenette. As I passed the sofa, my right foot brushed against a small object in my path. I glanced down and stopped.

"Verl," I said, "here's something you might want to bag as evidence."

"Whatcha got?"

"Randa's glasses."

They were the same ones she'd worn when we met Tuesday—red horn-rims with round, oversized lenses about a quarter inch thick. The three of us must have been blind to overlook them.

Verl picked them up. "These are what I'd call serious glasses. If the woman's eyesight is as bad as these spectacles suggest, why would she leave home without them?"

Herk and I both shrugged, although the answer was obvious.

"Guess they validate my foul-play theory," Verl said.

A validation, indeed. It gave me the willies. Since Monday night, two women had trusted me with possible incriminating information, and now both their lives were hanging in the balance.

"Right, chief," I said. "Now what?"

"You can start by telling me how you got this number," Verl snipped.

"I got her number from the caller ID after she called me

yesterday afternoon."

"She called you?" Verl's demeanor stiffened. "You just met the woman yesterday morning, and just like that—" Verl snapped his fingers. "—she calls you. Isn't that interesting?" He crossed his arms, resting them on top of his belly. "May I assume that she didn't call to exchange cookie recipes?"

"Yes, you may assume she didn't call to exchange cookie recipes."

"Then *what?*" Verl griped. "What did she want?"

"She called to tell me what I already knew, that Gertie had been cleaning the Baxters' house on Monday, and really that's about the extent of the conversation."

Verl arched a brow. "That's it? Seems odd that she would feel the need to set the record straight."

"That's what I thought, too," I said. "So now, in light of this development, obviously we've got some detective work to do." I paused to give Verl a chance to rebut my declaration. When he didn't, I asked, "Did anyone see anything?"

"Not that I know of," he said, "but I've got Chuck on it, checking with neighbors. It might be helpful if you happened to remember what time Miss Muridae called you."

"Of course, I remember," I said. "I'd picked up a late lunch and was just finishing it at my desk when she called."

"Time?" Verl said.

I needed to think about that for a moment, but a mere five seconds later, he said more insistently, "Do you recall the time?"

"Of course I recall the time," I said with exaggerated assurance to suppress my flummox over the order and times of the many stops I'd made Tuesday. After a quick estimate of the time spent at each, I said, "She called around four o'clock. The call was brief. I expected to see her today when I returned to the

Baxters' to interview Kathryn for my Coach profile."

"I take it Miss Muridae wasn't there," Verl said.

I sighed. "Do you not think I would have mentioned if she had been?"

"Just asking," Verl said.

"I did ask Kathryn about Randa, and she said she had the day off, which I didn't believe. I had a bad feeling then and a worse feeling now."

Turning to Herk, I asked, "How well did you know Miss Muridae?"

Herk scrunched up his receding chin and rolled his head side to side. "She rented this apartment three weeks ago. Paid her first and last, plus a deposit. All in cash. She seemed okay to me. Quiet. Polite. That's all I knowed."

"You didn't do a background check? References?" I said.

"Naw, you get a feel for people," he said. "I listen to my gut."

"Any visitors?"

"Not that I seen."

"Is this her furniture or yours?" I asked Herk.

"The apartment comes furnished," he said.

I opened both of the desk drawers—empty.

"Where's the bed?" I asked him.

"The sofa folds out," he said.

To Verl, I said, "I presume you will open it?"

A sliding door next to the bathroom turned out to be the combination linen-and-clothes closet. There wasn't much in it— a couple of uniforms like the one she wore Tuesday, a white cardigan, a white T-shirt, a pair of jeans, and a simple black dress. On the floor were two pairs of shoes—white sneakers and basic black flats. I found nothing remarkable about Randa's wardrobe until I checked the size of the jeans—two. I've had pimples larger than size two.

"Did she have a car?" I said, turning to Herk.

"Yeah, it's parked out back," he said.

"Have you run her license plate yet?" I asked Verl.

"Matter of fact . . . ," he said, inserting two fingers into his left breast pocket to extract a small slip of paper. Unfolding it, he went on, "It's registered to a Gloria Sparks, 526 Westmoreland Street, Earlville."

"Sparks? Earlville?" I echoed. The names struck a chord, but it took me a second to make the connection that the Pottsses' private investigator, Nolan *Sparks*, had been from *Earlville*. Coincidence? I thought not.

"Yeah," Verl said. "I figured I'd send one of the boys down there tomorrow. See what he can turn up."

I had a better idea. "Verl, do me a favor," I said. "Hold off on that until Friday. I think I've got it covered."

"You've got it covered?" Verl glared at me over the top of his readers and raised an eyebrow. I'm sure he thought it made him look debonair.

"Give me a day, okay?"

I figured he would. Organizing crowd control, traffic management, and security for Coach's approaching shindig was almost more than he could handle with his small staff. Considering the extra publicity the Indianapolis media had provided, Verl would be damned lucky if he pulled it all off without breaking into hives.

"Fine," he said, affirming my assumption. "I'll give you two days. But you better not be wasting time."

"Excuse me for a moment, gentlemen," I said. I headed down the stairs and out of earshot before calling Darcy.

"I need you to do something for me," I said. "Write this down."

A beat passed, and she said, "Crystal?"

"Good girl," I said. "I need you to get down to Earlville and check on a Gloria Sparks residing at 526 Westmoreland Street. I need to know who she is and why a car registered to her is here in Elmwood in the possession of a Randa Muridae, who's been working for about three weeks as Jack Baxter's nursemaid. Obviously, I need you to get everything you can about the Sparks woman as well as Muridae." I waited for Darcy's response. Several seconds passed. "Darcy, did you get all that?"

"Five-twenty-six West what street?"

I went through it all again, much more slowly, doling out the details of the assignment in smaller bites.

"When did you want me to do this?" Darcy said. "I've got a date in two hours, and there's no way I'm going to miss it."

"Dear," I said with the patience of an Olympian, "this morning you complained that your reporting assignments lacked substance. What I've given you is an assignment that not only has substance, it may well be tied to the biggest story ever to break in Elm County. I would go myself, but I am following other leads. We experienced journalists know that sometimes chasing a big story requires us to cancel our plans. No matter how cute and sexy they may be. So what do you say, Darcy? Are you going to be my Lois Lane or my Lindsay Loser? Your choice."

Still another pause. "Fine," she finally said, sans the enthusiasm I'd hoped to hear. "I'm on the clock. I get reimbursed for gas. And dinner."

"Take your pad and pen, dear. Make us proud."

28

VERLIN SHUTTLED ME BACK TO MY OFFICE shortly past three o'clock. I assured him I had a couple hours of work to do, then would head home for a quiet evening of TV and doing my nails. It seemed to pacify him. Perched on the curb outside the *Gazette*, I flicked Verl a wave as he drove away. The instant he rounded the corner, I made a dash for Clip's Corvette and split for the Whitfields'. I arrived ten minutes early for my three-thirty appointment.

Frank and Tammy still lived in the same place they had when their son, Lance, was alive, about five miles north of town in a rustic, two-story farmhouse roosting at the crest of a sprawling parcel of land. I drove up their private lane and parked next to the house. I stepped out of the car, and a blustery, frigid wind blew its chill straight through me. I folded my arms across my chest and tensed my muscles, as if that would fend off the cold.

A shoddy wire fence framed the perimeter of the residential portion of the property, which was flanked on the east with unplowed acreage extending as far as I could see. Dotted by patches of melting snow, the ground awaited the spring planting of beans and corn. On the opposite side of the main property, a weathered red barn lent the only splash of color within eyeshot. An old pickup was parked alongside it, and behind it was a grassy grazing pasture populated by about a dozen brown cows. The scene reminded me of an Andrew Wyeth painting.

The peaceful ambiance was in direct opposition, I was sure, to the despair my visit was about to evoke. As much as I hated to do it, I would ask Frank and Tammy about their son, forcing them to relive the days and circumstances surrounding his tragic death. Asking the tough questions meant first shedding my identity as "Crystal Cropper, the tenderhearted empathizer" and morphing into "Crystal Cropper, the relentless, hard-core newswoman, who's only doing her job." Whenever I forced myself to make the necessary transition for the sake of a story, I didn't know where the affable Crystal retreated to. I never evaluated it. I couldn't. I dared not risk over-analysis for fear I would lose that essential ability to separate. So there I was, "Crystal Cropper, the unswayable reporter," rapping lightly on the Whitfields' front door on a mission that would break their hearts.

"Miss Cropper," someone shouted from a distance. I turned. Frank was plodding up his expansive lawn, headed my way. He raised his right hand overhead and waved broadly.

"Hi," I shouted, returning the wave.

"Sorry to make you wait," he called out. "Been here long?"

"Nope. I just got here."

He was close enough by then for me to see the flush to his cheeks and hear his labored breathing—penalties, I assumed, for a sedentary winter and years of poor choices at the dinner table. That assumption was confirmed when the wind whipped open one side of his jacket to reveal a hefty roll of belly fat protruding over the waistband of his jeans.

"Tammy'll be along in a minute," he said, extending his right hand as he ambled up to me. "She's out back feeding the chickens."

I grasped his hand, cold and chapped, and gave it a shake. He was shorter than I expected. I felt like a giant looking down to meet his piercing blue eyes. "Thanks for making time for me."

I followed him inside through the side door, where he hung his sheepskin-lined jacket on a hook and led me to the kitchen. As we walked through the house, I sensed its warmth, both physically and viscerally. Heavy dark wood from the baseboards to the doorframes to the ceiling rafters contrasted soft, pastel furnishings and flowery wallpaper. A hint of citrus scented the air, and dozens of family photos, many of their deceased son, dominated every room.

Before our meeting, I knew the Whitfields only by sight. They turned out to be a lovely couple, warm, candid, and down-to-earth. After Tammy joined Frank and me, we sat around their kitchen table for the next hour chatting as we downed fresh coffee and munched on Tammy's famous German chocolate coffee cake, which had earned blue ribbons for her at the last seven county fairs.

A wholesomely attractive, perky blonde, Tammy couldn't have been much over five foot tall. She was the perfect hostess and made sure Frank and I had everything we needed, even before we knew we needed it, as if that was her purpose. She was in her element in the kitchen and one of those women born to be homemakers.

"Can I get you something else?" she said. "If you're getting hungry, I can put together a sandwich. It won't take but a minute."

"No, really, I'm fine," I said, although it was tempting. But, no, I also had a purpose, and so far I had skirted it by asking them nothing but soft questions about Coach. I swallowed my last bite of cake and moved on to the first of the hard questions. "Why do you think the boys Jack Baxter coached rallied around him with such unshakable loyalty?"

"I never did know," Tammy said. "It was almost like he cast a spell over those kids that took over their common sense."

She paused, and Frank jumped in. "They did whatever he told them to do."

"And drank whatever Kool-Aid he served," Tammy added, punctuating her comment with a titter and a shrug. "Right, honey?" She looked at Frank.

He smiled and shrugged.

Their answer caught me off guard and opened the door to a possibility I hadn't yet considered. "Wait a minute," I said. "Are you saying Jack Baxter abused his authority?" Unscrupulous coaches have been known to take advantage of the power bestowed upon them by their organizations, and even more so among unscrupulous *winning* coaches. In recent years, cases of coaches' abusive conduct had gained national attention, and some of them were at the high school level. So, it suddenly occurred to me, why not Elmwood? Why not Jack Baxter? "Do you think Baxter coerced his teams with emotional or even physical punishment?"

"Oh, no," Tammy said, shaking her head vigorously, "no, no, no, no."

Frank shook his head as well and echoed his wife's denial. "No, absolutely not! The boys idolized Coach. And we did too. Everyone did. He was a good and caring man, a natural with young people."

"To know Coach was to love him," Tammy said.

"I'm sensing that you remained supportive of Coach after . . ." I hesitated, groping for the gentlest lever to switch tracks and avoid the verbal train wreck I was headed for. Softening my voice, I continued, ". . . after Lance's . . . accident?"

Tammy jumped right in. "God, yes! You should have seen Coach at the hospital," she said, her tone falling to a murmur. "The way that man carried on, if you hadn't known better, you would've thought Lance was his own son. He didn't leave our boy's bedside for longer than ten minutes at a time. That whole day, he was there, crying with us, praying with us . . ."

"And mourning with us," Frank added as he wrapped an arm around his wife's shoulders.

"Sounds like he was a great comfort to you," I said, intoning what I hoped was appropriate empathy.

"Coach was our rock," Tammy said, her eyes filling with water and her chin quivering. "We couldn't have gotten through those days and weeks without him."

"I understand he spoke at Lance's funeral," I said.

"Yes, he gave a beautiful tribute," Frank said.

"Beautiful," Tammy echoed. "He had a lot of hope for Lance's future."

"Lance would have been courted by some of the Big Ten schools as soon as the season started," Frank said. "Our boy was an exceptional athlete, and he would've landed a full-ride scholarship to the college of his choice if . . ."

Frank's eyes glazed over again, so I jumped in to change the subject with another question.

"How long since you last spoke with Baxter?" I said.

Frank frowned and expelled a long puff of air out the side of his closed mouth. "Oh, gee, what do you think, honey?" He looked at Tammy. "Twenty years?"

"Twenty years?" I said. "Are you sure? I thought the three of you had grown close."

"Yes, we had," Tammy said, "but we haven't seen him since the stroke, and . . ." Her voice cracked and fresh tears filled her eyes. ". . . I'm sorry."

"No need to apologize," I said. I had done this to her, and it made me feel like crap. I was thankful when Frank picked up his wife's narrative.

"Coach suffered a stroke four months after we buried Lance, and after that, we never saw him again. It's my understanding that he never recovered the use of his faculties, and he's been a recluse ever since."

"Did you have a relationship with Kathryn?"

"We did not," Tammy snapped. "And I'll leave it at that."

"Coach was a saint," Frank said, "but that woman is some kind of snake."

"The poisonous kind!" Tammy added sharply.

"Did you have some sort of run-in with her"? I asked.

"Coach was in intensive care fighting for his life," Frank said. "It hadn't even been twenty-four hours since the stroke, and doctors didn't know if he would pull through or not. We called the hospital in Palm Springs, hoping for an update on his condition, and that woman grabs the phone and tells us she hired some big-shot defense attorney, and we'd be in for a lot of heartburn if we sued her husband for the wrongful death of our boy."

I was intrigued by Kathryn's blatantly insolent presumption that the Whitfields might sue. "Had you considered suing?"

"No," Frank said. "Why would we? We loved the guy. Filing a suit against Coach wasn't even on our radar screen."

"He was lucky to have friends like you," I said, "considering the role he played in Lance's death."

"What role?" said Tammy. "It was Eugene Potts who gave our boy the drug."

"Perhaps so," I said, "but Baxter was the adult and should have realized Lance was sick. Was Lance taking any sort of medicine before he left home that day?"

"It was the middle of summer, for Pete's sake," Tammy said. "We didn't have anything here for a cold." I sensed a subtle defensive shift in her demeanor. "He had the sniffles, and I gave him some vitamin C. If you're suggesting he was seriously ill, he wasn't."

"Maybe he wasn't, but it was over ninety degrees that day," I said. "Coach should have sent him home. Instead, he made your son suit up and get on the field. It's a wonder more boys didn't suffer heatstroke. Can you explain why no one held him accountable? Why didn't *you*?"

This was the question that crossed the line. The second it rolled off my tongue, Frank and Tammy's faces hardened, and what was left of their hospitality lost all its warmth.

"As an outsider, you couldn't possibly understand. Besides that," Tammy said tersely, "our son's death is none of your business."

After a prickly moment of silence, Frank said, "This conversation is over. We'll see you to your car."

I didn't argue. I appreciated the Whitfields' hospitality and admired them for tolerating my intrusive meddling for as long as they did. Even amid the bristling undertow of pain I had wrought for this gracious couple, they walked me outside and waited as I climbed into Clip's car and started the engine. As I shifted into reverse, I rolled down the window so I could ask them one final invasive question.

"I nearly forgot to mention that I spoke with Ray and Noni Potts yesterday. They said Eugene rode his bicycle out here to see you the morning before Lance's funeral, and I just wondered what the three of you talked about."

Tammy immediately turned and walked away, but Frank stayed put, his jaws clenched, nostrils flared. "Ray and Noni Potts," he said with a snarl, "are fully aware that their son did not show up at our house that day nor any other day. And you would know that too if you were any kind of reporter."

Point taken, I thought.

"Do you have a theory on what happened to Eugene?" I said.

And that's where the last grain of Whitfield hospitality exploded.

"You've got exactly thirty seconds to get off my property," Frank said, "and then I call the sheriff."

Point taken.

29

ALTHOUGH IT WAS ALMOST DINNERTIME, I drove straight home, bypassing all of Elmwood's fast-food havens. I was totally wiped out. It was only Wednesday, but I felt as if I'd already put in two weeks of hard time since Monday. I owed myself a little "me" time. I was going all lollipops and rainbows just thinking about it.

The second I walked through my front door, I threw off my coat, kicked off my shoes, and headed for the fridge. I had no more than opened the freezer door when the phone rang, and I scurried like Pavlov's dog to answer. So much for lollipops and rainbows.

"Crystal, for the love of God, can't you answer your phone when I call? I thought you had work to do at the office."

It was Verl. I fetched my cell phone, which showed three missed calls from Verl. The phone was on silent, which is how I usually kept it. I could have told Verl for the umpteenth time how much I dislike cell phones, hate what they've done to our society, and pity people who feel the need to be "connected" at all times, but I was in no mood for bickering. I answered with a simple, "What's up?"

"I just found out Gertie's assault might be connected to one of the biggest drug rings ever to operate in this country. The feds have been all over it for months."

Gertie Tyroo mixed up in a nationwide drug ring? Right. A bathtub ring, possibly. Ring around the collar, perhaps. But what Verlin claimed sounded utterly insane. I wondered if he had been hitting the sauce. "You're not making a lick of sense," I said.

"I beg to differ, Miss Smartypants," he said. "It makes a lot of sense. I know you think I operate in a vacuum over here, but I have friends beyond this department, outside this county, and some even extend past the state borders."

"The man who reads my electric meter might have friends in other states, too," I reasoned, "but that doesn't mean he's privileged to classified federal information."

"Look," Verl said, his tone suddenly sharp, "I'm not some guy who reads your meter. I'm the guy who reads your moods, or at least I try to, but apparently I'm not doing such a good job of it lately. So, forgive my ignorance. I'm sorry I bothered you, good night, good luck, and have a nice life."

"Verl, wait," I said, feeling a sudden pang of remorse. "I'm sorry. Of course you've got links to cases beyond this jurisdiction." I could be such a jerk. Verl was my best friend, and sometimes I treated him like stuff I had to scrape off the soles of my boots. "Look, Verl, I'm really sorry. I'm just tired."

"I know, I know. I'm sorry, too."

"Okay," I said, "what have you got? Do you really think Gertie's assault is related to a federal investigation?"

"I know it is. I talked to this fellow today up in Michigan with the DEA—"

"The Drug Enforcement Administra—?"

"Yep, and he told me they've been working for months with the FBI, the FDA, the IRS, and God-knows-who-all on some secret undercover probe called Operation Ring-a-Ding-Ding."

"Well, now, I guess it's not so secret anymore, is it?"

"No, smart-ass, it's not so secret anymore because the boys are swooping in all over the country arresting small-town racketeers for trafficking anabolic steroids, cocaine, and black-market pharmaceuticals imported from places like Pakistan, North Korea, and China."

"You don't say." I didn't believe a word he was telling me. I wondered if he was the butt of a practical joke, although his serious tone told me that he believed this was the biggest federal case since Abscam.

"*I* say," he said.

"And this is linked to the attempt on Gertie's life how?"

"I'm not exactly clear on that part . . ."

Why did that not surprise me?

". . . yet," he continued. "I'm not clear on that *yet*. But according to my Michigan buddy, there are FBI agents right here in Central Indiana homing in on suspects."

"That may be," I said, "but an international black-market drug ring operating here in Elmwood? I don't think so. Nobody in Elmwood is that smart."

Several seconds of silence passed between us. After an uncomfortably long moment, I jumped in and filled the void. "Verl? You still there?"

"Don't you see?" he said. "It's no coincidence that this Quigley clown shows up and starts snooping around."

"He's here to check on Gertie's well-being," I said, hopeful that I could use simple logic to diffuse Verl's crazy conjecture.

"Crys," he said, "how long have we known Gertie?"

I was going to say "decades," but he beat me to it.

"I've known that woman just about my entire life," he said. "As I recall, she showed up here while you and me were still in high school. What would that've been—'65?"

"That sounds about right," I said. "And your point is?"

"In all them years, how many FBI agents have we had poking around here?"

"I don't know. I wasn't here for all 'them' years."

"Well, I was, and I'm telling you, this Quigley is not here for the reason he stated. He's a part of this drug sting. Mark my word."

"Okay, duly marked," I said. "Now, if you will excuse me, I'm going to get off the phone, fix myself a bite to eat, and get my beauty sleep."

"You do that," he said, "and I'll send one of my boys over to keep an eye on your place."

"Verlin, you're a peach."

"I guess that's why they call me 'the fuzz.' G'night, Crys."

Verl had a gift for getting under my skin like nobody else, but he was the only person I could stand talking to first thing in the morning and last thing at night. After I hung up the phone, I flopped onto the couch and switched on the TV. I had planned to relax with a *Law & Order* rerun, but two nights of sleep deprivation finally caught up, and I promptly nodded off. Shortly past 2:00 a.m., I was awakened by the grating voice of aging-but-still-glamorous former sex kitten Sylvia Goldstone peddling her battery-operated, anti-wrinkle zapper, which frankly, if you asked me, looked an awful lot like an adult toy. Curious whether Verlin had fulfilled his promise to send over one of his men, I peeped out the window into the still, dead night. Sure enough, parked directly across the street was one of the county's patrol cars containing the lucky public servant assigned to protect me.

I stirred up a cup of instant coffee and deposited a cherry-flavored Strudel Pop into the toaster. When it was done, I threw my coat over my shoulders and scurried across the street with my offerings for the deputy. As I approached the driver's side of the car, Deputy Riley Paxton, the department's newest rookie, a sweet, fresh-faced kid all of twenty-one, rolled down the window and stared at me with huge, saucer-shaped eyes.

"Ma'am," he said, "is everything all right?"

I quickly assured him that all was well and handed him my meager offerings. Had I known it was Paxton out there, I would have fetched him a glass of warm milk and a sock monkey.

"I was about to fix myself a little midnight snack and thought you might like something too," I explained. "If there's anything in particular I can get you, just ask."

"Thank you, ma'am," he said in his soft, boyish voice. "This here is fine."

"You haven't seen any suspicious-looking bad guys lurking around here in the shadows, have you?"

He smirked a silly half-grin and snorted. "No, ma'am. No bad guys."

"Right, but if you saw any, you'd call the dispatcher, right?"

"Yes, ma'am. I'd radio the dispatch center, and they'd have a backup team over here in nothing flat."

"Thanks, Deputy. Hearing that makes me feel real safe."

"No need to thank me," he said. "It's my honor to be here for our elderly citizens."

I actually gasped. Had he really said what I thought he said? Had he just called me "elderly"? Yes, he had, and for a moment, I entertained reporting the snot-nosed little bastard for police brutality. But who would believe me? He had a face like an angel and was barely out of training pants. It was a losing proposition.

"Well, thanks," I said, imagining the satisfaction I'd get dumping the coffee over his head and stuffing the Strudel Pop up his nose. "I'm honored that you're honored. Take care of yourself, and I'll see you tomorrow night with *two* Strudel Pops."

Proud of my anger management, I hustled my wounded elderly pride back inside, heated up a frozen dinner entrée—angel hair pasta topped by orange-colored sauce and four raisin-sized tomatoes—and flopped back onto my couch, balancing the plastic platter on my knees. Between bites, I punched the TV remote and surfed the cable channels. I was less than thrilled to find more infomercials featuring perky, small-boned blondes selling an assortment of can't-live-without wares on all but two of the channels. Of the two, I passed on the documentary exploring the heartache of spontaneous human combustion—my years of menopausal hot flashes long behind me—and settled on a riveting episode of the *You-nique Antique Boutique*. And that's where I found my first real break in Gertie's case.

Bleary-eyed, I watched a string of antique-bearing guests describe their objects to the show's host, Antique Andy, who made a quick assessment of each item as "valuable treasure" or "worthless piece of junk."

My attention tottered on the brink of unconsciousness by the time a fragile-looking Vermont antique dealer, an antique himself, shuffled across the stage and pointed to a chifforobe—a six-foot-high, oak wardrobe. Elegant in its practical simplicity, its front was divided into halves, one side containing eight drawers and the other a hinged door concealing a clothes closet. It looked exactly like the wardrobe in Gertie's living room.

The old man explained that the Ohio Shakers had

handcrafted it more than a hundred years ago. And, while many of the chifforobes they constructed during that period appeared identical, a few of them contained a built-in, hidden compartment in the back for secure storage of precious family heirlooms. Persons outside the Shaker religion who owned the wardrobe, he said, often used the secret space to hide valuables or private papers. *Or incriminating evidence in a murder case?* The realization struck me like a giant fist.

I'd forgotten about the dinner entrée on my lap and bolted upright, unintentionally launching a glob of spaghetti two feet straight up. What goes up must come down, and when it did, it hit the coffee table with a soft plop. Grumbling but energized, I wiped up the stringy orange mess with a wad of paper towel, the quicker picker-upper, and crafted my plan for first light.

30

I AWOKE SHORTLY PAST 6:00 A.M., just in time to catch a glimpse of Deputy Paxton's squad car driving slowly up the street. Good boy. He'd stayed on Crystal Watch until dawn. Wasting no time, I jumped into a pair of sweat pants and a zip-up hoodie and headed for Gertie's. The early bird catches the worm, and I was going to catch mine.

Gertie's lavender, yellow, and peach-colored cottage was nestled amid a half-dozen mature trees on a puny piece of land in the four hundred block of Hoover Street. Its steeply pitched, slightly off-kilter double-gable roof, white-lace trim, and dilapidated condition made it one of Elmwood's more unusual properties. Its construction predated World War II, and I could only guess that the design had been inspired by a Grimm's fairy tale. To the neighbors' chagrin, Gertie was the solitary holdout in a recent redevelopment project that populated the area with unspectacular, look-alike, single-family dwellings representative of the Clinton-era construction boom. The street screamed for character, and Gertie answered the call with a cavalier "up yours" defiance that I had to admire.

I parked Clip's Corvette two blocks up the street and scanned the surroundings for busybodies. Seeing not a single soul, I stepped out and pretended to be on my morning walk, striding purposely toward the alley that ran behind Gertie's backyard. Except for the crunch of gravel beneath my sneakers, I made a stealthy procession up the narrow lane. As near as I could tell, I attracted no attention. That is, until a drooling, giant set of teeth with four legs—for an apt visual aid, let's call him Cujo—stepped into my path, locked his eyeballs with mine, and dared me to take another step.

The stocky mutt appeared to be a sort of hybrid devil-dog, perhaps part Rottweiler, part St. Bernard. When he started to growl a low, guttural warning, I assumed that I inadvertently had infringed on his doggy territory and presented some sort of threat. And indeed, I did. I vowed to call animal control and have the beast locked up—if I made it out alive. I hate being intimidated, but the situation appeared to be a no-winner, for me anyway, unless I stopped in my tracks and made nice with the portentous pooch.

I forced a wide grin and, in my cheeriest little-girl voice, I cooed, "Hello, you ugly fleabag." Raising my pitch an octave, I added, "Now, why don't you go chase a semi and let the nice lady pass?"

Demon dog did not budge. Instead, it slunk lower and growled even deeper. I was screwed. I could feel my teeth start to sweat. For once, I didn't know what to do. Should I stand my ground and hope this canine bully would give up and leave? Inch backward? Make a mad dash for the car? Lie down and play dead? It was then that my savior, in the form of a small child, stepped into the scene.

"Tiny, you bad boy," she said. She whacked the dog's haunch

gently with an open palm. In her other hand, she carried a triangular, black-and-white plaid scarf. Looking up at me, she said, "I found this over there." She pointed to Gertie's patio. "Is it yours?"

"Nope," I said.

She draped the scarf over Tiny's head babushka-style and secured it with a fat knot under his chin. "Come on, Tiny. It's time for school."

Smiling sweetly, the raven-haired moppet flashed her waifish, Keane-like eyes up at me and led her humiliated hound out of my path. In a way, I could relate to Tiny's wounded pride.

Grateful for the intervention, I shook off the adrenaline rush and proceeded on my way. My press pass in hand, I ducked under the yellow tape strung around Gertie's back door and rushed up the steps. Unfortunately, something had changed since my last visit. The door had been secured with a heavy-duty padlock that not even I could pick. It had a combination. Damn. I shuffled down the steps and tried raising the two windows that overlooked the backyard. They wouldn't budge, probably long painted shut from the inside. The only other back windows led to the basement. I dropped to my hands and knees, crawled to the nearest window, and pushed. To my relief, it opened easily. I poked my head in for a look-see, and that's when I heard, "Crystal?" coming from somewhere behind me.

I withdrew my head, banging it on the top of the window casing and gazed upward into the contorted face of my favorite county sheriff.

"I knew it," he said. "I'd recognize that hind end anywhere."

"Morning, Sheriff," I said. So much for early birds. "What brings *you* here?"

"What brings *me* here? I'm here because two people called 9–1–1 to report a burglary in progress. What in tarnation brings *you* here?"

"Well," I said, my mind scrabbling for a halfway-convincing story. I had already used my lost-can-of-mace excuse to get in there Tuesday. Since nothing came to mind, I supposed the truth, if told in a compelling way, might hold the key, figuratively speaking. And literally, too. If we lived in an ideal world, I simply would have told Verlin I needed a look around inside and he would have helped me to my feet, led me to the door, and let me inside the palace walls. And happy little bluebirds would have serenaded me, and a pair of frolicking mice would have strung me a pearl necklace. But life is no Disney cartoon, I'm not Cinderella, and Verlin is no Prince Charming. But then again, sometimes when I least expect it, he can be a pretty good guy.

"Well, what?" he said. "What did you leave here this time?"

"Nothing," I said. "I think I figured out where Gertie may have stashed a critical clue about who attacked her, and I want to check it out."

"Why didn't you say so?" Verl said, offering a hand. "Come on."

Although no caroling bluebirds or pearl-toting rodents materialized, Verlin graciously helped me up and walked me inside Gertie's palace.

The house was unchanged since my last visit. I stepped carefully through the mess of papers, books, knickknacks, and broken glass as I approached the wardrobe, its doors and drawers still open and its contents strewn this way and that.

"So what's this big clue?" Verl said.

"I'll let you know in a minute," I said. I slipped my right arm into the slim space between the chifforobe and the wall and blindly patted down the rough back panel in search of a secret drawer. I felt nothing but nail heads and splinters. I needed to take a look.

"Lend me a hand with this," I said, grabbing hold of the wardrobe's left front corner, "will you?"

Without hesitation, Verl stepped forward and helped me swing the wardrobe forward several inches. Thanks to a thick felt pad attached to the bottom of each of the four paw-like feet, it slid out as if the floor were coated with ice.

Once I got a clear view of the back panel, I didn't find a drawer, but what I saw confirmed that my hunch was on the right track. Inset at the lower right corner was a wood tile measuring approximately five by five inches. It was barely noticeable, thanks to a snug fit. Drilled into the tile's center was a teeny-tiny hole, about the size of a pencil lead. I inserted the tip of one of my hairpins, and with some fiddling, loosened the wood square and extracted it, exposing a secret compartment behind it.

I smiled at Verl and sang, "Ta-da."

"What?"

"A drawer," I said.

"You suppose she knew it was there?" he said.

"We're about to find out."

I slid the foot-long box into the open. Eureka! My hunch had been right on. Stashed in the drawer were a letter-sized brown envelope, a black-and-white photograph, and a rolled-up sheet of parchment. Exhilarated, I carried the drawer to the kitchen table.

"Let's see what we've got," I said, picking up the photo by the top edge of its fluted border. The picture showed a professional-looking couple, somber and stiff, dressed in attire typical of the 1960s—she attractive and young, he droopy-faced, pudgy, and easily old enough to be the woman's father. The setting appeared to be an office, an assumption I based on the dark, wood-paneled walls decorated with an assortment of official-looking government seals, a heavily populated bookcase, a spacious, uncluttered desk, and a large American flag. The couple each held onto their respective corner of a sheet of paper, which appeared to be some sort of certificate. At first, I thought my eyes were playing tricks. It took a moment before the identity of the two people fully registered. "Oh my God," I croaked.

Verl snatched the picture from me, muttering, "What? What?" He also needed a moment to digest it. "You've got to be kidding."

I didn't think anyone was kidding, even though what we were staring at contradicted everything we thought we knew about Gertie Tyroo. She was the young woman in the snapshot, and the man standing beside her was J. Edgar Hoover.

I snatched the picture back from Verl and flipped it over. Scrawled on the back in nearly translucent blue ink was, "12–12–63." I shrugged one shoulder and gave Verl an I-don't-know grimace. "Do you suppose Quigley was telling the truth about her?" I said.

Verl's unruly eyebrows converged to a V. "Hell if I know. What else is in there?" he said.

I carefully unrolled the parchment. "Oh, my God."

"What?" Verl said.

"It's a commendation," I said, "and it looks like the one in the picture. It says, 'Awarded to Special Agent Geraldine Gertrude Bridges in appreciation for courageous and meritorious service beyond the call of duty on behalf of the United States of America. Awarded this twelfth day of December in the year of our Lord, nineteen hundred and sixty-three,' and it's signed by J. Edgar himself."

"Let me see that," Verl said, taking the paper from me. "Who is Geraldine Gertrude Bridges?"

"Apparently she's *our* Gertie," I said.

"Can't be."

"Take another look."

He studied the photo for at least a full minute. "All these years," he said, "and we never really knew her. How do you suppose she ended up in Elmwood?"

"I can't even imagine, but I'll tell you what. Once we close this case, we're going to find out."

Verl nodded. "What else have we got?" he said.

I took the envelope and turned it over. "Crystal" was scribbled across the front in pencil. My curiosity shot up like a missile. I immediately straightened the metal clasp that secured one end of the paper sheath and withdrew a news clip from the August 13, 1994, edition of the *News Tribune* of Millersburg, Kansas. The story, entitled "Woes Stacking Up in Cemetery," revealed the town council's proposal to bury the dead three to five levels deep in a single plot to save room for new arrivals. Why Gertie thought the article would interest me, I couldn't imagine. I handed the page to Verl as I tossed the envelope to the end of the table, where it landed with a soft clunk. My eyeballs locked on Verl's for a millisecond, then I lunged for the envelope. Verl got to it first and shook the open end over his palm. A stainless steel pendant, about the size of a quarter, tumbled into his grip.

"Well, I'll be damned," he said.

He held up the medallion for my inspection, and my thoughts flashed back to Ray and Noni Potts. They claimed

Gertie contacted them two weeks before asking about their son's medical alert pendant.

"Eugene's?" I said.

Verl handed the pendant to me, and I read the engraving out loud. "Eugene Potts, DOB 6-7-76, Phone 765-555-1212, Allergic to pseudoephedrine." I looked at Verl. "This is exactly what Ray and Noni told me."

"If this thing is legit," Verl said, "it's a major breakthrough. It could tie the kid to somebody who knew what happened to him. Plus it backs up the one key piece of evidence in Potts's favor that we didn't release to the press during the investigation."

The significance of these discoveries was enormous. My optimism about bringing the case to a swift conclusion should have been bubbling over. Unfortunately, where to go from there was bewildering to me. With Gertie out of commission for God only knew how long and possibly forever, the chances for mining meaningful answers were only marginally better than Gertie's chances of full recovery.

31

WHEN I STOPPED AT HOME to freshen up and change into my editor garb—a knee-length brown skirt in a houndstooth print, a black turtleneck, and a rust-colored cable-knit cardigan—I took the opportunity to call Dr. Bannerjee for a Gertie update. In his absence, the ICU nurse on duty reported that Gertie showed neither signs of improvement nor decline. "She's holding her own," the nurse said. I found the continued use of the term annoying, and yet, it was the only positive data about her I could cling to.

I whisked through the *Gazette*'s front door at nine o'clock sharp. Darcy sat at the front desk, where she was typing up announcements for that day's briefs column.

"Good morning," she said. I thought I detected a slight edge to her tone.

"Tell me about your trip to Earlville," I said. "What did you get?"

"I got nothing, but—"

"What do you mean, you got nothing? You didn't find that Sparks woman? Are you telling me you went down there and it was a bust? Is that all you've got to report?"

"Hold on a second," Darcy said, raising her voice and her hands, palm-side out. "Yes, we found Gloria Sparks, but—"

"We? What's this 'we' stuff? Don't tell me you dragged someone along with you, and I bet I know who."

"So what?" she said. "Harold's a trained law enforcement officer, and besides, he said it might be dangerous, and I shouldn't go by myself."

I crossed my arms and drummed my fingers against my elbows while I arched one brow and stared daggers at her. I was hoping I could make her squirm. Secretly, however, I celebrated the success of my little ruse. While I hadn't directly asked Agent Quigley to go down to Earlville to look for Randa Muridae and her possible connection to the Pottses' private investigator, Nolan Sparks, I was certain sending Darcy would accomplish the same result. Not that she had the skills for the detective work, but over the past couple of days, she and Quigley had gotten rather cozy. Considering the FBI resources at his disposal, I'd have wagered that within hours, he would have Randa's whereabouts nailed down and perhaps gathered bits of information tied to Gertie and even to Eugene Potts.

"All right," I said, "what did *Quigley* get?"

Darcy shrugged. "I fell asleep in the car while he was knocking on doors," she said.

"But you eventually woke up," I said, "right? Didn't he tell you what he got?"

Darcy shook her head.

"You were a reporter on assignment," I said. "Didn't you ask questions?"

"Yes, but not about *that*."

"I see." And did I ever. This wasn't going quite as I had envisioned. "When do you expect to hear from him? When can I expect a report?"

"I'm not exactly sure," she said sheepishly, "but I'll keep you posted."

I sighed to convey my annoyance. "Any calls? Anything else I should know about?"

"Judge Stillwater called to remind you about lunch today."

Auggie and I had been meeting for lunch every Thursday for years. Even so, she still called every Thursday morning as a reminder, just in case. It was good that she did because, occasionally, it did slip my mind. As it had today.

"Of course," I said to Darcy. "I knew that."

With roughly three hours before lunch, I sequestered myself in my office. I spent the rest of the morning on routine work for that day's *Gazette* and started on my feature story about Coach for Saturday's morning edition.

• • • •

The Country Corner Café sat on the opposite side of the courthouse square. I arrived right on time. Auggie was already there, seated at our favorite booth next to the front window. We always enjoyed watching the townspeople pass by, since they provided us endless opportunities for entertainment, speculation, and gossip. She had ordered for me, bless her, so my usual—a nutritious pecan-tuna salad on a fresh croissant—was waiting for me. The instant Auggie spotted me, she flashed her butter-melting smile. As I slid into the booth across from her, she tipped her head to the left and mumbled, "Who's that over there with Kathryn Baxter?"

"Where?"

Auggie waggled her thumb in the direction of a cozy table

across the dining room, where an attractive, well-tailored man was seated with Kathryn. She was all gussied up in a smart black suit, which she accessorized with a red scarf, red stiletto-heeled pumps and black lace stockings. *Always a nice look*, I thought, *for a hooker*. Draped over the back of her chair was a black-and-white coat, and something about it niggled at the back of my head like an itch I couldn't quite reach.

"I don't recognize him," she said. "Do you?"

"Yes," I said. "That's Ted Carlson, the anchorman from Channel 16 out of Indianapolis."

"What's he doing here?" asked my imagination-impaired friend.

"I imagine he's here to do a feature about Coach's hall of fame induction," I said.

"If you're right, why would he want to be seen with Kathryn in a place like this?"

"I believe you have that backwards," I said. "Why wouldn't she want to be seen with him? Being in the company of a TV celebrity feeds her ego. And why not here? The Country Corner Café is, after all, Elmwood's finest—the hometown version of Spago."

"I suppose you're right. But poor Coach. I pity him for marrying that self-aggrandizing witch."

I wanted to say, "You don't know the half of it," but since I may have broken the law the day before with my trespassing and window-peeping, I merely nodded.

"His first wife was a saint, a real gem," Auggie said. "Nobody didn't like Ginny Baxter. It devastated Coach when she passed. He was just a shell of his former self without her. "

"I never really knew her," I said. "My loss."

"Did I ever tell you that at one time, back in the '70s, when I was starting out, I practiced probate?"

I shrugged a shoulder. "Sounds familiar."

Auggie leaned forward. Lowering her voice, she said, "I had just been hired by Little, Gillam, Herschfield, and Gnome, the law firm that had handled the Dewer family's legal affairs for years. Ginny, as you may recall, was the last of the Dewer line."

I nodded.

Auggie continued. "Shortly after I was brought in, I was told she was having the lawyers write up her will, leaving the family fortune to Coach if she died first."

I asked, "How much would that have amounted to?"

"Better than ten million is what I was told," she said, "but that's what was left *after* she set up her charities and scholarship funds, plus handed out large chunks of change to several universities."

The batteries powering my mental calculator were on fire.

"Now get this," Auggie said. "The ten million dollars Ginny bequeathed to Coach was all tied up in strings."

"What kind of strings?"

"This is where it really gets good." Auggie rubbed her palms together and grinned conspiratorially. "She stipulated that it was his to spend as long as he was alive, but upon his death, all remaining funds were to go to PETA."

"PETA?" I clasped my mouth shut with both hands to stifle my laughter.

"Shhh," Auggie said with obvious glee. "Ginny specified that none of the remaining estate was to be transferred to any other organization, cause, or person, and particularly not to subsequent wives or heirs resulting from those marriages. And we're talking stocks, bonds, real estate, personal property, cash—all of it. Everything else was to be liquidated or auctioned off and the proceeds given to People for the Ethical Treatment of Animals."

"So," I said softly, "for Kathryn this means what?"

"It means she better enjoy herself while Coach is still among the living because the minute he draws his last breath, she's on her own."

"Beautiful," I said. "There's cosmic justice after all."

"Yeah, that Ginny Baxter, she was something else."

"What do you know about Kathryn Baxter's past?" I said.

Auggie made a grunting noise. "Apparently, before Coach married her, she didn't have one. Since then, however, she's created quite a stir, what with her lavish wardrobe and jewelry, a new luxury car every year, rumored dalliances with younger men, and her condescending, nasty personality. That and how protective she is of Coach are really all I know about her."

"Did I mention that I dropped by the Baxters' place yesterday and interviewed her for a feature story I'm writing about his hall of fame induction?"

Auggie shook her head. "Sounds amusing. How'd it go?"

"About what you'd expect," I said, "but things went south fast once I asked her about Coach's stroke."

"Did she say it was a stroke?" Auggie asked.

"She called it a massive cerebral hemorrhage. Same thing. Why?"

"Oh, I don't know," Auggie said. "There's never a shortage of gossip in this town, so I never put much stock in it. But there were some folks around here who swore Coach didn't have a stroke."

"What made them say that?"

Auggie sighed and rolled her eyes. "It's like this," she said. "When a guy has a stroke, his family doctor is called in. Even if the guy has his stroke while he's on vacation in another state, like Coach did, his doctor typically gets a call. At the very least, when the guy comes home, someone informs his doctor. Right?"

"Sure, I guess so."

"Coach's former doctor is my doctor," she said, "and he told me that after the alleged stroke, Kathryn never called him again. He hasn't seen Coach—either as a patient or socially—since. In fact, nobody I know has seen Coach since the day he and Kathryn headed off for Palm Springs." Auggie shook off her darkening demeanor with her typical jolly laugh. "But, hey, I never said I believe that rubbish."

"But, then again," I said, "there could be something to it."

Staring over my shoulder, Auggie clamped her lips together and motioned to the left again with a small tip of her head. I looked in that direction, and I, like Auggie and most of the Corner Cupboard's other patrons, watched with overt fascination as Kathryn and her anchor buddy promenaded through the restaurant toward the front door. Kathryn conspicuously waved across the room at acquaintances, pausing twice to introduce her companion to them. Just before the two made their exit, they stopped while Ted unfurled Kathryn's coat and helped her into it. I nearly choked on my tuna salad sandwich. The fabric, a distinctive Scottish tartan black-and-white plaid, appeared to be an exact match to the scarf I'd seen that very morning, draped babushka-style over the head of my humiliated, ferocious canine friend, Tiny.

32

AUGGIE AND I HAD JUST TAKEN OUR FIRST BITES of the Country
Corner's famous apple-cinnamon crunch pie when my phone
rang. I checked the incoming number. "It's the sheriff's office,"
I told Auggie. "Verl will be so pleased I turned on the ringer."

"Answer it," she said.

Elsie, Verlin's secretary, dispensed with any preliminary nice-
ties. "Sheriff Wallace suggested you come down here right
away," she said. "He's questioning the mayor and wants you
there."

For once, I didn't balk, didn't argue, didn't complain. I didn't
even ask for a to-go box. I immediately threw a ten on the table
and dashed out the door. I knew Auggie understood.

I burst into Verl's office but was totally unprepared for the
scenario underway. Elmwood's illustrious mayor was on the hot
seat, a metal folding chair positioned in the middle of the room
under the spotlight of a single, bare halogen bulb screwed into
the top end of a five-foot pedestal. The poor schlub looked all
mixed up. His teeth chattered so loud, I half-expected a wood-
pecker. At the same time, he was sweating like a potbellied pig. I

wasn't sure where Verlin had picked up his new interrogation technique, but my guess was some old pulp fiction novel.

"What's going on, boys?" I said.

Dick Head was apparently speechless. The corners of his mouth twitched, but I wasn't sure if he was trying to say something or show off his Humphrey Bogart impersonation.

"Verl, you mind telling me what you two are up to?"

"Sit down," Verl said, pointing toward one of the vinyl chairs reserved for important guests. "Here's what's going down. I got a call this afternoon from Cara Beckwick. You know Cara, don't you?

"Of course, I know the city auditor," I said.

"She came over to see me," Verl said, "and she had a bunch of paper work with her, and it's all documented."

"What?" I said, glancing at Dick, who had stopped chattering and appeared ready to cry. "She has all *what* documented?"

"Seems that our good mayor here has been selling off the city's improvements, things like . . ." Verl started to fan through the stack of papers ". . . like razing the old Moose lodge, the former town hall, and the abandoned drugstore up the street, and then paving the empty lots for extra parking. He also re-roofed all the city buildings, landscaped the park, and put up that damned wrought-iron fence around the cemetery."

"Yeah, I know," I said. "He's been awarding no-bid contracts to his friends and family since he was elected."

"Hold on, Sheriff," Dick sniveled, "according to our city charter, I don't have to get a bid for every little job."

"Put a clamp on that mouth," Verl snapped, "or I'll charge you with resisting interrogation. Understand?"

Deflated, the clueless mayor obediently settled back into his chair.

Verl's eyebrows relaxed, and he smiled smugly at me, obviously fully plugged into his hard-boiled detective personification. "But you didn't know about the bribes," he said.

"Bribes?" I said.

"Every job he awarded had an extra ten percent tacked onto the bottom line, which showed up on the contract as consulting fees or reinforcement scaffolding and bull pucky like that. But what he did was pad the contractors' charges to line his own pockets. He even had work done on his own house on the city's dime."

I always knew the mayor was a Dick. I just never realized how big of one.

"Assuming Cara's figures are correct," Verl said, "this yahoo cost the city in the neighborhood of three-quarters of a million dollars," Verl said. "The prosecutor's already drafted a probable cause affidavit with a list of charges as long as his arm. As soon as Chuck and Ernie bring me that paper work, we'll be calling Judge Stillwater for an arrest warrant."

"Now just a minute, Sheriff," the mayor spat. "You said you'd cut me a deal."

"Relax, hotshot," Verl said with a tone of annoyance. "Don't get your liver in a quiver. I said I *might* be willing to cut you a deal. But it all depends on how much of your cockamamie story about that old Potts case checks out."

"Old Potts case?" My interest rocketed. I looked to Dick and prodded, "What about it?"

Verlin harrumphed and ground his lower jaw. After pausing a moment longer for effect, he answered for Dick. "The mayor claims he was with Potts the day he went missing and knows all about it." Sneering at Dick, he baited, "Right?"

"Look," Dick said, "I'm not telling you a thing, not until I know what charges you're filing against me."

"Oh, you can be sure," Verl said, "once I get that arrest warrant, your ass will be toast. And then, I'm gonna use it to sop up the three eggs over easy I have for breakfast every morning." Verl looked over at me and winked. "Most mornings, anyhow."

I glanced at Dick. He didn't appear amused.

"If I were you," Verl said, "and I thank my lucky stars I'm not, I'd cooperate. I'd cooperate to give the prosecutor a reason to ease up on me during the punishment phase of my trial. In fact," Verl paused to harrumph again, "I'd cooperate on the long shot it might get me a good plea arrangement."

"Okay, okay," Dick sputtered. "I'll talk, but you need to remember, Bobby and me—"

"Bobby." I said. "Bobby who?"

"Markle," Dick said. He held up his right hand and crossed his first and second fingers. "Him and me, we used to be like this."

"Used to be?" I said. "I thought you two were still tight buddies. Isn't that why you appointed him parks and cemetery supervisor?"

"Well, yeah, we're friends. But when we was kids, we was practically *imseparable*."

Verl rolled his eyes. "Knock off the trip down Memory Lane, and tell me what you know about Potts."

Dick shot me a dirty look. "As I was trying to point out," he said, "this incident happened twenty-one years ago, when Bobby and me was just *se'mteen*. We didn't know our hind ends from our front beginnings . . ." A goofy grin spread below Dick's bushy mustache, ". . . as they say."

I never knew "they" said any such thing, but I let it go, underwhelmed by Dick's imaginative way with words.

"You want to tell us about Eugene Potts, or should I go ahead and get your cell ready for you?" Verl said. "I believe Crystal brought her Nikon along, and a page-one picture of our high-and-mighty mayor locked up behind bars ought to guarantee record sales for tomorrow's *Gazette*."

The smirk on Dick's face flattened. "All right, but you're going to have to stop interrupting me."

Verl raised his hands to signal his surrender.

"All right," Dick said, "as I was saying, when Lance passed away, me and Bobby lost our other best friend, the third leg to our tripod. The three of us was EHS's three musketeers. Hell, it started long before high school even. We started out in kindergarten. So when Lance up and died, me and Bobby was sort of in shock, as you can imagine."

"Yes," I said, nodding. "Teens have a hard time processing the death of a peer. Your close friendship with Lance must have made the tragedy even more excruciating."

That comment got me a long, blank look from the mayor. "Like I said, we lost a bud," he said.

A beat passed, and Verl said, "Is there more to this story?"

"Hell, yes, there's more to this story," Dick said. "It was the Thursday after Lance died, and Bobby and me had been out to visit the Whitfields."

"What time of day would that have been?" I asked.

Dick scratched his chin. "I don't remember. Around noon, I guess."

I wrote that down. "Why did you boys go to see the Whitfields? Seems like a good time to give those poor people some space," I said.

"Yeah," Dick said, "but me and Bobby thought we might help them somehow. You know, do some chores around the farm."

"A noble gesture," I said.

Verl gave me a look and shook his head almost imperceptibly.

"Uh-huh," Dick said, "that's what Bobby's granddad said, too, when he sent us out there. He thought we might help them, considering Lance's funeral was that afternoon."

"At the high school, correct?" I said.

"Yes," Dick said. "Grady said Lance's folks might find comfort if we showed up."

I wrote that down, too. "Go on."

"Bobby was driving and—"

"What was he driving?" I asked.

Dick huffed. "Do you want me to tell this or not?" Crossing his arms across his belly, he looked up at Verl. His eyes blazed with anger, his lips tightened, and he snarled, "If you do, tell that woman to keep her freakin' trap shut."

Verl turned to me and said, "Keep your freakin' trap shut, Crystal." Then turning back to Dick, he grumbled, "What was Bobby driving?"

Dick sucked in a deep breath and exhaled it quickly. "Bobby was driving his grandfather's Chevy 4x4, and we was cruising up the Whitfields' road, headed back to town, when we passed Eugene Potts riding his bike. Bobby slammed on the brakes and told me we was going to have a talk with 'Eugenie'—that's what the kids always called him. Bobby wanted to talk to him because we'd heard that Eugene might've been the one that give Lance the *legal* dose of that medicine."

"*Lethal* dose," I said. Dick looked at me blankly again. "Never mind."

"So Bobby stopped the truck," Verl said, "and you both got

out?"

"Yeah, and right off, Bobby started in on Eugene, razzing him, saying everybody knowed he killed Lance and couldn't wait for him to fry in the electric chair. Bobby said we could save everybody a lot of time and trouble if we gave Eugene his punishment right then."

"What'd Potts do?" Verl asked.

"I think he about messed his pants, but he didn't say a word. He just stood there," Dick said. "And that set Bobby off. He laid into Eugene, pounding him with both fists, smacking him again and again in the gut and upside the head. I never seen nothing like it 'cause Eugene just took it. He didn't even try to defend hisself. Then Bobby hauled off and punched him in the nose. Broke it too. I never saw so much blood pour out a nose."

"And all this time, what were you doing?" I asked.

"Watching," Dick said.

"Uh-huh," Verl said, "and I assume you didn't lay a hand on Potts."

"Not a finger," Dick said. "Not till Bobby needed help getting Eugene into the cab."

"Where'd you two plan on taking him?"

"Bobby said we were going to see Coach," Dick said. "But at that point, I didn't have a clue what he really had in mind."

"What about the bike?" I asked. "There were no reports of Eugene's bike ever being found."

"We threw it in the truck bed and took it with us."

"Okay," Verl said, "the three of you headed to Coach's. What happened there?"

"I don't know," Dick said. "My mom told me to be home by one o'clock to get ready for Lance's funeral, so Bobby dropped me off on the way. What happened after that, I have no idea."

"Bullshit," I said. "A minute ago, you told us that you and Bobby were like this." I held up my right hand, first two fingers crossed. "He told you what happened."

"Crystal's right," Verl said. "Your stay-out-of-jail card is only valid if you tell us what happened."

Dick's expression turned smug. "If I told you what happened, it would be meaningless hearsay."

"Hearsay is only useless in a courtroom," Verl said. "In an interrogation room, it's what might keep you a free man."

"All right, but don't take this as gospel 'cause it's just what Bobby told me. Got it?"

"Got it," Verl said.

"Okay, he told me that the three of them—"

"The 'three'?" Verl said.

"Bobby, Eugene, and Coach. They had a good talk, and Eugene promised to turn hisself in. He left, we never heard from him again, and that's all I know."

"That's it?" Verl said with a renewed air of annoyance. "That's your story?"

"That's my story."

"Pathetic," Verl said. Grabbing the telephone receiver, he held it to his ear and punched zero. After a few seconds, he said, "Elsie, did Ernie and Chuck come back from the prosecutor's office yet?" He paused. "The second they do, fax the papers to Auggie Stillwater and ask her to rush an arrest warrant." He paused again, nodding. "Yes, when the warrant's filed, send Chuck and Ernie in to escort the subject to a cell." He hung up the phone.

I kept an eye turned to Mayor Dick throughout Verl's brief exchange with his secretary. He fidgeted uncomfortably in his chair, and reminded me of a little kid afraid to ask permission to go pee, but when Verl mentioned the arrest warrant, he froze. His face twisted into a pained expression and his complexion paled. I thought he might be having a coronary. Then he spoke.

"Okay," Dick said, "here's the truth." He inserted a finger under his button-down collar and slid it around the inside, loosening the starched band from around his throat. He twisted his head about forty-five degrees, first one way then the other. I heard his neck crack. Avoiding eye contact with both Verl and me, he focused somewhere on the ceiling—or somewhere way past it—and went on speaking. "The truth is, both of us was beating Eugene up pretty bad. What I told you about breaking his nose and knocking him out was true. But what happened to him after that, like I told you, I don't know. I honestly don't know. Bobby never told me, and I never asked. I figured the less I knew, the better. Could be Bobby finished him off. We never talked about it again."

The smug confidence Dick displayed moments before was gone. In its place was a kind of pathetic diffidence, an uncharacteristic submissiveness. Hunching over, he began to slowly rock, pressing the inside of his knees together and wrapping his arms around himself. "All these years, I tried to put it out of my mind," he said, seemingly to no one in particular. "It's why I pushed myself the way I did."

"Pushed yourself?" I said.

"The harder I worked—" His voice cracked, and he stopped to recalibrate his composure. "—the more deals I made for the city, the busier I could keep my head thinking about other things."

What a bunch of bull, I thought. *The deals he made cost the city hundreds of thousands of dollars.* My disgust for the very aptly named Dick Head was only growing stronger as his soul-baring continued.

A knock sounded at the door, and Verl grunted, "Come in." The door opened, and in walked Chuck and Ernie. Ernie handed Verl a sheet of paper. Verl read it over quickly and said, "Okay, boys, go ahead and arrest Mayor Head and read him the warrant."

"You can't do this to me," Dick protested as each deputy latched onto one of his arms. "We had us a deal, and I'm warning you, Wallace. You'll be sorry if you mess with me. So will that snitch of yours, and you can be sure I know exactly who it is."

"I'm shuddering, Richard," Verl said, "but you might want to remember that you've got the right to remain silent, and anything you say now can be used against you in a court of law—"

"Blah, blah, blah," Dick said, as the deputies escorted him from the room. "I watch TV, too, and you don't scare me with your legal mumbo-jumbo. If it's the last thing I do, I'll have your job for this."

The office door slammed behind Chuck, leaving Verl and me alone, shaking our heads.

"Well?" I said. "What now? Do you think he knows about Gertie?"

"I don't know, but I intend to find out. Among other things. Right now, I'm going to pay a call on Bobby Markle." Verl adjusted his gun belt and walked toward the door. Passing me, he said, "You comin'?"

"Not so fast," I said. "Let's give this some thought."

Verl stopped and turned to look at me. "Let's give *what* some thought?"

"Head's tale. Do you believe it?"

"Don't know." Verl's tone dropped an octave. "That's why I

want to talk to Bobby."

"Okay, but before we go off half-cocked," I said, "let's think about this: if Bobby roughed up Eugene, as Dick Head suggested, and then took him to see Coach, let's imagine for a minute what might have gone down."

"They built a campfire and sang 'Kumbaya'?" The corners of Verl's mouth twitched like it wanted him to smile. He didn't. "Why are you asking me, when we should be asking Bobby Markle?"

"Not necessarily," I grumbled, "not yet. What good will it do us to tip our hand and let him know we think he was involved in Eugene's disappearance? Need I remind you that we don't have any proof?"

"That's why we need to talk to Bobby."

"Exactly," I said, "but not until we've laid the groundwork. We go rushing in before we've done our homework, we're going to spook him. No telling what we'll set off."

"You have any ideas?"

"Yes, of course. You should follow up on the one potential piece of evidence we do have."

"Eugene's medical alert tag," Verl said.

"Yes, if indeed it belonged to Eugene," I said. "Have you shown it to the Pottses yet for a positive ID?"

"I was planning to stop by their place later this afternoon."

"The sooner the better," I said. "If that tag belonged to Eugene, it's got to be the missing link Gertie was talking about."

"And somebody's motive to want her dead," Verl added.

"Bingo. But the sixty-four-dollar question is, *which* somebody?"

"Bobby'd be my guess."

"Maybe," I said, "but we can't be certain where or when

Gertie found that tag."

"I thought you said she found it Monday."

"Nuh-uh. Her exact words were—" I drew imaginary quota-tion marks in the air. "'—a few days ago.' There's no telling how many days that really was. Three? Ten? Thirty?" I shrugged. "Then she said, 'after today'—meaning Monday—she was posi-tive."

"What do you think she stumbled across that day to confirm her suspicions?"

I shrugged again. I had racked my brain. I knew whose hous-es she cleaned Monday, but her big revelation could have come from anywhere. I couldn't simply assume her big "Ah-ha!" had originated at Grady's or the Baxters'. I could appreciate how fun it was to make assumptions, but in law enforcement, assump-tions were good for hedging bets but not so good for building airtight cases.

"I just don't know," I said. "That's why I suggest we step back and make sure we're heading up the right path."

"Yeah," Verl said, "you're probably right. C'mon then. Let's go see Ray Potts."

"I can't. I need to get back to my desk. Now that Head's in jail, I've got a major story to write for tomorrow's paper, plus I haven't finished my piece about Coach for Saturday's edition. You go by yourself. You can give me a call later to let me know what you find out."

Verl eyed me with suspicion. "You'll be at your office?"

"Yep."

"Nowhere else?"

"Nope."

"And you'll give me your word on that?"

"Cross my heart," I said, tracing an X across my chest. Of

course, I crossed my toes to neutralize the oath.

Verl walked back to his desk. From the top drawer, he pulled out the sealed plastic bag that contained the medical alert tag. "Okay," he said, "I'll call you when I get back. But keep this in mind—if Ray identifies this thing, all hell's gonna break loose."

We walked outside, and I sent Verl off on his mission, encouraging him onward like a proud mother sending her child off for his first day of scout camp. With him fully occupied and out of my hair, I scurried around the corner to the *Gazette*'s parking lot, climbed into Clip's Corvette, and headed for Bobby Markle's.

33

BOBBY LIVED ALONE on the west side of town in what amounted to a run-down shack, not where you'd expect to find the son
of a wealthy businessman. According to rumors, Bobby cut ties
with his family long ago for reasons they kept to themselves. As
for his past, I knew few details. He attended Indiana University
for three years and played football for two of them, but never
achieved status beyond third string and the scout team. Quitting
college at the start of his senior year, he returned to Elmwood
and never quite lived up to his promise. Although his friend,
Mayor Dick Head, gave him a chance by appointing him the
parks superintendent, a position he still held, as near as I could
tell, the job required little effort and zero accountability. Over
the years, a string of bar fights, drunken-driving arrests, and re-
straining orders filed by a former wife evidenced his instability
and short fuse and helped explain his present reclusive state.

Even in bright daylight, I felt a little uneasy standing on
Bobby's front stoop waiting for him to answer the door. I
tapped a series of four knuckle raps before conceding to the
obvious—he wasn't going to answer. I considered tucking one

of my business cards into the screen, but thought better of it. When I talked to him, I wanted to catch him off guard so he would have little time to fabricate a line of bullshit. Since Bobby wasn't home, though, I wasn't going to waste the opportunity to find out something that had nettled my curiosity since Tuesday night.

I walked around to the back of the house to Bobby's garage. I had to know if Bobby owned a pickup truck, a light-colored one with mismatched taillights—one red, one orange—and a banged-up front fender.

Finding the side door locked, I pressed my nose against its window and peered inside. My pulse quickened. I did see a truck, a white one, but my vantage point did not allow me to see either its back end or its front. I had to know. I forced my press pass into the thin space between the doorframe and the lock and joggled it about. The lock quickly disengaged, allowing me to push the door open. Sometimes, I even amazed myself. Perhaps I should have pursued a life of crime rather than one of crime reporting. It would have been far less work, and the financial rewards far more satisfying. But then again, both professions demanded a certain *je ne sais quoi*, evidenced by the tap on the shoulder I received the exact moment I pushed open that door.

"Hey, lady, what the hell do you think you're doing?"

I jumped about two feet off the ground and spun to face an unshaven, unkempt Bobby Markle leering at me with an expression of depraved curiosity. In his hands, he clenched a chain saw. The sight of him standing inches from me wielding a pernicious power tool indeed made me wonder, too, what the hell *did* I think I was doing? Because I could think of no good way to answer him and get out of there in one piece, I assumed an "I'm-a-certified-self-defense-expert-so-don't-even-think-about-messing-with-me" persona.

"Oh, there you are," I said, steeling my spine as I fixed my eyes on Bobby's, the way Velcro balls stick to felt. "After I banged on your front door for ten minutes and no one answered, I thought I might find you back here." Thrusting my right arm forward, I offered him my hand. "Crystal Cropper. Pleased to make your acquaintance."

He hesitantly took my hand and gave it a limp shake. Before he had a chance to say word one, I pressed on, talking fast, hoping it would get his mind off the fact that I had just broken into his garage.

"I'm-with-the-*Gazette*-and-I'm-here-to-speak-with-you-about-Coach-Jack-Baxter-and-as-you-know-he's-being-inducted-into-the-Indiana-High-School-Football-Coaches-Hall-of-Fame-on-Saturday-and-since-you-were-on-his-team-back-in-'93-just-before-he-retired-I-would-love-to-get-some-comments-from-you-to-use-with-our-coverage-of-this-historic-event." I inhaled. "So what do you say?"

Bobby scowled and huffed, "Huh?"

"I would like to talk with you about Coach Baxter for an article I'm writing. Would you have a couple minutes?"

"Coach Baxter?" he said less than enthusiastically. "What do you want to know?"

Turning from him, I pushed the door open just wide enough to insert my head into the opening and steal a look at the truck. A twinge of disappointment washed over me. His pickup was in pristine condition, not a ding on it. Besides that, it was a much smaller truck and not at all what I was looking for. "Can we go inside?" I said. "I'm getting a tad chilled standing out here."

34

"HONEST TO GOD, VERL, when I asked Bobby if he had any idea what had happened to Eugene Potts, he cried. The man broke down like a baby and cried. What do you think?"

Verl had phoned me at the office shortly past five o'clock to report the outcome of his visit with Ray and Noni Potts. They both identified their son's medical alert tag, and he was feeling pretty chipper. That and Dick Head's confession were the first real breaks in the case, he said. When he mentioned that he was about to go see Bobby Markle, I admitted what I'd done and braced for a chewing out.

"What do I think?" he said. He sounded miffed, and I almost didn't blame him. "What do *I* think? I think you shouldn't have been questioning a possible material witness, at least not without me being present and certainly not without my permission. Because of this little stunt, you may have blown this whole case."

"Stunt?" I shot back. "You didn't see the guy come at me with a chain saw. Fortunately for you, thanks to my quick thinking and cool head, I was able to extract some valuable information. I have no doubt that had it been you standing nose to nose with Bobby Markle and his chain saw, some Hollywood mogul would already be scripting *The Indiana Chainsaw Massacre*, and it wouldn't be a work of fiction. So you'd best be cooling your jets, buddy."

I expelled a long, pent-up breath. First he wanted my help, then he didn't. The man's equanimity was as rickety as a three-legged ironing board. Then I had a different thought: he was probably right. I had pulled a stunt. I had stopped by Bobby Markle's for one reason only—to satisfy my suspicions that he had been the erratic truck driver who'd tried to kill me Tuesday night. And when that hadn't panned out, rather than waste an opportunity to smoke out a good story, I took advantage. Maybe I had been wrong to try to shake out Bobby without Verl's knowledge, but what I did reap surely neutralized my transgression.

• • • •

Bobby and I had stepped inside his garage, where I was even colder than I had been outside. He fired up a small gas heater that instantly threw out enough heat to defrost my bones. For effect, I pulled my reporter's note pad from my handbag and positioned my ballpoint pen at the top of a clean sheet. Then I asked him what he remembered best about his football days under Coach Baxter. He stunned me with his response.

"What was *best?*" Bobby said with an obvious tone of incredulity. "Well, ma'am, since Jack Baxter was a first-class prick, what I remember best was how happy I was when he had that stroke."

"Happy?" I said, taken aback. "I thought the boys worshipped him."

"I don't know who you've been talking to, lady," he said,

"but for all I cared, the man could've dropped dead."

"I'm not sure I understand," I said, although I was beginning to. Coach's reputation as a beloved, surrogate father and pillar of the community was a lie, crafted by coercion and perpetuated in fear. "What makes you say that?"

"Because he wrecked my life. I had a football scholarship to IU—full ride. I was supposed to be a starting player as a freshman, but Coach poisoned the IU coaching staff against me, and I never got further than the bench. For two years, I was sidelined, until I finally had enough, until the day I threw in the towel and came back to Elmwood. So yeah, screw Jack Baxter. May he rot in hell."

"What did he do that turned the IU coaches against you?"

"He told them I was gay," he said.

I rarely find myself at a loss for words, but for once my ability to form an articulate sentence failed. Generally, I try not to antagonize a man bearing a power tool, so I sidestepped the IU matter entirely and turned to Dick Head's claims concerning the old Potts case.

"And what about Lance Whitfield and Eugene Potts?" I said. "What did you think about that whole episode?"

Bobby lowered his gaze and waited a long beat before answering. "Pitiful," he said. "A goddamned—" His voice cracked, but he went on. "—a goddamned pitiful shame." His breathing quickened, and I could see his chest quickly rising and sinking, rising and sinking beneath the bib of his overalls as he grappled to maintain his composure. After a moment, he looked up at me with tear-filled eyes. "They were good guys. Both of 'em. And I won't ever understand how the good Lord could've let it happen." Bobby pulled a filthy red bandanna from his back pocket and blew his nose into it. "One thing's for sure, though. The

Lord works in mysterious ways."

"So, are you telling me you think Jack Baxter had something to do with those tragedies?"

"Is the pope Catholic?"

• • • •

"That may be interesting, Crystal," Verl said, "but did you ask Bobby about him and Head meeting up with Potts on their way to the Whitfields'? Did you ask him about the fight? Did you ask him if he'd taken Potts, like Head said, to see Baxter?"

"No," I said. "I thought about it, but the man was so upset he was blubbering like a squeaky toy in a bubble bath. Besides, I knew that was a job for a law enforcement official."

I was fibbing of course, and I almost felt guilty about it. The truth was, I had opened the door to that line of questioning and, after a peek inside, I promptly slammed it.

• • • •

"There was talk that the morning before Lance's funeral," I had said to Bobby, "Eugene Potts was seen pedaling his bike up the Whitfields' road headed in the direction of their house. What do you know about that?"

At that moment, my congenial little chat with Bobby Markle took an abrupt turn south. Something dark and menacing enveloped him like an electrostatic nylon net.

"Horseshit," he fired back. "Who told you I knew anything about that? I'll freakin' kill 'em."

I believed him, too, which is why I tucked my note pad and pen back inside my purse and surreptitiously wrapped my hand around my canister of mace.

"Where did you hear that?" he demanded, taking a step toward to me.

"Back off, Bobby. Settle down," I said in what I hoped was a firm, but non-threatening, tone. "Nobody told me you knew anything about it. I was just asking the question, you know, in case you did. That's how we reporters are, always probing, always looking for a story."

"Yeah," he said, "always sticking your big noses into places they don't belong."

Big noses, indeed. People always told me my nose was cute, but I let Bobby's insult go. Our interview having reached an impasse, I thanked him for his time and excused myself. I didn't look back, not even when I heard the chain saw motor roar to life. However, I did pick up my pace.

• • • •

"Hey," I said to Verl. "Would you like to come by tonight for a pizza or something? I'm buying."

"Actually, no, I wouldn't like to," he said. "I feel some heartburn coming on, and you and pizza would just make it worse. Besides, I've got some things to do."

"What kind of things?"

"For one thing, I've got to question Bobby, if I can find him, and for another thing, I've got to find out where Gertie Tyroo came up with Eugene Potts's medical alert tag and see where that leads."

"What can I do to help you? I'll be free in about fifteen minutes."

"What can you do to help? Go home. I've got this one."

And then he hung up.

I might have gotten a little depressed about making Verl mad enough to hang up on me if my phone hadn't rung almost immediately. I grabbed the receiver and ventured forth into unfamiliar territory.

"Verl," I cooed, "I'm really sorry. I screwed up. You're right. I should have waited for you."

But the voice that came from the other end wasn't Verl's.

35

"CRYSTAL CROPPER?" the male caller said.

"Yes."

"I hope I haven't phoned at a bad time. This is Sherm Hollingsworth, and as long as we're doing apologies, let me extend mine for taking so long to get back to you."

Sherm Hollingsworth had played football for Elmwood High from 1987 to 1991. A phenomenal lineman, he was one of those iron-man guys, who played offense and defense with equal poise. His high school athletic skills earned him a football scholarship to the University of Kentucky, and afterward, he went pro, playing for the Carolina Panthers. A knee injury at the tender age of twenty-nine meant the end of his NFL career and the simultaneous start of his high school coaching career.

For the past couple of days, I had heard conflicting reports about Elmwood's esteemed Jack Baxter: The man was a saint; the man was a demon. Which was he? It depended on whom you asked. I was interested to hear Hollingsworth's take.

"The guy was likable enough off the field," Hollingsworth said, "but frankly, on the field, his disciplinary tactics crossed the line. By today's standards, they would be classified as abuse—physical, verbal, and emotional, which is why I won't be attending any of the hall of fame festivities. It wasn't unusual for Coach to train his team to the point of exhaustion. God forbid if a kid made Coach angry—he would withhold breaks, snacks, even water, and on the rare occasion that a player found the courage to object to the treatment, Coach came down even harder, using fear, intimidation, humiliation, and coercion."

"Not exactly sportsmanlike, was it?" I said.

"No, it wasn't. But here's the rub. For a lot of the guys, Coach Baxter was this larger-than-life, surrogate dad. They looked up to him and wanted to please him. But as a coach myself, I can guarantee there's a fine line between discipline and abuse, and Coach Baxter crossed that line again and again."

"Did anyone ever report him?" I asked, although I was fairly certain what his answer would be.

"I know it sounds crazy," Hollingsworth said, "but no." Apparently anticipating my next question, he pressed on. "Let me explain it this way. There was an incident while I was a junior at EHS. One of the kids on the team missed two after-school practices due to the death of his grandmother. The boy took it real hard, and when he returned to school on Friday, he was having problems coping. In the locker room a half hour before the game, Coach verbally attacked the boy and backed him in a corner, yelling obscenities, calling him names like sissy, mommy's boy, queer, until the kid literally broke down and cried. That made Coach all the more angry, and he ended up smacking the kid in the face so hard he broke his nose."

I gasped. "Don't tell me Baxter got away with it."

"Oh, he got away with it, all right. He claimed the boy got his nose broken during the game, and the school board lapped it up.

The school didn't give him so much as a warning."

"But what about the other boys? Surely, one of them witnessed what happened."

I could hear Hollingsworth's gentle, humorless laugh. "Did you ever hear of a code of silence?"

"You mean where people quietly look the other way while an authority figure breaks the law?"

"Right," Hollingsworth said. "During Coach's reign at Elmwood High, no one dared speak out against Jack Baxter—not an athlete, not a parent, not a member of the school administration. No one."

"Is that illegal?"

"I don't know if it's illegal," he said, "but it's certainly unethical. As long as Coach won games, it brought prestige to the county and a lot of money to the coffers. The man was untouchable."

"What do you know about Lance Whitfield's death?" I asked, coaxing the questioning toward my investigation into Gertie's assault.

"He died of heatstroke during football practice, and Jack Baxter should have been indicted," he said, "but that's just my opinion."

"Did you know Eugene Potts and Bobby Markle?"

"Oh, sure. Eugene went missing after police blamed him for Lance's overdose on some drug—I can't remember the details. And after Lance died, Bobby became Coach's best hope for a Big Ten school to recruit one of his boys."

"Interesting," I said. "I hadn't heard about that."

"Bobby was good," Hollingsworth said, "just not *that* good. His grandfather was obsessed with getting Bobby into Notre Dame to play for Lou Holtz, but there was no way that was going to happen. I always felt sorry for Bobby because of the pressure."

Hollingsworth was a gold mine of information, and I enjoyed talking with him. We were about to say goodbye, when I remembered to ask for one detail he hadn't given me.

"Who was the boy with the broken nose?" I said. "Do you remember his name?"

Hollingsworth wheezed a humorless laugh. "No way I could ever forget that," Hollingsworth said. "The boy was me."

After my chat with Hollingsworth ended, I sat there in the solitude of my office and mulled over what I'd learned. Jack Baxter was a fraud. Not only was he unworthy of the glory showered on him over the years by an adoring community, but his forthcoming induction into the High School Football Coaches Hall of Fame would be unadulterated folly. My head was pounding. I needed to focus on someone else.

36

I PULLED A CHAIR UP TO GERTIE'S BEDSIDE. She was still hooked up to every plastic tube known to mankind and a heart monitor that registered a series of numbers with no meaning to me. An IV drip of sugar water, vitamins, and minerals kept her body nourished, while another IV delivered her meds. She appeared even smaller than she had Tuesday. Tiny and drawn, she looked like a delicate, wrinkled porcelain doll. Nurse Becky was on duty again at the nurses' station, and she smiled in recognition as I passed. I asked her how Gertie was doing, and she reported that, although there still had been no measurable change, Gertie was holding her own. It was the same answer she'd given me Tuesday, and the standard line uttered by every other member of Elmwood Hospital's medical staff. I suppose it beat the alternative.

"Hey, Gert, guess what," I said. "Nurse Becky tells me you're holding your own. Holding your own what, I'm not sure. Your tongue? Your nose? Your bladder? Your horses? I honestly don't know. When I find out, I'll let you know, but apparently it's to your credit."

I looked around the semi-darkened room. There was one modest bouquet, which I had sent Tuesday, and not a single get-well card.

"I have some good news," I said, feigning excitement as you would to a child. "I found the medical alert tag you hid in your secret drawer. Are you impressed? Yeah, pretty good detective work, if I say so myself. I found it this morning, and Verlin has already talked with Ray and Noni to confirm that it belonged to Eugene. Now, if I can just figure out where you found it, we might find out who did this to you.

"Hey, I've got an idea," I said, infusing my fake enthusiasm with extra elation. "Why don't you just wake up and tell me?" I shut up for a moment, just in case, but Gertie didn't stir. I went on.

"It's sure been a weird couple of days around this town. I met that young FBI friend of yours, that Harold Quigley, when I broke into your house Tuesday morning. Actually, he broke in first, and after I got him settled down, we had a nice chat. Honestly, Gert, why didn't you tell me you used to work for the FBI? All these years and you never breathed a word. Who could have guessed it?"

"Guessed what?" The question came from a woman behind me. I quickly turned and found Nurse Becky entering the room.

"I was giving Sis a weather update," I said. "Who could have guessed that we'd have thunderstorms forecasted so early in March?"

She pulled the clipboard from its place at the foot of the bed. "It's going to take one more good drenching to wash away the rest of the snow," she said, checking the IV lines. "But it won't be long now."

I kept quiet as Becky took Gertie's temperature and pulse,

recorded the readings, and smoothed out the blanket.

"Don't you agree?" she said.

"About what?"

"That spring is just around the corner. One more hard rain, and we'll be seeing crocuses."

"Oh, sure," I said, but I couldn't have cared less about spring.

"I'm glad you're talking to her," Nurse Becky said. "Some folks think it's silly to talk to a person in a coma, but I've seen too many cases where patients regain consciousness and say they were completely aware of everything around them. So you just keep it up."

Nurse Becky offered to bring me a cola, and I declined. "Well, then, I'll leave you two to your visit," she said and left the room, pulling the door closed, all but for a crack. I resumed my one-sided conversation, bringing Gertie up to date on the investigations her phone call launched, news about the mayor, Coach's induction, the disappearance of Randa Muridae, and certain Elmwood citizens' connections to a possible drug ring.

"And that about sums it up," I said, several minutes later. "Verl is all atwitter about security and traffic control for Saturday's big event for Coach, and I still haven't heard who's delivering the keynote address at his dinner. No doubt, it will be some old football celebrity I've never heard of, but I'm sure the males of the species will be thrilled."

I stopped talking and glanced at my watch. My mouth had been barreling along at IndyCar speed for thirty minutes.

"So, Gertie—" I picked up her limp right hand and cradled it in both of mine. It was cold and colorless and felt like death. It made me sad. "—when are you going to open those baby blues and start cussing me out again? Things aren't right around here without you." I gave her hand a gentle squeeze. "I know you're in there fighting to come back. And you will. I know you will."

Although never one for a gooey show of affection, I felt compelled to give Gertie a sisterly peck on her cheek. The instant my lips brushed across her soft flesh, I sensed the slightest tremor flow from her hand into mine.

37

THE SUN HAD SET LESS THAN AN HOUR BEFORE, leaving the western horizon awash in streaks of cool, sherbet-colored pastels. I cruised through town on my way home. I needed to work on Coach's feature story. It was due the next day, and I hadn't written the first word. I wasn't in panic mode yet though, since I always did my best work on deadline. I could get my writing done at home the same as I could at the office, provided there were no unexpected interruptions.

Turning onto my street, I was delighted to see that Deputy Paxton again occupied the parking spot across from my house. I pulled up beside him and cranked down my window.

"You're here kind of early, aren't you?" I said. "It's barely dark."

When he saw who it was behind the wheel of the vintage Corvette, his eyes literally bulged. He rolled down his window and blew an approving whistle. "Nice wheels," he said. "I think Clip Parker has one almost like it."

"Yes, I know," I said. "How long are you on Cropper duty tonight?"

"My shift just started. I'm here until 6:00 a.m."

"That's comforting to know," I said. "I'll bring you some co-coa before I hit the sack."

Once inside, I settled in, nuking a frozen entrée of two cheese enchiladas, rice, and beans, and getting started on Coach's profile. The biggest chunk of time I spent producing a major feature story involved sifting through my notes for the best material and quotes. "Organizing the chaos," I always called it.

The evening seemed to fly. I stopped work around eleven o'clock, after having written fifty pretty good inches of copy. Before hitting the sack, I delivered two toasted cherry Strudel Pops and a cup of hot cocoa to Deputy Paxton. He seemed ap-preciative. It was the least I could do for the man who guarded my life.

• • • •

Paxton was long gone, of course, when I looked out the front window at seven o'clock the next morning. After I spent an hour polishing the story I'd written the night before, I showered and got ready for the day. I styled my hair, applied a layer of un-derstated makeup, and dressed, selecting my tan slacks, a white turtleneck, and red cardigan. At straight-up nine o'clock, I strolled through the *Gazette's* front door. Darcy handed me the sealed envelopes containing our weekly paychecks. I stopped, handed her back the envelope marked "Darcy" and said, "Have we heard from Quigley? I thought he would get back to me by now."

"I never said that."

"Maybe not, but I wouldn't expect a simple task like driving to Earlville for an address check to take more than a few hours."

Annoyed, I lowered my voice and erased any inflection that could be misconstrued as warmth. "I gave you the assignment Wednesday afternoon, and today is Friday. If you want any more reporting assignments, I suggest you get Quigley on the phone. Now. I need to know what he found out." Darcy stared back at me blankly, her mouth half-open. "What's wrong?" I said.

"Nothing," she said, the light suddenly snapping on in her eyes. "Give me a few minutes."

"Don't take too long. I want that information in today's paper."

I marched into my office, closed the door, and called Verl. Elsie put me right through to him.

"Good morning, sunshine," I said. "How'd last night go?"

"With regard to what?" he said

"Did you pick up Bobby for questioning?"

"No, I didn't pick up Bobby," he said, mocking my question with exaggerated mimicry. How very mature.

"Oh," I said, "so you found where Gertie scrounged up Eugene's medical tag, right?"

After several seconds of dead air, he grunted, "Nope."

"Oh, well, today's a new day."

"What do you want, Crystal?"

"I want to apologize for trying to break new ground without you yesterday at Bobby's. I want you to tell me not to worry about it. And I want to see what you're doing for lunch."

"Accepted. Don't worry about it. I'm on my way to Pendleton to meet with the state police, so I can't do lunch. Now I've got a question for you."

"If I've got an answer, it's yours. Shoot."

There was a tap at my door, and it opened just wide enough

for Darcy to insert her head and mouth the word, "Quigley," gesturing behind herself with her thumb.

I nodded and she left, closing the door behind her.

"But first," I said, "have you had any luck finding Randa Muridae?"

"Not yet," Verl said. "What did you find out about her car?"

"I'll have something for you ASAP," I said. "I've been waiting to hear back from Quigley—"

"What do you mean you've—"

"—and he's in my office right now. I'll get right back with you." I hung up the phone, cutting off any further protest from Verl.

I punched the intercom to Darcy's desk. "It's about time," I said. "Tell him to get his keister in here."

There were some whispers from the hallway before the door opened and Quigley sauntered in. He walked up to my desk and pushed a large manila envelope across it. "You know," he said, "I'm not obligated to give you any of this."

"Then why are you?"

"Because I need to know how this fits in with what you've turned up."

"Ah," I said, "it's the media to the rescue. I scratch your back, you scratch mine?"

"Something like that."

I pulled the contents from the packet and ruffled through a variety of papers, mainly photocopies of official-looking records. "What have we got here?"

"First, Earlville," he said. "Gloria Sparks is Randa Muridae's aunt. She lent her car to Randa about three weeks ago and hasn't heard from her since."

"You told her the girl's gone missing?"

Quigley shrugged. "Of course, but she seemed more concerned about her car."

"What else did you get?"

"Gloria's deceased husband, Nolan, was a private investigator who worked cases all over the state, including one in Elmwood back in—"

"1993," I said. "Ray Potts hired him to find his son."

"Yeah, you'll find a copy of Sparks's report in there somewhere."

I pulled out a file from the Paducah, Kentucky, police department. "What's this?"

"I was hoping you'd ask," Quigley said. "It's a little messy to explain," he said, "so you'll have to listen."

I looked up at him. "You have my undivided attention."

Quigley pulled over one of the wooden chairs and straddled it. "While Sparks was on the Potts case, he got a wild hair and headed down to Paducah to snoop around," he said. "Apparently, before Jack Baxter married his second wife, she was involved in some trouble that may have been the catalyst for her timely meeting with Baxter. Sparks found out that prior to meeting Jack Baxter, Kathryn was a private-duty nurse going by the name of Kathy Lovejoy. In 1984, Charles Kronkite, an uberwealthy Kentucky Colonel who raised thoroughbred racehorses on about a thousand acres outside of Paducah, hires her to care for his ailing wife. Early the next year, the wife dies of a massive stroke, and about seven months later, Kronkite marries Kathy, despite being at least fifty years her senior. Within a year, unfortunately, he too suffers a massive stroke. In this instance, he survives but is totally incapacitated."

"And dependent on his wife?" I said.

"Exactly, until he dies in October of '92." Quigley paused

and cleared his throat. "Now, as I said, Charles Kronkite was a rich man, which put Kathy in an excellent financial position."

"How convenient," I said. "Kathryn inherited her husband's estate."

"She would have," Quigley said, "except his children put up a big stink."

"She showed up here with Coach in the spring of '93," I said, "so can I assume the children won?"

"Yep, they won. They proved she had forged his signature on a phony will that left her everything, and they were this close to getting her arrested for fraud—" Quigley measured off about an inch with his thumb and forefinger. "—when she skipped without leaving a trace."

"That's when she skipped into Coach's heart at a French Lick resort," I said.

"That's right," Quigley said. "And now you know the rest of the story."

When I interviewed Kathryn two days before, she called it "fortuitous" that she and Jack had picked the exact same French Lick hotel on the exact same weekend to mourn their respective dead spouses. After hearing Quigley's story, I realized their meeting was not simply "fortuitous"—"for gold digging" was more like it.

"Are the Paducah police still interested in her?" I said.

"Crossing state lines to avoid prosecution is a federal offense," he said. "I expect to get Paducah's attention as soon as I get the arrest warrant."

Arrest warrant? The thought of Kathryn Baxter donning an orange jumpsuit made me almost giddy. "What can I do to help?"

"Do you know where I can reach Sheriff Wallace?" he said.

"He's on his way to the state police district office in Pendleton."

Quigley checked his wristwatch and gnawed at his lower lip. "Did he locate the Muridae woman?"

"Not yet," I said, "but I know he's doing everything he can. The information you turned up should help."

Quigley stood. "I'll catch up with him later," he said, fumbling for the buttons on his coat. "How's Miss Tyroo?"

"Holding her own."

"Holding her own," Quigley echoed. "What the hell does that mean?"

"I think it means they don't know what else to say," I said.

"Any leads in her case?"

"Maybe a couple," I said. "Sit back down and I'll bring you up to speed."

In return, Quigley spilled some inside poop on Operation Ring-a-Ding-Ding, which wasn't nearly as much as I'd gotten from Verl, and laid out a ridiculously far-fetched tale about Gertie's distant past that I'd have to be nuts to believe. And yet, it was just nutty enough to make me think it might be worth checking into. If it panned out, Verl's reaction would be priceless.

When Quigley left, it was almost noon. I had the rest of my profile on Coach to write for Saturday's morning edition, as well as an update on Dick Head's arrest. There were new leads to pursue concerning Gertie's attacker and Randa's disappearance, and I couldn't ignore Quigley's report on the former Kathy Lovejoy or, more importantly, his confirmation that Elmwood was the target of a federal investigation. On top of that, the activities surrounding Coach's induction would begin in less than twenty-four hours. While a lesser editor might have felt overwhelmed with her plate so full, nothing helped me cope quite so effectively as a good cliché: a journey starts with the first step . . . along with several dozen grams of carbs.

38

I WAS STILL WORKING on my Mr. Happy Burger when I steered Clip's car under the iron arches of the Pleasant View Gardens Cemetery's main gate. I was hoping the caretaker, Otis "Digger" Fossor, could shed some light on Gertie's clip from the August 13, 1994 Millersburg, Kansas *News Tribune*. She must have had a good reason for saving it all those years, but whatever it was eluded me. I skimmed the article again while I sucked up the bottom of my vanilla shake. Under the headline, "Cemetery's Woes Stacking Up," the story read:

With occupancy at the Millersburg Cemetery nearing maximum capacity, the city council introduced a plan this week that it says prevents the town's beloved historic graveyard from ever hanging a "No Vacancy" sign.

"Rather than turn people away," said Council President Jack Morrison, "we're proposing that groundskeepers dig deeper holes and arrange the caskets they bury three, four, even five deep."

Although several area residents expressed ethical concerns over the councilman's suggestion, he pointed out that the practice of stacking coffins is not new.

"Take any potter's field, for example," he said, referring to charity cemeteries maintained by a few large cities where the unidentified, unclaimed, and indigent dead are interred in mass graves. "New York City has buried its residents three and four deep for decades."

As word spreads about the Millersburg City Council's advocacy for burying the county's dead in stacks, outrage has followed. To counter the anger, Millersburg Cemetery's chief caretaker, Horace Spitznagle, assures the public that burials will proceed with the same honor and dignity that have prevailed since its founding in 1864, one body per gravesite.

I climbed out of the 'Vette and traipsed across the front lawn of the cemetery toward the garage-sized building that housed Digger's equipment and his office. I saw him watching me through the window and gave him a wave. Before I reached the front door, he stepped outside. He was a short, squat of a guy in his late fifties, decked out in denim coveralls over a white thermal undershirt. A plaid cap with insulated earflaps topped his ensemble. He wore a pair of half-frame reading glasses pushed down to the end of his red, bulbous nose and squinted at me over the top of the lenses.

"What can I do for you, Crystal?" he said out of one side of his mouth, the side that didn't have the mostly burned down stogie plugged into it.

"I'm not sure," I said, "but I'm curious about something and think you can help me."

"Am I being quoted for the newspaper?"

"Naw, this isn't for the paper. What I'm after is personal."

"All right, then," he said, "lay it on me."

"How long have you had this job here?"

Digger bit down on his cigar stub and stroked his chin. "I started here right after high school in 1979, so I guess that makes it about thirty-three years."

"That's a long time," I said. "So if anybody knows where Elmwood's bodies are buried, it would be you because you've buried them, at least those that died since you've been here."

"Assuming they're buried in this cemetery, I reckon I would."

"Of course," I said. I made an obvious visual sweep of the cemetery. I was stalling. I needed to ask him the next couple questions without raising his suspicions. "A friend of mine sent me an article about some Kansas graveyard that proposed burying its dead three deep. Have you ever heard of such a thing?"

"Oh, sure. It's happened," he said. "It ain't right, but before we had laws against it, such things wasn't all that unusual, particularly in cemeteries for prisons and mental institutes, or special city plots reserved for vagrants. But nowadays no graveyard would do something like that. It's flat out disrespectful."

"That's what I thought you'd say, Digger, particularly knowing that in your tenure here, you've buried so many of our friends and neighbors."

"Oh, yeah," he said with a scowl, "I've taken care of each grave with the same respect I gave my own mother, God rest her soul." Digger tilted his head and flashed me a knowing grin. "I guess it's that time."

"That time?" I said. His comment puzzled me. "What time do you mean?"

"I get questions like this all the time, especially when older folk like yourself start to preplan their funerals. I can't imagine that it's easy."

I clamped my lips together and faked a smile as a hot surge of indignation flared in my gut. With all the restraint I could muster, I said, "Thanks for that compassionate understanding."

"Hey, I'll get there myself one day."

Right, I thought. *You keep smoking those cigars and ingesting all those deep-fried Twinkies, and your day will be here quicker than you know.* But again, I kept my lips sealed.

"Digger, just so I understand you correctly, you have dug every single grave in this cemetery since you came to work here?"

He squinted one eye and looked skyward. "That's correct," he said. He poked a finger under his cap and scratched his head. "I have personally dug or helped dig every single grave since the first day I come to work here."

"Okay," I said, "and you're positive of that."

"Yes indeedy," Digger said. "But there was one I didn't close."

"Oh?" I said. "Why not?"

"Well, sir, it was the damnedest thing," Digger said. "It was after that Whitfield boy died. Grady Markle told me him and his grandson, Bobby, would fill in the grave."

The alarm started to clang in my head until I thought I'd go deaf. "Why would they want to do that?" I said.

Digger shrugged. "Grady said on account of the boys being such good friends, it'd be good for Bobby. Seemed pretty odd to me, but I figured he knowed what he was talking about. So I let 'em. I didn't see any harm."

Something was very wrong with that little scenario, and I could hardly wait to share it with Verl. I thanked Digger and turned to leave, but he kept talking.

"So, I guess after tomorrow, there'll be two I haven't closed."

I turned back to him. "Two? Whitfield and who else?"

"Yesterday, a guy stopped by here asking if he could close

227

the grave for a woman I'm burying tomorrow."

"Didn't that strike you as odd?" I said. It did me.

Digger shrugged. "If it made him happy to bury her, I figured, why not?"

"Who's the woman?" I couldn't recall running any obits this week.

"An old gal by the name of Violet Hornsby," he said.

"Hornsby?" The name had a familiar ring, but I couldn't place it.

"She's from over in Hart County."

"I see." It was interesting, but I couldn't see how the unusual request might have any relevance to Gertie's case. "Who contacted you? A member of her family, I presume."

"I can't rightly say what relation he was," he said, "nice feller though . . . for a pretty boy, if you catch my drift."

I did a mental eye roll and played dumb. "No, actually, I don't catch your drift," I said.

Digger pulled at his left earlobe, batted his eyelids, and answered, "The guy was wearing the sweetest little diamond earring you ever seen."

That sounded like Kathryn's gentleman caller. "Did he have blond hair?" I asked.

"I believe he did."

"Was he wearing a brown leather jacket?"

"He sure was. You know him?"

"Nope," I said, "lucky guess—if you catch my drift."

39

AS MUCH AS I WOULD HAVE LIKED TO CALL IT A DAY, I had a few hours of work left for me at the office. I checked the final proof of Saturday's paper, but my attention kept drifting to the silent phone on my desk.

I'd called Verl twice already earlier in the evening and gotten no answer. I picked up the receiver and tried one last time before I headed home. I really wanted to know what, if anything, he had turned up about Randa Muridae, plus I wanted to talk to him about what I'd learned from Digger. Damn it all anyhow. With a best friend like Verl, who needed a hemorrhoid? His phone rang four times before it rolled over to voice mail. Typically that's where I would have disconnected, but for once, I waited for the beep and started talking.

"Verl. I really like the way you always criticize me for not using my cell phone like you do. But really, let me ask you something. What's the difference between me not turning on my phone and you refusing to answer my call? Either way, we aren't talking. It seems to me, though, that your behavior is much more rude. But I digress. Look, I have something urgent that I need to speak with you about. It's going on nine thirty, and I'm heading home. Give me a call. If I don't hear from you tonight, I'll look for you at the parade in the morn—" And that's where Verl's voice mail cut me off.

• • • •

The Corvette's burly engine purred to the playful Tony Bennett and Barbra Streisand duet wafting from the radio. After one hell of a week, it was finally Friday night, and I was bound for my comfy bed. The prospect of sleeping in past dawn made me almost giddy, even though I knew better than to indulge in such frivolous jollity. It always came back to bite me in the butt.

In this instance, my butt bite arrived shortly after I pulled up beside the brown-and-tan sheriff's car parked across the street from my house. I peered through the 'Vette's passenger-side window at Deputy Paxton slouched to one side in the driver's seat. He appeared to be sleeping like a baby. Fond as I was of Paxton, I was not amused by his lack of discipline. He was supposed to stay awake and alert to keep me safe.

Irritated, I wrapped my sweater cape around my shoulders to fend off the chill and marched around the front of the 'Vette to the cruiser. I tapped on the driver's window, but when Paxton didn't stir, I opened the door and shouted his name. When he didn't respond, I poked his left shoulder, and he slid sideways across the console without a murmur and lay face down in the passenger seat. I dove inside, grabbed him with both hands and gave him a shake. I shouted his name again, but he was as unresponsive and limp as a 150-pound bag of flour. It was as if he were . . . dead? I could hardly bear to think it. I yanked the cape from my shoulders and spread it over him. I was about to pick up his hand-held radio and call for help when a pair of slowly approaching headlights lit the cruiser's interior. I left the radio where it lay and scrambled out of the car, waving my arms at the driver in the pale-colored pickup truck with the battered front fender. I wanted desperately for it to stop. And it did, after it rumbled slowly past, revealing two glowing, mismatched tail-lights—the left one red, the right one orange.

My heart sank into my stomach and hissed like an ember immersed in a bucket of water. I turned and bolted, but I had taken no more than a half dozen steps when something slammed into my right cheek like a wrecking ball. The flash of fireworks behind my eyelids was the last image I saw before my lights went out.

40

SOMEONE GROANED. It was me. My side stung, my face was numb. My cardigan was too thin to keep me warm. I was freezing. I wanted to speak, but my mouth was taped. I opened my right eye. The left one didn't seem to be working. Where the hell was I?

I struggled to get up, and discovered my hands were bound together at the wrists. I couldn't yet figure out where I was, but the ground beneath me was lumpy and rock hard. The dormant grass was wet. Digging my right elbow into the ground, I propped myself up and scanned the surroundings, so dark, so quiet . . . so near the permanently sleeping residents of the Elmwood Pleasant View Gardens Cemetery.

Gravestones in all shapes and sizes surrounded me. The closest, engraved "Violet Hornsby," ascended from the earth at the far end of a mound of dirt. My thoughts raced. Graves were generally intended as single dwellings, but I feared unless I acted soon, Violet's would be a duplex.

Someone grabbed hold of my hair from behind and yanked so hard I thought my head might disconnect from its neck socket. My assailant's face was indistinguishable, blending with the darkness. "Get up," he said.

My mind raced, assessing the wisdom of resisting versus playing along until an escape route presented itself to me. I took my sweet time struggling to my feet, mostly as a stalling tactic, but also because my body ached all over.

Something hard pressed into my back, and I shuffled forward a few steps. Lacking the use of my hands and my mouth limited my options—even if I could've found a weapon, I wouldn't have been able to wield it.

The only weapon I had was myself.

Just short of the open pit, I dropped to my knees and rolled onto my back.

"What the hell are you doing?" my attacker said.

He stopped directly in front of me and grabbed for my ankles. Applying all the force I could muster, I rammed the sturdy soles of my oxfords into his groin. He doubled over, clutching his crotch. As he rocked back and forth like a Bozo the Clown punching bag, I scrambled to my feet and rushed forward, crashing into him full force with my shoulder, bulldozing him into the hole.

A string of nasty expletives emerged from the grave behind me, so I knew he'd survived the fall. Certain he would come after me, I ran, heading deeper into the cemetery. Darkness was my only ally.

• • • •

With nothing but a sliver of moon lighting my way, I stumbled through the garden of tombstones with no sense of direction. My attempts to break the duct tape that bound my hands proved futile, but by rubbing my taped mouth against my shoulder repeatedly, I managed to peel loose the adhesive strip that covered my lips.

Something hooted. It was the only sound I'd heard since my friend in the hole stopped his bellyaching and became strangely silent. A semblance of peace settled over the cemetery, lending me a small sense of irrational hope that pushed me forward. I muddled about the old boneyard for several minutes before I accepted that I'd lost my bearings. I thought if I kept going in what seemed a straight line, eventually I would arrive at Dick Head's newly installed, fifty-thousand-dollar wrought-iron fence that lined the cemetery's perimeter. But where was it?

The March wind kicked up, rustling bare branches in the trees around me. With only my thin office attire to fend off the late-night chill, I picked up my pace, advancing several yards before I noticed the soft whoosh of footsteps sweeping through the grass nearby. I stopped, and so did they. I resumed, and so did they. I stopped again, and so did they. I turned, straining for a glimpse of my stalker. It was useless. The night was too dark. My eyes were too tired. I would have to try another tack.

"Excuse me," I said in a flat, apathetic tone that I hoped would cover the knocking of my knees, "is this the way to the ladies' room?"

"Crystal, darling," came from the shadows.

I whirled toward the source and was at once blinded by a flashlight beam. The dark shape behind it said, "You naughty girl."

"Takes one to know one," I said.

The unmistakable, cloying voice belonged to Kathryn Baxter. Funny how you could never tell who you might run into at a cemetery. Like Grandpa Cropper used to say, "Folks are dying to get in."

Ignoring my comeback, Kathryn went on speaking in that phony, pseudo-intellectual tone she could only have acquired by listening to the BBC. "Tsk. What are we going to do with you?"

The light deflected off the headstones around us, casting an eerie glow over Kathryn and revealing the small pistol she aimed at my chest.

"Your little prank has cost us all quite a bit of time and trouble," she said, her tone brittle and condescending, as always.

"Oh, gosh," I said, buttering my syllables with mock astonishment, "I am so sorry." Smiling sweetly, I added, "But I'll tell you what. Let's all head out to Bud's for a burger and fries. My treat."

"You never stop, do you?" she sniveled. "There's never an end to your sarcasm."

"What can I say? I'm a natural wit."

"Unfortunately, dear, you're almost at your wit's end." She gestured with the gun, directing me back toward the void from which I'd escaped. "Let's go."

Trekking through the cemetery grounds was considerably less trouble with the aid of Kathryn's flashlight pointing the way. How thoughtful of her.

"What brings you out to the graveyard this evening, Kathryn?" I said, making small talk as I racked my internal hard drive for a way out. "*Ghouls* night out?"

We advanced several steps. She offered no response.

"Oh, I see," I said conversationally. "Just out for a breath of fresh *scare*."

Kathryn contributed more of the same bristling silence as we forged onward, growing closer with each step to the fate awaiting me in that bloody hole.

"Feeling a little stiff?" I said. "Me too. This is a great way to *exorcise.*"

I was using my best material, but still the woman wouldn't crack. "Hey, I know," I said. "How 'bout a friendly game of 'Name That *Tomb*'?"

"You're really quite amusing," Kathryn said, at last caving under the pressure of my relentless jibber-jabber. "Almost likable. Pity you couldn't keep out of matters that don't concern you."

"Hey," I said, making an abrupt stop. I turned and took a step toward her. "You realize, don't you, that you're talking to the press?" I took another step forward. She inched back. I stepped forward once more, shrinking the distance between us to a couple feet. "You should never threaten someone who buys her ink by the barrel."

Her pinched, overly made-up face projected conceit. Smiling smugly, she said, "And you should never *misunderestimate* someone who's pointing a loaded gun at an old lady's heart."

Old lady, indeed, I thought.

Why Kathryn had worn makeup to a graveyard caper eluded my mental acuity, but whatever her reason for also wearing a tight miniskirt and spike-heeled slingback pumps, it was singularly to my benefit. I clumsily slammed into her, but managed to gouge her left kneecap with the toe of my right oxford and burnish her shin with the edge of my shoe's hard, leather sole. Squealing like a banshee, she dropped the flashlight and clawed the air for my throat. Mindful that her right hand was still wrapped around that bothersome pistol, I drove my right hip into her mid-section, gaining leverage and compromising her balance. Wobbling, she grabbed my arm and took me down with her, hitting the earth on her back and pulling me on top of her soft, furry coat. The gun slipped from her grip and fell to her side, freeing her hands to pummel weakly at my back as she buckled and writhed under my weight.

"Get off me, you stupid cow!" she bellowed. "I should have killed you the first time I had the chance."

The little hairs on the back of my neck prickled. I've tolerated numerous threats and insults during my reporting career. They came with the territory, and I typically sloughed them off. However, being called "stupid" was an affront to my intelligence, and one I simply could not tolerate. However, for now, that insult took a backseat to Kathryn's offhanded comment about wishing she'd killed me the first time she'd had the chance. *The first time?* Inadvertently, she had revealed who attacked me at Gertie's back door the night this whole mess started. It touched off my anger like a Molotov cocktail, and even with both my hands taped, Kathryn Baxter was still no match. Straddling her, I sat upright, pinning her arms under my knees.

"So," I snarled between my gritted teeth, "you should have killed me 'the first time'? You mean after you broke into Gertie Tyroo's house and almost killed *her*?"

Kathryn stopped her futile squirming and met my gaze. The glow of the abandoned flashlight lying on the ground revealed the rancor in her mean, dark eyes. My mind raced to connect the dots. Besides the break-in at Gertie's and the attempt on her life . . . and mine, there was the road rage assault, Randa's disappearance, the attack on poor Officer Paxton, who may well be dead, and now this. I was certain Kathryn was involved in them all, even though I didn't know exactly how. Had Gertie's call to me Monday night set this string of violence in motion? Was it all about Potts, or was there more? Kathryn's actions proved she had a stake in something. But what?

"Surely you know the authorities are monitoring you," I said, bluffing. "You think I'm the only one who's figured out what you're up to? If you think getting rid of me is going to save your ass, you're in for a rude awakening."

Kathryn's lips parted, but she didn't speak.

"The FBI has been watching you for months," I continued. "They're looking for any excuse to haul you in. And you think you're going to kill me and get away with it?" I feigned a laugh. "Wrong, sister. Wrong on both counts."

Kathryn twisted and arched her back, trying to buck me off. She was feistier than I'd expected. In a fair fight, I could probably take her, but I was still operating without my hands, and had already had enough of a workout for one day. I pressed down again with my knees, but my quadriceps were starting to go wobbly.

Kathryn went still, and I relaxed a little, which I realized— too late—was a huge mistake. With one final thrust, Kathryn toppled me off of her. We both lunged for the gun, and as we did, the top of my noggin slammed into her perfectly sculpted snout. For the second time that night, stars exploded in front of my eyes, but I managed not to pass out this time. I felt the cold metal of the pistol at my fingertips. I grasped it with my bound hands and rolled myself into a ball with the gun under me. I fought a wave of nausea.

I'd expected Kathryn to jump me to try to wrestle away the gun, but after seconds passed and nothing happened, I lifted my head to look for her.

Kathryn was flat on her back. It appeared that I'd inadvertently pulverized her rhinoplasty. Her eyes were rolled back in her head, and she was limp. I hoped I hadn't killed her, but it wasn't like I had many choices.

I sat for a moment, catching my bearings and hoping my

head would stop spinning. Getting back on my feet was a monumental struggle. I wasn't accustomed to close-quarter combat, and the batterings I had endured lately were taking a toll on my body. I was tired, I was winded, I probably had a concussion, and, damn it, I hurt everywhere. Kathryn was out of commission, and my kidnapper was nowhere to be seen. I tucked my hands and the gun beneath my cardigan. My solitary goal was to get the hell out of that cemetery. But which way was out?

I attempted another three-sixty scan of the turf, but when I turned halfway around, I faced a tall, dark figure whose hooded sweatshirt obscured his identity. He was within spitting distance. And just as Kathryn had done a few moments before, the stranger greeted me with a firearm—some kind of rifle—pointed at me. Shit!

41

"YOU'VE BEEN QUITE THE PAIN IN THE ASS," the man said, pushing the hood off his head to reveal his face, "nothing but trouble the whole time I've been back in town."

I wasn't exactly surprised. It was Kathryn's mysterious visitor, the one who had called on her while I spied on them from behind some trees.

"What kept you?" I said. "Have trouble finding a parking spot?"

"You don't recognize me, do you?" he said.

"I can't say that I do."

"Ned," he said. "Ring a bell?"

My adrenaline rush was watered down by a surge of confusion and disbelief. "Friendly?" I gasped. "Ned Friendly?"

"You seem so surprised," he said, his tone slathered in arrogance.

Aside from spying on him Wednesday at Kathryn's, I hadn't seen Dr. Ned Friendly for six years—not since the state revoked his medical license for treating overweight patients with frog urine and other equally nasty animal excretions. Ironically, back then, Friendly tipped the scales at more than four hundred pounds. But the stud standing before me that night was less than half the man I remembered.

"Well, I'll be damned," I said. "Look at you, all buffed up. Bravo, doctor. You finally nailed the balance between fraud and desperation. I guess that makes you Elmwood's reigning biggest loser." I was stalling again. My muse had gone AWOL, and I hoped like hell she'd return and whisper an escape plan in my ear. "What brings you back to Elmwood? Planning to reopen your Friendly Neighborhood Clinic?"

"Sorry," he said, "I left my clinic days long ago. I'm into much bigger ponds now."

Bigger ponds, indeed. Verl's theory about an international drug ring tied to Elmwood might have merit after all. "So I've heard," I said.

"Oh, yeah? What have you heard?"

"Rumor is, you've branched out into the world market."

He stomped his left foot like a spoiled child. It only called attention to his pristine white athletic shoes, likely made by slave laborers in one of the third-world countries from which he imported his drug inventory.

"Ah, yes, of course," he said. "You've heard the gossip that's being spread by that meddlesome, old cleaning woman. But guess what. I've heard rumors about *her*." He grunted a humorless laugh. "Pity about her accident. If you like, I could stop by the hospital and check on her. In a professional capacity, of course."

"That would be lovely," I said. "Be sure to let me know before you do, so I can alert the sheriff."

"Under normal circumstances," he said, "I'd be more than happy to do that. But regrettably, by the time I get to Miss

Tyroo, you'll be dead." Friendly jerked the barrel of his gun to the left. "Let's get going. We've wasted enough time. I need you back at that hole."

Tightening my grip on the pistol, I looked toward Kathryn and said, "What about her? Aren't you going to see if she's all right? She could be dying. Or dead."

Friendly crouched and placed his right ear a few inches above Kathryn's broken, bloody nose. He listened for a few seconds and rose. He was grinning. "Looks like I owe you one. You took care of her for me."

I felt nauseated. And scared spitless. "I thought you two were partners," I said, dialing back the horror in my tone.

"Were," he said. "We *were* partners." He sighed loudly. "All right, if you must know, without her I'd still be catering to an endless line of marshmallow-assed morons who foolishly believed I had the magic cure for blubber. With her, I've made a fortune."

"Well, isn't that interesting?" I said. "Please tell me more."

"Maybe later," he said, "Let's get going. Time's a'wasting."

He waved his rifle at me again, and I got going, shifting my body to keep Kathryn's pistol concealed from him, although it was worthless without the ideal opportunity to use it. I hadn't fired a weapon for years, and I dared not risk discharging an aimless shot. I needed to get Friendly into the perfect position. Holding back tested my patience as we moved quietly through the cemetery, passing row upon row of chiseled headstones shrouded in the murky night. My head throbbed, which made formulating a coherent plan even more difficult.

After traveling for what seemed like a country mile, he ordered me to stop. We had reached our destination. The four-by-ten, six-feet-deep opening in the ground lay a few yards to my right. If I were to make my move, it had to be soon, and it better be good.

"So," I said, "looks like this is the end of the line."

"I'm afraid it is," Friendly said.

"You're going to shoot me?"

"You're very perceptive."

"Uh-huh," I murmured agreeably, then swirled on my heels to the right, then to the left as I squinted deep into the darkness. "Where's the other guy?"

"Other guy?" he said, playing ignorant.

"The guy with the muddy cowboy boots, the guy whose family jewels I crushed before I knocked him into Violet's grave."

Friendly shook his head. "That was my *other* partner," he said, "the silent one—well, silent now—and waiting for you right where you left him."

"Down there?" I said, jerking my head toward the grave. "He certainly has simmered down, hasn't he? What's he doing down there? Napping?"

"Let's just say he's made the transition out of this life."

"Of course," I said. I strained my neck for a glimpse at the silent partner lying in the grave, but I couldn't see a thing. "Anyone I know?"

"I believe it is," Friendly said.

"Oh?" I said. "Would you mind telling me?"

Friendly heaved another deep sigh. I suppose it was meant to convey his boredom with the conversation. "Suffice it to say that somebody's going to have to find Elmwood a brand new citizen of the year."

Glenn Markle? If thoughts could scream, mine were bellowing, *No! It couldn't be!* Glenn was one of the good guys, not some sociopathic thug involved in a murder cover-up. Friendly had to be lying. "Well, sure," I said as casually as I could, "makes perfect sense."

Friendly gave me a placid smile. Under normal patient-doctor circumstances, a smile like that would follow with good news, like the tumor was benign or the test strip didn't turn pink. Not so in this circumstance. Friendly pulled a tubular device from his sweatshirt's kangaroo pocket and screwed it onto the rifle's muzzle. He must have interpreted the fear on my face as puzzlement, prompting him to explain, "It suppresses the sound of the blast," as he gave the muffler a few more twists. Finally, gripping the weapon with both hands, he asked, "Have any last words?"

The grains of sand in my hourglass were rapidly trickling away. If I ended up dead in that hole, come tomorrow afternoon the truth would be forever buried with me and Violet Hornsby. No one would ever know what happened here tonight. I would turn up missing, and no one would ever guess I was the filter for Violet's rotting remains. *Think*, I told myself. *Think!*

"Soooo," I said, the cylinders in my brain spinning, "do I have any last words? Matter of fact, I do . . . *steroids*."

"Steroids?"

"You didn't think it was a secret that you and your partners were running a little steroid-import business, did you?" If my bluntness unnerved him, he hid it, except for the slight twitch above his right eye.

"Steroids are where the money's at," he said with a shrug. "The entire sports world is hooked—and not just the pros. Performance enhancement drugs have been prevalent in high school and college sports, even the Olympics, for more than a half century."

"What about Coach's teams at Elmwood High?" I said.

"Back then," he said, "I supplied Coach with all of his, shall we say, *pharmaceutical needs*, which he quietly distributed as special vitamin supplements."

"Who did he give them to?" I had a feeling I wasn't going to like his answer.

"His athletes, of course," Friendly said. "Who do you think?"

My disgust manifested as an angry groan. "Those boys may have been athletes," I said, "but first and foremost, they were kids—*children* actually." Jack Baxter was even more deplorable than I thought.

"Relax," Friendly countered. "Coach was selective. He saved his so-called vitamins for the boys with potential."

"Boys like Lance Whitfield?

Friendly nodded. "As I recall, Whitfield was a pretty good quarterback. All the Big Ten schools had their eyes on him."

If Whitfield had gone on to play for one of them, it would have been another feather in Baxter's legacy. Is that why he pushed Whitfield so hard? Why he gave him steroids? In 1993, when Whitfield died, Baxter had been coaching for at least thirty years. He had to have known the potential hazards of mixing steroids and pseudoephedrine during a strenuous workout in sweltering heat. It was a formula that could play havoc with a kid's health, causing hypertension, dehydration, convulsions, stroke, and yes, even death.

"Baxter knew the dangers when he made Whitfield suit up for practice that day under a ninety-five degree sun. In my book, he was at least complicit in that boy's death and possibly guilty of manslaughter."

"Maybe," Friendly said, "if indeed Coach were the one who supplied the pseudoephedrine."

"If you're saying Baxter didn't offer Whitfield that drug and you know who did, this might be a good time to quench my curiosity. It seems safe to assume I'll take the news to my—" I glanced into hole beside me. "—my grave."

Friendly squinted one eye and appeared to toss my suggestion around in his air-filled head. "Okay," he said, "listen up. I'll give it to you . . . consider it payback for taking care of Kathryn for me."

"You have my undivided attention," I said.

"As you know," he said, "Whitfield showed up for practice that day with a head cold. He was in no shape to play ball, and Coach should have sent him home but didn't. To make matters worse, Whitfield took a double dose of Mucxyphed."

"The over-the-counter cold medicine which contains pseudoephedrine," I inserted, "and is now regulated by the FDA because of its health risks." So far, this clown hadn't told me anything I didn't already know. "What led the police to search Eugene Potts' locker?"

"Let's call it 'an anonymous tip,' " he said.

A tip of the iceberg, I thought. "A tip no doubt phoned in by who?" I said. "Let me guess. Kathryn? Did she also plant the Mucxyphed in his locker?"

"No, our partner down there was happy to take care of that little detail."

I wondered what Glenn had to gain by pulling a stunt like that. I pressed on. "We both know Eugene was deathly allergic to that drug. He didn't give it out to anyone, but who did? Who would want to harm a nice kid like Whitfield?

Friendly cracked a bemused smile. "No one."

"No one?" I echoed. "Really? You don't think there was malicious intent?"

"Not an ounce," Friendly said.

"Then who gave Whitfield the drug?"

"You're so goddamned smart, you figure it out," Friendly said. "I'll give you one minute more before we say goodbye."

One minute indeed. I positioned my feet at right angles and bent my knees ever so slightly. Under my sweater, I choked the pistol butt and curled my right index finger around the trigger. Other than keeping Friendly talking, I didn't yet have a plan, but I was hoping against hope that my white knight was on his way.

"Okay," I said, pulling a half-baked theory from thin air, "here's what I figure. It was Bobby, wasn't it?"

I took Friendly's silence as affirmation. That was encouraging. The pieces were falling into place.

"Bobby gave the pseudoephedrine to Whitfield, and Potts had the bad luck of seeing him do it."

Friendly maintained his silence.

"That's it, isn't it? Bobby was simply trying to help a buddy when he gave the Mucxyphed to Whitfield," I said. "No malice intended, no crime committed. Potts's fate, however, is another matter."

Imagining Bobby Markle as Eugene's murderer was not exactly a stretch. My own experience with Bobby the day before certainly left the impression of a homicidal maniac, and Dick Head said as much in Verl's office, even though he claimed it was accidental.

"Bobby killed Potts," I said, "but he didn't mean to. According to my source, the boys got into a scuffle, but Eugene's death was an accident."

Friendly shook his head. "Your *source*? And who might that be? Richard Head?"

I answered with a halfhearted shrug.

"You reporters never cease to amaze," Friendly said.

"Clearly, your esteemed source was pulling your leg. I gave you more credit than to believe anything coming from that dimwit. My bad. Turns out you're stupider than you look."

There's that word again. Nothing got my panties in a twist faster than being called "stupid," but under the circumstances, I decided to redirect my burst of rage to shore up my stamina for the coming showdown with Mr. Friendly. "Busted," I said. "My secret is out. I'm actually quite thick, so you're going to have to tell me outright who killed Eugene Potts."

Through a smug, self-satisfied grin, Friendly said, "Markle did it."

"Isn't that what I just said? Bobby Markle killed Eugene Potts."

"Not *Bobby* Markle, you twit," Friendly said. "*Glenn* Markle."

"No," I gasped. Until he tried to kill me about thirty minutes before, I had always known Glenn Markle as a charming, soft-spoken humanitarian. Now, Friendly had told me Markle was a cold-blooded child killer. It was like trying to imagine Kathryn Baxter as a brain surgeon. "You're lying."

"Ask him yourself," Friendly said, gesturing toward the open grave with his gun barrel, "when he meets you in hell." He looked almost euphoric as he aimed the gun at me.

"Wait!" I shouted. I was the only person alive, aside from the Friendly gang and Gertie Tyroo, who knew the entire truth about Whitfield and Potts. In case Gertie didn't wake up, it was up to me to get the facts to Verl. Alas, my window of opportunity was almost closed, my moment to act had arrived, and my trigger finger was itchy.

"This case would have remained Elmwood's greatest unsolved mystery if Gertie Tyroo hadn't figured it out," I said. "Once you heard that an odd, eighty-year-old woman was about to bring you all down, you sent Kathryn and Glenn to shut her up. What you don't know is how badly they failed. Early this evening, Gertie woke up, and she's already given her statement to the sheriff. So, regardless of what you do to me, you're going to jail."

Even in the absence of light, I could see Friendly's jaws lock, his nostrils flare, and his eyes narrow—signs that he had bought my big fib. *Whew.* In a dramatic show of exasperation, Friendly glanced skyward and stomped his foot. It was the wedge I needed. In one swift move, I took a short step forward and made a slight turn to the right as I squeezed the trigger and fired off a round. Damn it! I missed.

In retaliation, Friendly bolted straight at me, positioning his rifle like a lance. In a split second, it was within a hair's breadth of my hipbone, and I instinctively jumped aside, landing on my left foot as I extended my right one, tripping Friendly. Stumbling forward, he grabbed a handful of my sweater and yanked me to him. He held fast, while we teetered this way and that at the edge of the open grave.

I attempted to ram a knee into his sweet spot, but he was squirming and squealing like a frightened pig. I tried with all my might to loosen his grip and pitch him into what, in the dark of night, looked like a bottomless pit. But he held on fast until, finally, unable to gain the leverage I needed, I lost my balance and tumbled into the hole, taking Ned Friendly with me. The deep voice yelling obscenities was mine. The high-pitched screams were his.

42

I'D ALWAYS HEARD it's not the fall that does the damage, it's the landing. My landing, on top of Friendly, was surprisingly soft. My proximity to Markle allowed me an up-close look at his bloody face, his left eye puffed up like an overripe plum, and his nose flattened. I shuddered. I assumed he was dead until I heard him groan.

Friendly's gasps assaulted my ears. Apparently the landing had been harder for him—perhaps knocked the wind out of his lungs, perhaps broke his back. I could hope, but in the darkness, I couldn't be sure of much. The only thing I knew for certain was that the direction of freedom was up.

I scrambled off the mound of men and pressed my back to the earthen wall for leverage. Digging my heels into the dirt floor, I pushed myself up and onto my feet. I desperately wanted out of that hole, but the last time I needed to scale six feet, I had a rope strung from the rafters of the high school gym and two free hands. That was fifty years ago. I had none of those amenities that night. Compounding my disadvantage, in the chaos of the tumble, I had dropped my gun. I wasn't sure where. But Ned's rifle was definitely down in this hole, and I wanted it for myself.

"Friendly?" I said. I poked the tip of my right shoe into his midsection. "You alive?"

He didn't respond. Underestimating his condition could be fatal, however, so I played it safe. I presumed he was merely stunned and would regain full use of his faculties at any second. I strained my eyes to see where the rifle could be.

Markle groaned again. He was fighting for each shallow breath as he propped himself up on one elbow, revealing his grip on Kathryn's pistol, which was pointed in my direction.

"Glenn!" I shouted. "You don't stop, do you? First you try to run me off the road, and now you want to shoot me?"

"Sorry," he said softly. "You got in the way. It wasn't personal."

"Wasn't personal? You almost killed me. It's *personal.*"

"You're still in the way," he panted. "Move aside. This is between me and him now."

I promptly obeyed, sinking into the nearest corner to make myself small.

"Why, Ned?" Markle's voice was weak. He spoke barely above a whisper. "Why'd you do this to me? To all of us? After all these years, it all came down to the money, didn't it?"

Friendly didn't answer. He only grinned as he pushed himself to a sitting position. I followed his gaze and spotted the rifle lying inches from his right hand.

"I was your chump," Markle said, his breathing more exaggerated, heavier, "your deal maker, order taker, distributor, banker, risk taker . . . Why? So you and Kathryn could take the money and disappear?"

"How much money are you talking about?" I asked Markle.

251

Even under deadly circumstances, it was impossible for me to stifle my reporter's curiosity.

"Roughly a hundred million," he said.

"Dollars?" I said.

"That's right," Friendly said, "stashed in several off-shore accounts."

"And only I know where they're at," Markle said, his chest heaving under his strain to breathe.

"That's not entirely accurate," Friendly said.

Confusion creased Markle's face.

"The boss was more than happy to assist," Friendly said with a patronizing tone. "He'd do anything for his girlfriend."

"He has a girlfriend?" Markle said.

Friendly sighed as he shook his head in a show of condescending exasperation. "Kathryn, you idiot."

Faster than a blink, Markle's confusion turned to rage. "And this is for you," he hissed. Then he pulled the trigger.

Gunshots erupted, setting off a burst of sparks that illuminated the grave like a strobe light. Glenn Markle went limp and fell sideways before me.

A stream of intensely bright light bobbed overhead and then swept the grave. The ringing in my ears muffled the shouting from overhead. "Police! Drop your weapon."

Friendly clenched his rifle and aimed it at me. His broiling hatred seared my soul.

43

THE LIGHT SWEPT THE GRAVE and hovered over Friendly, bathing him in its harsh white glow. From the blackness above, a voice commanded, "Drop it . . . *now*."

Friendly cowered pathetically, pressing his body into the wall of dirt behind him as he staved off blindness with his forearm. I would be lying if I said I hadn't enjoyed seeing the asshole go down. After an interminably tense moment, Friendly dropped his weapon onto the ground.

"Crystal? Are you hurt?" came from the detached voice at the top of the grave.

I squinted into the blinding light. "Verl?"

"No, it's the Lone Ranger," he grumbled. "Are you all right?"

"I think so," I said.

From some distance away came a shout. "Is she okay?" The voice was Quigley's.

"She thinks so," Verl hollered over his shoulder.

"What about the two men?" The question came from Quigley. He sounded closer.

Verl waved his light over Markle, who lay next to me, still and silent, blood oozing from his face, chest and abdomen. "Markle's in bad shape, maybe dead," Verl called out, glancing behind him. "The other one's headed for jail."

"I found a woman back there," Quigley said. "I think she's alive. The ambulance is on the way."

"Excuse me," I said, shouting out to anyone not too busy to get me out of that goddamned grave. "Remember me?"

The next thing I knew, Quigley slid into the hole. After he undid the duct tape from around my wrists, he gave me a boost up. Verl offered a hand and pulled me out. Quigley followed, toting both Markle's and Friendly's guns.

Verl slipped his jacket over my shoulders and wrapped an arm around my waist. It was at that moment that my knees buckled and my intestinal fortitude went weak.

"I've got you," said Verl. "Let's get you over to the car where it's warm." Turning to Quigley, he said, "Do me a favor and keep an eye on our friend in the hole until backup arrives. Then get hold of Chuck and Ernie. Tell them to go get Grady and Bobby Markle and bring them to the office. I'll get there as soon as I can to break the news about Glenn to them."

Each step I took taxed a different muscle group and shot raw hurt through my weary body—a stabbing pain like a drill bit bore deep into my right shoulder blade, a pulsating throb hammered at my shins, my right cheek was badly swollen and numb where it had intersected with Glenn Markle's fist, and my head ached. A wince escaped my lips, and Verl's grip on me at once strengthened and grew gentle.

As we made our way through the cemetery for the cruiser, I took in the scene around us. How different it had become since I last walked through it with a rifle pointed at me. Now blue, red, and amber lights spun atop a half-dozen police cars, while a dozen or more local and state police officers milled about. The previously bleak darkness took on a carnival atmosphere, while still more police arrived with their sirens shrieking.

"What," I said, "no FBI?"

"They're coming," Verl said, "but let the record show who was here first."

"You can count on it," I said.

Verl and Quigley had performed stellar police work with precision timing. I understood that better than anyone, and when my report came out in Monday's paper, I would give all the credit and praise due them.

"What about Deputy Paxton?" I said.

"He's been airlifted to Methodist for observation," Verl said, "but he's going to recover."

"Thank God."

Verl patted my arm, and my jitters ebbed a bit. More astonishingly, so did my reservations about leaning on another human being for support, both physically and emotionally. It was a breakthrough for someone whose self-reliance and autonomy were tantamount to her identity.

I smiled at him, and he mumbled something that sounded a little like ". . . proud of you." *Surely not*, I thought. "Come again?"

"I said I'm proud of you," he answered with a tenderness I didn't often hear in his tone. "You done good." Verl hooked his arm around my shoulders and gave me a squeeze.

"I guess I've still got it," I said.

"Hey," Verl said, stopping in his tracks and locking his eyeballs with mine. "You never lost it."

"Thanks," I said, drinking in our little moment. To avert the impression I'd gone soft, I changed the subject in short order and nuzzled into him as we resumed our slog toward his cruiser. "How did you figure out where I was?"

"For now, let's just call it a lucky hunch."

Lucky hunch? A chill ran through my body. "If you hadn't shown up when you did," I said, "I'd be dead, and tomorrow no one would know Violet Hornsby was sharing her final resting place with a party crasher."

"I'm not so sure of that," Verl said with a chuckle. "Knowing your capabilities, I'd say Ned Friendly was damned lucky Quigley and I showed up when we did."

Verl helped me into his car. Adjusting the heater, he said, "Let's get you to the hospital."

"No," I said, "we've got to get to the Baxters'. Coach is there by himself, and he's in trouble."

44

VERL SHIFTED THE CAR into drive and looked at me. "I want to get you checked out at the ER," he said, his eyes pleading.

"Honest, Verl," I said, "there's nothing wrong with me that a shower and a few hours' rest won't cure. Coach is who we need to worry about. He's alone in that house, and he could be dead."

Verl floored the gas pedal, and the cruiser shot forward like a bullet along the narrow cemetery lane, slowing only to give right of way to one of the county's two ambulances as it soared past us toward the commotion. Turning onto the residential street, he radioed the dispatcher.

"This's Sheriff Wallace," he said into the hand-held mic. "I'm headed for Jack Baxter's house, and I need an ambulance to meet me there ASAP. Crystal Cropper's with me, and she's fine."

"Thanks, Verl," I said.

He patted my knee. "Dang it, Crystal. You had me scared to death."

Although I wouldn't admit it to anyone, I had been pretty scared too. I had always played a pretty mean game when I had to defend myself, but this time I not only had taken a nasty walloping, I had come close to cashing in the chips.

"What am I going to do with you?" Verl said.

For once, I had no smart-ass comeback. I rode the balance of the ten-minute drive in silence. When we arrived at the Baxter house, Verl broke the lock on the front door and we rushed in, darting from room to room looking for Coach. We found him in an upstairs bedroom lying in his urine-soaked bed, unconscious, ghost white, and emaciated. An acrid stench dominated the air. A length of twine tied around each of his wrists and secured to the side rails bound him to his bed. Even without the cruel restraints, the man couldn't have escaped. The ambulance arrived a minute later, and Elmwood's paramedic twins rushed in. Without a second's hesitation, they set to work on Coach, tending to his most urgent needs as they readied him for the ride to Elmwood Memorial.

Typically, I would have insisted on staying behind to poke around for evidence. That time, I didn't. In fact, I didn't even protest when Verl drove me to the hospital emergency room. The resident on duty, who looked not a day over fourteen, dressed my wounds and admitted me for the night. After a cocktail of pain meds and a mild sedative, I succumbed to my fatigue and lapsed into my first six hours of glorious, uninterrupted Zs in almost a week.

45

I AWOKE TO A CHORUS of muffled chatter wafting into my room from the other side of the half-closed door. My eyelids fluttered open and slammed shut, thanks to a nearly blinding sunray that breached the edges of the window shade. I had to pee. I attempted to rise, but I couldn't quite make it. Every part of me hurt. Even my earlobes ached. I gave myself a couple minutes and tried again. This time, I ignored my body's protests and pushed on. I forced myself off the bed and limped to the bathroom. When I had finished, a perky young nurse's aide twirled into the room bearing good cheer and a tray of hospital cuisine.

"Good morning, Miss Cropper," she chirped. "How're we doing?"

"We're doing grand," I chirped back. "What's that?"

"It's your breakfast," she said. "A bowl of mush, three strips of turkey bacon, a sausage patty, a hard-boiled egg, two pieces of toast, two pats of margarine, eight ounces of orange juice, a cup of yogurt, a carton of milk, a pot of hot tea, a tub of creamer, a packet of sweetener, a dish of strained prunes, and a stool softener."

"Sounds delightful," I said. "Just leave it on the bedstand, would you, dear?"

"Sure thing, Miss Cropper," the girl said most pleasantly. "You enjoy that meal, okay?"

"Okay," I said, returning her annoying sprightliness.

Rather than breakfast, what I wanted most was to go home, clean up, and get myself to the parade. It was the biggest event to hit Elmwood since I'd been running the paper, and I'd be damned if I would let another paper scoop us on our own news. The parade was scheduled to begin at 11:00 a.m. It was already 8:00. I had no time to waste.

There was a phone next to my bed. I lifted the receiver and punched in Verl's office number. Elsie answered. Verl was on traffic patrol, she said, but he had given her instructions to pass on to me: "Stay put." Elsie reminded me that the hospital admitted me for twenty-four-hour observation, and there were still almost sixteen hours to go. I thanked her and ended the call on a cordial note, but I fully intended to get myself out of there.

I opened the closet door and found that my mud-covered, bloodstained clothing I'd worn the night before had been stuffed into a plastic bag. Extracting them, I brushed at the stains on my ripped slacks and shook out my mud-encrusted turtleneck. No, I told myself, these filthy, torn duds would not do. I picked up the phone again and dialed Darcy. On the third ring, Harold Quigley answered. A half hour later, he and Darcy arrived, delivering what I would generously call an "interesting" ensemble composed of a pair of pink tights, a huge, gray cable-knit sweater that draped loosely over one shoulder and exposed the other, a pair of argyle socks, and black leg warmers. They also brought a light-colored trench coat. I couldn't say if I was supposed to look like the girl from *Flashdance* or Inspector

Gadget. At least the outfit, kooky as it was, bore no cakes of dried mud or blood.

"Thanks, Darcy," I said. "You are a lifesaver."

"It's all I had that would fit you," she said. "The coat belongs to Harold."

I nodded my thanks, scooped up my borrowed wardrobe, and hobbled into the bathroom to change. "Quigley," I said, through the door, "what's the word on the street about last night?"

"Glenn Markle is dead, Ned Friendly's in jail with charges pending, Jack Baxter was admitted to intensive care, and his wife is critical but stable at Methodist Hospital in Indianapolis. Her face is so messed up, she may need a transplant."

"Are you joking?" I said, tugging on the tights, stretching them to cover my long, stiff legs.

"Yes," Quigley said, "I'm joking. Once she has surgery to fix her busted nose, she'll be fine. But I hope she can afford a lawyer half as good as the surgeon."

"For what she did to Coach?" I said as I pulled on the socks.

"That," he said, "and her antics in Paducah, not to mention her involvement with Friendly's illegal drug business."

"Ah-ha!" I said, slipping the enormous sweater over my head. It hung loosely over my torso, its hem stopping mid-thigh. I felt as attractive as a humpback whale. "Do you think the authorities can tie her and Friendly to Lance Whitfield's death?"

"I can't say," Quigley answered, "but we'll certainly be looking into the possibility."

"I knew it," I said. And I had. My nose for solving crime was as keen as ever. The only unknowns left for me to ferret out were who, besides Glenn Markle and Kathryn, helped Friendly and why. I quickly pulled on the leg warmers, draped the coat around my shoulders, and limped out of the bathroom. "Well? How do I look?"

Darcy gave me a paltry smile and quickly changed the subject. "What's the plan?"

46

THE PLAN WAS SIMPLE. I was going to escape Elmwood Memorial.

"There's a lot going on that needs my attention," I said.

"Like?" Darcy said.

Shards of pain tore through my body, and the right half of my face throbbed. Ignoring the discomfort as best I could, I perched on the edge of the bed and answered Darcy's obtuse question.

"Like . . . Coach's parade is starting in—" I glanced up at clock. "—two and a half hours. A mob of spectators is probably already pouring into town, and a few hours after that, another mob will flock to the high school gym for the induction dinner. Since this is the biggest wingding to hit Elmwood in years, it might be nice to be there to cover it for the *Gazette*."

I had pushed myself to my feet and toddled a few steps toward the door, when a charley horse suddenly seized my left calf. Stopping, I let out a yelp and kneaded the spasm.

"Crystal," Darcy said with a hint of pity, "I have it all covered."

I looked up at her. "You do?"

"Yes," she said. "You taught me that the first rule to becoming a good reporter is showing up. So you go home, get your rest, and leave everything to me."

And all this time, I doubted the girl was paying attention. My chest swelled with pride. Or maybe it was gas. "Good girl," I said. I grabbed the bag containing my soiled clothes. "Shall we go?"

A lone nurse was seated at the station with her back to the hallway as she engaged in a subdued phone conversation interspersed with giggles and moans of pleasure. Darcy, Quigley, and I tiptoed past and proceeded quietly up the hall. At the elevator, Darcy reached for the "Down" button, but I interceded and mashed "Up." She looked at me quizzically.

"I need to check on Gertie," I said. "I'd appreciate it if you two would wait for me in the lobby."

I stepped off the elevator at the third floor and headed for the ICU. Passing the unattended nurses' station, I hurried on and entered Gertie's dark, dismal room. Tiny specks of light emanated from the various monitors, streaking a crisscross of miniature beams across the tiny woman in the bed. I was disheartened that she seemed unchanged since my last visit two days earlier—no worse, but no better either. She lay on her back, her eyes closed, her breathing shallow, her hands curled at her sides.

I brushed a wisp of her hair off her forehead. "Come on, Gert," I said, barely above a whisper. "You've got to pull through this and wake up. We caught the people who did this to you, and I know you're going to want to be there for the trial. After that, you and I have our work cut out for us. There's a lot more corruption to clean up in this town, and I can't do it without you."

"Excuse me." The words came from behind me as something hard jabbed at my right shoulder blade. I turned and found myself staring into the squinty eyes of a platinum-blonde, full-figured, mustached nurse—female I presumed, although she bore an uncanny resemblance to Hulk Hogan. But far less friendly. Her finger was pointed an inch from my face. "How did you get in here?" Without giving me a chance to answer, she went on. "This patient is not allowed visitors, and I'm going to ask you *just once* to leave."

"Oh, I'm not just a visitor," I said, ramping up the charm. "I'm Miss Tyroo's sister. You can ask Nurse Becky. She knows me."

"Nurse Becky isn't here," the nurse said fiercely. "So leave right now. Otherwise, I'll call security to have you escorted out. Do I make myself clear?"

I'm not one who takes kindly to threats, but I was in no shape for another hassle, especially not with *this* woman. I obliged, but not without noting the nurse's nametag, Pat. *Hmmm.* I could feel Pat's eyes burning holes in my back as I shuffled down the hall toward the elevator. Passing Coach's room, I paused. It, like Gertie's room, was somber and murky, illuminated only by tiny lights that glowed from the various medical contraptions attached to the bedfast patient. Based on what I'd recently learned of Jack Baxter's coaching techniques, though, I couldn't summon him much pity.

47

SOME TEN HOURS LATER, the Elmwood High School gym was packed for Jack Baxter's induction into the Indiana High School Football Coaches Hall of Fame. As much as I wanted to yield to my aching body and stay home, I simply could not blow off the event. I'd be damned if I let the *Indianapolis Times* or even the *Logan City Ledger* scoop me on the story that was mine. I'd earned it and had the battle scars to prove it. Darcy had covered the morning's parade like a seasoned journalist, so I told her to go have a lovely evening with Quigley. Then I accomplished a feat I hadn't attempted for at least twenty years—I dressed up.

My mind was busy spinning the yarn from the previous night's events and weaving it into a single cloth. While most of the strands intertwined as I expected, a few discordant loose ends defiantly dangled. First, who murdered Eugene Potts, disposed of his body, and kept it secret for twenty years? And second, who could orchestrate a successful, illegal drug-importation business? I was never convinced that the known players—Kathryn Baxter, Ned Friendly, and Glenn Markle—possessed the smarts to mastermind such complex crimes. Was it the "boss" Friendly mentioned just before he killed Glenn Markle? If it were, was said "boss" living here in Elmwood right under my nose? The final loose strand was Randa Muridae. She almost certainly was dead, and I wouldn't rest until we found her. Neither would Verl.

"Crystal, you look magnificent," said Auggie, who gave me a lift to the gym. "I've never seen you wear anything so festive. You look positively radiant, even with the shiner."

Who was I to disagree with a judge? Auggie was right. I did stand out. I had dug out my old formfitting, above-the-knee, black-knit sheath from the back of my closet. I accessorized its plunging neckline with a strand of pearls, real, not fake. I had slipped my feet into a pair of three-inch black heels and swept my hair into a French twist. I applied actual department-store makeup—eye shadow, mascara, blush—the works. Subconsciously, I think I was going for a contrast to my mud-caked, near-death appearance of the night before, and it felt good to feel attractive. Auggie looked great in a filmy red tunic and tight zebra-print slacks. We met Shay and Richelle at the dinner, and they also stood out, although both had opted for classic business attire, having donned dressy pantsuits.

The chicken and noodles were superb, and as my three BFFs and I savored the last bites of our New York-style cheesecake, I was at one with the universe. As much as I'd wanted to stay home and yield to my aches and pains, I was glad I hadn't. I was still looking for Verl. I hadn't talked with him since we parted at the hospital the night before and knew he had been busy since dawn with traffic and crowd control, but I was eager to see the old coot. Or more accurately, I was eager for the old coot to see me.

I scanned the faces throughout the gym for the umpteenth

time. The crowd of approximately five hundred was composed of an almost even mix of Elmwood residents and complete strangers. I almost didn't recognize the cleaned-up and polished model of Clip Parker when he stopped by my table to report that the truck I asked him to look for—one with a bashed-in front end and mismatched taillights—belonged to Glenn Markle. I thanked him for the information, but I planned to have a chat with him about his timing when Nellie was ready for me to pick up.

Frank and Tammy Whitfield were seated several tables away, and I wondered why they were even there. The head table was placed on a makeshift stage at the front, where the town's illustrious mayor, who had been granted bail since I last saw him, was seated with his wife next to Grady Markle, whose presence surprised me, considering his only son had died the night before. With them were eight other people, whom I recognized from the printed handout as officials from the Indiana High School Football Coaches Association. The dignitary I was most curious about, however—the keynote speaker—was missing.

At exactly eight o'clock, the gentleman in the center, the association's president, Chester Morgan, walked to the lectern and greeted the crowd. After the requisite opening remarks, he said, "We've all been concerned for our beloved Coach Jack Baxter's fragile health for quite some time. Many of you may not know that last night, Coach was admitted to the hospital, where he remains in stable condition with his devoted wife, Kathryn, at his side." Gasps erupted followed by a wave of chatter throughout the gym. Morgan stopped talking and raised his hands, signaling everyone to quiet down. When the noise began to wane, Morgan resumed his speech. "While the Baxters cannot be with us here tonight physically, they are here in spirit. They instructed me to express their immense appreciation for this honor. Coach personally told me how humbled and grateful he is to all of you for your support. So before we get started with tonight's program, please join me in a moment of silence and ask God to push our great Coach Baxter across the goal line for one more glorious victory. After that, I will introduce our very special, surprise keynote speaker, direct from Hollywood, California, adored by fans for his much ballyhooed, award-winning, 1974 football film. And with having said that . . ."

Morgan closed his eyes and bowed his head. The audience followed his cue. A blanket of silence fell upon the room, and I took the opportunity to compose the opening paragraph for my story for Monday's paper:

Jack Baxter and his wife, Kathryn, were no-shows Saturday night for the former Elmwood coach's induction into the Indiana High School Football Coaches Hall of Fame. The IHSFCA president blamed Baxter's absence on a minor health problem. In reality, Baxter was fighting for his life in the local hospital's intensive care unit, while his wife was recovering from surgery some fifty miles away as she awaited indictment for a list of felonies that includes neglect, battery, drug dealing, kidnapping, and attempted murder.

Several seconds into the silence, the ambiance of the solemn moment was shattered when the doors of the main entrance suddenly banged open, and Ray Potts stomped into the room wielding his long-handled barbecue fork as if it were a samurai sword.

"Stop it! All of you, stop!" he bellowed. "Jack Baxter doesn't deserve your prayers. Or your praise. The man's a finkin' fraud. He murdered my son!"

The audience's collective gasp cascaded through the gym. "And them," Potts shouted, pointing his double-pronged prod toward the head table, "how many of them were in on it?"

Potts held his threatening pose, locking the terrified head table dignitaries in their place as Frank Whitfield snuck up from behind and smashed a plateful of chicken and noodles into Potts's face. Undeterred, Potts wiped the doughy strings, globs of mashed potatoes, and bits of succotash from his eyes and quickly retaliated, jabbing his fork toward Whitfield's belly and screaming curses that were almost too indelicate for my seasoned tolerance. Nearby, a few men jumped from their seats, trying to restrain the two adversaries while avoiding the sharp tines of the fork.

Throughout the gym, diners scattered like a herd of startled wildebeest. Some stampeded for the nearest exit; others bolted toward the action for a better view.

While I was distracted by the pandemonium, I let one of the honored dignitaries slip away, but my gut told me where he'd gone. I dove into the human stream flowing toward the exit. If I hurried, I figured I might beat him to his destination. Spike-heeled pumps were not the ideal footwear after all.

The current carried me past Auggie, Richelle, and Shay. I called out to them, asking if they had seen Verl. Auggie waggled her thumb toward the main entrance and shouted, "He went thataway!"

I spotted him stopped on the interior side of the doorway. "Verl!" I shouted, waving an arm.

Miraculously, he heard me and turned in my direction. I elbowed my way toward him, and he met me halfway. I fell into him.

"Gertie!" I sputtered. "We've got to get to her. She's in danger."

Verl clasped my arm and led me through the gym's clogged

entrance to his waiting patrol car. "What is it?" he asked.

"Trust me," I said. "I know this all looks crazy, but I know who's behind everything that's happened. Gertie does too, and that's why we need to get to her."

Verl stomped the gas pedal, and his tires squealed to life. We careened through the parking lot, the car's siren blaring and its emergency lights awhirl, prompting startled pedestrians to jump from our path and motorists to slam on their brakes.

The hospital was only a few blocks from the high school, and we arrived in less than a minute, barely time for Verl to radio the dispatcher to send a couple of deputies for backup. The instant the car stopped outside the hospital entrance, we threw open our doors and bolted for the elevator. As it groaned its way to the third floor, Verl asked me if I was all right. I replied with a nod.

"You've got no business being out after what you went through," he said, "let alone running back into a burning building. You don't know when to stop, do you?"

I placed a finger to his lips. I knew he meant well, but I was in no mood for another bawling out. When the elevator doors parted, I kicked off my high heels and sprinted down the hall, Verl right behind me. Passing the nurses' station, I nearly collided with Nurse Becky as she skittered around the corner.

She stopped abruptly, grabbed her heart, and snorted, "Mercy me! First your brother, and now you."

"My brother?"

"He's with your sister right now," she said. "What a comfort he must be to you."

Verl and I made a dash for Gertie's room at the end of the hall. Her door was closed, and parked alongside it was a medical walker; a miniature football covered the foot of each of its front legs. I slammed into the door full force, but it didn't budge. It was barricaded from the inside. As if our moves were choreographed, I jumped aside and Verl bulldozed the door open with his shoulder.

Muted, indirect light from the hall infiltrated the dark room, revealing the intruder, a man. His back to the door, he bent over Gertie, pressing a pillow over her face. Instinctively, I bounded onto him and latched on. Wrapping my left arm around his neck, I doubled my right hand into a fist and hammered his chest and bald head, each whack triggering sputters and groans. In short order, he drooped and fell to his knees. Verl snapped a pair of handcuffs onto the man's wrists behind his back, while I flicked on the light to reveal the identity of the would-be assassin.

"Hello, *boss*," I said to Grady Markle. Turning to Verl, I said, "Believe it or not, *this* is the brain behind the Potts disappearance, the drug ring, and who knows what else."

"Brain?" Verl said, shaking his head. "Only in Elmwood."

I leapt to Gertie's side, fearful that Grady's attempt on her life had worsened her condition. Thankfully, her breathing was steady, and her electronic monitors were undisturbed. She looked okay, but just in case, I yelled for Nurse Becky.

Grady whimpered as Verl yanked him from the floor to his feet.

"You're goddamned lucky we got here when we did," Verl said. "Had you killed that woman, I would've gladly asked the prosecutor to seek the death penalty. Frankly, I couldn't care less who you are or how many birthdays you've chalked up, but I will say this: things might go easier if you cooperate."

Grady said nothing. He only glared at Verl below his colorless, hooded lids. After a long, bristling moment, he broke down and wept, dousing his silence with an outpouring of incoherent blubbering.

"That woman had no right," he said, gesturing toward the bed. "She ruined everything."

"Because she found Eugene Potts's medical alert tag at your house?" said Verl.

"Thanks to her, we figured out it was Glenn who killed Potts and buried him with Lance Whitfield," I added.

"Hogwash," Grady said. "Glenn couldn't kill anyone. He had no stomach for death." Grady's sorrowful expression twisted into a snarl. "Whoever heard of a kid growing up in a funeral home and being scared of a dead body? Why, he couldn't even touch one, let alone commit murder."

I rubbed my swollen, bruised cheek. Perhaps Grady hadn't known his son as well as he thought. "So, are you saying *Bobby* killed Eugene?" I said.

"Bobby?" Grady barked. "Hell no. My grandson doesn't have the sense of a squirrel. Or the nuts." His snarl curled into a smirk, then flattened back to sadness. "Look at me. I'm a tired old man. I just lost my son. My grandson hates me. I don't even know why I'm here." Grady lowered his head. "Bobby's sake, I guess. I'd have done anything for him. He always was the apple of his grandpa's eye. "

"How much of a part did he play in Eugene's disappearance?" I said.

"Zero," he snapped.

"You expect us to believe that?" Verl said.

Grady scowled first at Verl, then at me. "I don't give a rat's ass what you believe. I'm telling you my grandson had no part in any of that business."

"Bobby didn't beat Eugene Potts to death?"

"Hell no," he said as he wiped his runny nose across his sleeve. Who told you that? Richard Head? He's an idiot. Besides, he only knowed half of it."

"And the other half is what?" Verl said.

"What happened after him and Bobby knocked the Potts kid around a little bit."

"A little bit?" I said. "That's not what Head told us. He was under the impression he and Bobby killed Eugene."

Grady cracked a smile and shook his head. "Head never was the sharpest needle in the haystack, so I figured he would be more apt to keep quiet about it if he thought he helped kill the boy. It was understandable why he thought that. Potts sure as hell looked dead when Bobby brought him to me."

"Wait a second," I said, "Bobby didn't take Eugene to Coach and ask for help?"

Grady shook his head again. "Bobby brought him to *me*. Other'n what was printed in the paper, Coach never knowed what happened."

"Are you saying that nobody but you knew what really happened to Potts?" I said.

"That's the long and short of it," Grady said. "The boys whupped Potts pretty bad, but he was nowhere near dead. Matter of fact, if he'd woke up, he would'a been fine."

"I don't understand," I said. "If he was fine, what happened to him? Where did he go?"

"The problem was," Grady said, "the Potts kid knowed Lance got the cold medicine from Bobby. I still thank the good Lord that Potts didn't tell anybody. If he had, folks would've held Bobby responsible for Lance's death, and Bobby's chances for a football scholarship to Notre Dame would have been ruined, just like mine were thirty-five years before when my dad made me go to mortician's school. I could've been a bigger star than Knute Rockne. I wasn't about to let that happen to Bobby, so I did what was necessary."

"Necessary?" I said. "What exactly are we talking about?"

Grady stroked his dimpled chin and gazed at me for a long moment through watery, bloodshot eyes. "To make sure Potts kept his trap shut about my grandson."

"*You* murdered Eugene?" I wasn't exactly surprised, but I felt like the definitiveness of the logic had just knocked me over the head.

Grady responded with a half shrug.

"Let me make sure I'm understanding you correctly," I said. "You killed Eugene to guarantee he couldn't mess up Bobby's non-existent chance for a football scholarship to Notre Dame?" I felt nauseated. I was furious. "Your grandson received a full-ride scholarship to an excellent state university. What was wrong with that?"

"IU is *no* Notre Dame," Grady said with disdain.

"Did it ever occur to you that Bobby couldn't have gotten in-to Notre Dame if he'd been the pope's son? To satisfy your own twisted ego, you snuffed out a young boy's life in cold blood."

"I did it humanely," he said, lowering his voice.

"*Humanely?*" I shouted. I couldn't even imagine where he was going.

"The boy was out cold when I embalmed him. He never knew."

Something in me snapped, and I lunged at Grady with both hands. I intended to wring his wrinkled neck, but my impulsive move was thwarted when Verl stepped between Grady and me and gently took hold of my wrists. He subtly shook his head at me, and I conceded with no objection.

"And after you murdered him," I said, "you buried his body with Whitfield's. You did all of this to cover up Bobby's mistake."

Grady nodded weakly. "I wanted only the best for my grandson. I had to make sure our lives weren't destroyed."

I gave Grady a long, penetrating glare. I felt nothing but contempt.

"You mind telling me why you held on to the boy's medical alert tag all these years?" Verl said.

"He lost it in the truck bed when Bobby brought him to me. I hadn't noticed it until weeks later. I kept it in my catch-all drawer all these years. I'm a compassionate man, and I planned to send it back to the Pottses when the time was right, anonymously of course."

The slap of rapid footfalls sounded from the other end of the hall and grew louder as they neared Gertie's room. Two deputies I recognized as Craig Steele and Wade Huffman stormed into the room, their guns drawn, their eyes darting about. The radios on their shoulders crackled static.

"Sheriff, we responded as quick as we could," Deputy Huffman said. "Is this the only situation? Are there other suspects?"

"No, this is the only one," Verl said. "You can take him in for me, and I'll be in directly to file a report."

"Sheriff," Huffman said, "there's been a development in the Muridae case."

"Randa Muridae?" I said, my hope spiking. "You found her?"

Huffman shifted his focus to Verl. "Sheriff?"

"Answer the lady," Verl barked. "Did you find the Muridae woman?"

"Yes, sir. We found her in a back room at Markle's Mortuary.

She's deceased, sir."

I cringed. Although I feared Randa was dead, I had naively hoped to be proven wrong. "You bastard," I said to Grady. My rage reached the boiling point, and I lunged at him again. Fortunately for Grady, Verl pulled me back.

Grady's thin lips stretched into a mocking grin, and he said, "You think I killed her?"

"Before you say another word," Verl said, "remember that your words can and will be used against you in a court of law. You have the right to an attorney. If you can't afford one, the court will appoint one for you. Okay?"

"Okay," Grady said, "but I didn't kill her. Kathryn Baxter and Ned Friendly shot her. I was only going to bury her in—"

"In the next available grave," I said. "You son of a bitch." My self-control snapped, and I stepped up to him, my right hand poised to slap that arrogant sneer off his shriveled, pleated face. But before I could consummate the intended act, I was stopped by a wee, but mighty voice speaking out behind me.

"For God's sake, people," it said, "what does it take for an old woman to get a little peace and quiet?"

Stunned, we all turned to the source of the caustic admonition—the tiny woman at the crux of the commotion. Gertie. She was sitting upright in the bed, her blue eyes wide and alert, her pale lips pursed.

"What the hell are you people looking at?" she said. "You were expecting Sleeping Beauty?"

48

I⊤ WAS LATE WHEN VERL AND I LEFT THE HOSPITAL. Gertie's sudden awakening was such a relief. But the real cherry that topped my friend's delicious development was Dr. Bannerjee's report. After a couple months of physical therapy to strengthen her motor skills, she was expected to make a total recovery.

"You comin' in?" I said to Verl when he stopped his cruiser in front of my house. "I've got some fresh blueberry muffins. I'll fix you a decaf to go with them."

Verl patted my knee. "Thanks, Crys, but I'll take a rain check. It's late. There's been enough lewd gossip about us for one week, and we don't need to rekindle those fires. Not just yet."

"Agreed," I said. "But you've got to admit, it's been one hell of a week."

"Yeah, we done good," Verl said. "We solved us a twenty-one-year-old murder case, stopped a serial killer, took down an international drug ring, and exposed the mayor's corruption."

"I can hardly wait to start working on Monday's paper," I said. "Maybe I'll win us one of them *Poolitzers*."

"Beg pardon?" Verl said.

"Never mind," I said. "Let's not forget that while we're reveling in our triumph, for the Pottses it's a bittersweet ending."

"At least now they know what happened to their son," Verl said, "and they can finally bury him where he belongs."

"Yes, there's that," I said. "Let's not forget about Randa Muridae either. She didn't deserve what happened to her."

"Neither did you," Verl said. "I shudder to think what else could've happened to you if Digger hadn't called in that report."

I flinched. "Digger Fosser?"

Verl nodded.

"Called in what report?" I said.

Verl picked up my hand and squeezed it gently. "It's the damnedest thing. He went back to the cemetery around eleven o'clock last night to make sure he'd locked the tool shed. He saw people with flashlights near that open grave and phoned in to report vandals. I was still at the office, so I took the call, figuring I'd bust me some kids for curfew violation.

"On my way there, I swung by your house to check on Paxton, and the second I saw the 'Vette double parked, I knowed something was wrong. My first thought was for you."

"For me?"

"Yeah, I don't care how tough you think you are, you're no match for a homicidal maniac."

Actually, I was a superior match for the homicidal maniac, but I was too tired to spar with Verl. I let it go and merely said, "Uh-huh."

"Then I found Paxton, but when I saw your black cape thrown over him, I knowed you'd been there and would never've left him if you could've helped it. My gut told me there was a connection between what happened there and what Digger reported."

"Good thinking, Verl."

"I called for an ambulance and backup and hightailed it to the cemetery. Then I called Quigley."

"Why would you call Quigley? You haven't wanted him here the whole time."

"Because," he said between clenched teeth, "as much as I hate to admit it, he's a better-trained officer than any of my deputies. I didn't know what I'd be walking into at the cemetery, and I needed the best-trained officer at my side. I wanted to be ready in case it came down to an SAR op."

There he went again with the fancy police lingo he learned at the law enforcement academy. "Search and rescue operation, I presume," I said.

"Uh-huh. And thank God we found you when we did."

I gave Verl's hands a gentle squeeze. Next, catching him completely off guard, I planted a warm peck on his left cheek. I let him fluster for a moment and said, "In case I forgot to mention it previously, thank you. I guess there really are white knights." This I pronounced with all the biting sarcasm I could scrape up. I could not risk letting him know I was dead serious.

"Oh, for corn sake, Crystal. I was just doing my job. I couldn't let somebody shoot the newspaper editor. What would folks have to complain about then?"

I let that one go, but not without a little tit for tat.

"Okay," I said. "That reminds me. I've got some startling information for you."

"Dare I ask?"

"Harold told me," I said. Then I gave it to him fast. "Gertie was an FBI operative under J. Edgar Hoover and helped bring down Lee Harvey Oswald."

Even in the dark, I could see the color drain from Verl's

chubby cheeks.

"Let's go inside," he said.

• • • •

Verl took me up on my decaf and blueberry muffin offer, and we sat at the kitchen table talking for almost three hours. The numbers on my bedside clock radio glowed two forty-five when I finally settled in for my long-overdue sleep. I was past exhaustion and planned to stay in bed all of Sunday. Independence was the cornerstone advantage to being single.

And then the telephone rang.

"What?" I grunted into the receiver of my bedside Princess phone. "This better be good."

From the other end came, "Crystal? Crystal *Crapper*?"

It was a male voice that joggled certain old, but pleasant memories. It was a voice I'd not heard utter my name since my Hollywood days. My pulse quickened. "Yes, this is Crystal *Cropper*," I said.

"Well, I'll be damned," he said. "It *was* you at that free-for-all last night."

"*You*? *You* were the surprise keynoter!" I said, clamping a hand over my mouth to stifle my gulp of astonishment.

"Talk about surprises," he said. "What the heck are you doing here in Toadstool, Indiana? No, wait. Don't tell me. I've got a better idea. I'll send the limo by to get you, and you can tell me in person. How's twenty minutes? Goddamn, Crys, it's sure been a long time."

I propped myself up on one elbow and shook my tousled hair. "Burt," I murmured as I undid the top button on my flannel pajamas. "Indeed, it *has* been a long time."

About the Author

Janis Thornton is a freelance writer, personal historian, and award-winning journalist. She is the author of two local history books, *Images of America: Tipton County* and *Images of America: Frankfort.* She is a member of Sisters in Crime, the Indiana Writers Center, Association of Personal Historians, and the Midwest Writers Workshop Planning Committee. She lives in a small Indiana town not unlike Elmwood. *Dust Bunnies and Dead Bodies* is her debut cozy mystery. You may connect with her via her website at www.janis-thornton.com.

Now available from Cup of Tea Books

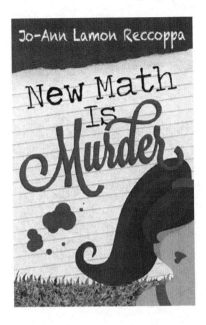

Reporter Colleen Caruso was never good at math.

A stingy ex-husband, a teenage daughter, and a rusted-out Ford Escort have multiplied her troubles. Tripping over a dead body while on her morning jog seems like another incident for the minus column.

But then her new editor at the newspaper gives her a regular column detailing the investigation. He's handsome, single, and just a bit mysterious. Suddenly, Colleen's life is on the plus side.

Unfortunately, 1 dead algebra teacher + 2 secret affairs + 4 suspicious suspects quickly adds up to 3 perilous "accidents" for Colleen.

Which means Colleen needs to come up with the solution to the murder . . . before the killer removes her from the equation.

www.cupofteabooks.com

Now available from Cup of Tea Books

Recently divorced, forty-something Vicky Andrews desperately needs a life.

Finding her boss naked and dead at an open house she's hosting was not what she had in mind.

Wishing she'd spent more time reading Nancy Drew in her formative years, Vicky calls upon her own intuition and various investigative skills to try to find a piece of incriminating evidence the murderer thinks she has—before the murderer finds her.

She might decide that the world has it in for her if not for Detective Nick Carson, who shares frustration, information, and more than a few fantastic kisses as he tries to solve the case.

Throw in a rescued miniature dachshund, a skeleton named Max, and a coven of well-intentioned neighbors, and maybe, just maybe, Vicky has found exactly what she needs.

www.cupofteabooks.com